LORD OF FIRE

The Dragon Demigods

CHARLENE HARTNADY

CHAPTER 1

AVA

It feels like someone has their hands around my throat.

I can't breathe.

I'm trying but I can't seem to get it right.

And yet, I can hear the air rushing in and out of my lungs. I can hear the sobs coming from my mouth as I run towards the block of apartments. The apartments where he lives. Or used to live. I fight back another sob as the realization hits again. My eyes are stinging. My chest is so tight it hurts.

Red lights are flashing. Uniformed officers are moving in and out of the building, which has been cordoned off.

"Ava!" A woman screams my name. She is on the pavement, about thirty feet away from where the action is. Her eyes are wide. Her face is too pale. She's much thinner than I remember. A waif, really. It's been a good couple of months since I last saw her. Even from across the street I can see that her eyes are red-rimmed. Tears are streaming down her face. Her hair is an unkempt, stringy mess. It doesn't look like she's washed it in weeks. What a thing to notice at a time like this. It's clear that nothing has changed since I left.

That's not true.

Everything has changed.

Everything.

"Lee," I choke out. "What happened?" I yell, my voice is shrill. Thankfully, I still have the good sense to check for oncoming traffic. My purse strap almost falls from my shoulder as I pick up a panicked jog. Gripping the leather in my hands, I close the distance. *Shit.* I'm crying now as well. Tears are coursing down my face.

Lee is sobbing in earnest. She's shaking her head and saying something I can't quite make out. Between the sirens, our combined racking sobs and my thumping heart, it's hard to hear anything else. Her eyes have this look. It's terrible. It makes me pick up the pace even more.

"I found him…" I finally hear her choked words. "I found him…I found him…" she keeps saying the same thing over and over. It looks like she's about to lose it. Her eyes are wild now. Filled with…fear. *Why fear?*

I grip her wrists in both my hands and force her to look me in the eyes. She flinches as our gazes lock. Her nose is running. Her eyes are not just red but puffy as well. Tears are still streaming down her face. I can sense that a sob is lodged in her throat.

"What happened to him? What happened to my brother?"

Lee shakes her head. "He…he…"

I squeeze her arms. Not hard enough to bruise but enough to anchor her. To keep her focused. "What happened to Bruce? How did he die?" I choke on the last word. I still can't believe this. My little brother is dead. Gone.

Her face crumples and fresh tears fall.

"Did he OD? He overdosed, didn't he?" My fingers are digging into her arms now. I need answers. I make a noise of frustration. There is underlying anger there too. "Forget it! I'll find out soon enough anyway." I turn to walk to the closest uniformed person I can find. A middle-aged man. He looks to be guarding the entrance to the building. There is less activity outside.

"He killed himself," Lee says behind me, her words making my blood run cold.

I turn, facing her. Lee is chewing on the quick of her nail. It's bleeding but she doesn't seem to notice. Her eyes are directed at the asphalt at her feet. "An H overdose but it wasn't an accident." Her big blue eyes lock with mine. "He left a letter," she mutters. "It was addressed to you. An apology." A tear trickles down her face. "He didn't know what else to do." She starts to cry all over again.

"Why?" I shake my head, unable to comprehend what I am hearing. "Why would he do such a thing? I thought the two of you were doing better." I'm frowning, unable to comprehend. "Bruce told me he had a job. He said he was working for a local courier company. I…" Swallowing down the lump in my throat, I stop talking. My mouth falls open.

Lee is laughing. She's damn-well laughing. The laugh quickly turns into an all-out bawl. She is shaking her head so hard her greasy hair is swishing. "A courier. Yeah, that's exactly what Bruce was, only it wasn't regular packages he was transporting. He was—" Her eyes lift, and she stares at something over my shoulder. Whatever it is has Lee freezing. It has her eyes widening in...terror. *This strange reaction again...why?* Her lip trembles. Her face drains of any vestiges of color. "I'm sorry." Her voice is high-pitched.

I can't be sure if she's talking to me. I don't think she is. Lee turns and runs. She stumbles and almost falls. Once she finds her feet, she picks up the pace again. The police officer calls after her but she isn't listening. Something has her spooked. Something or someone.

The hairs on the back of my neck stand up. My whole body becomes rigid. I slowly turn. I almost take a step back but catch myself. "Mr Herms?" I sound incredulous. "What are you doing here?"

He smiles. It's warm and kind but I'm not taken in. I don't know very much about this man, but I do know his type. Herms owns the casino I work for. With inky black hair and startling blue eyes, he's extremely attractive. He is rolling in money. Has women falling at his feet. He's also taken a keen interest in me of late. I don't know why, but I don't like it. My heart should beat faster when he flirts with me. I should have jumped at the chance when he asked me out some weeks back. It's not just about losing my job, there is something about him I don't like. Herms is a player. He's used to getting what he wants, when he wants it.

My boss arches a brow. "I heard that an employee

just lost a family member. I thought I would come see if you needed anything."

My eyes prick with fresh tears as I remember why I'm here. That Bruce... I swallow thickly, trying hard to dislodge the lump of emotion forming in my throat. For a moment I'd forgotten why I was here. I'm reeling inside, working hard to keep my feelings under wraps. I don't want this man to be privy to any of it. His explanation doesn't sit right with me. There is no way Sly Herms, owner of The Winged Palace Casino, drops everything whenever one of his staff members has a family crisis. No damned way! I want to tell him that he's full of crap, but I bite my tongue. I nod once. "Thank you but I can manage. I will need a few days to..." I clear my throat. wishing he would leave, "to make arrangements."

"Of course, take all the time you need."

"Thank you. I need to go...I..." *Shit!* A tear runs down my cheek. I catch it with the tips of my fingers, sniffing and blinking to stop myself from crying.

"Here..." Herms pulls a crisp handkerchief from his suit pocket. Always dressed to the nines in expensive, designer suits, tailored to fit his built frame.

I take the hankie, mumbling my thanks.

"You shouldn't have to deal with this alone." He shakes his head, those deep blue eyes never leaving mine. *How do I make him go away?* It makes absolutely no sense that he is here. I don't want him here.

I need to speak to someone. I need to see my brother. I need answers. More tears run down my cheeks.

"Let me..." the casino owner begins but is interrupted.

"Ava...oh my god! I can't believe this." It's my best friend, Trudy. She'd been my first call after I got the news, and it's no surprise she dropped everything and raced to be here with me. She hooks an arm around me. "I'm so sorry." Unable to hold back any longer, I cling to her and sob. It's a good couple of minutes before I'm able to come up for air. "You poor thing. I'm so sorry." Trudy's cheeks are wet too. She's known my brother for almost as long as I have.

"Thank you for coming." My voice is choked.

"How did this happen? Did he...?"

"He killed himself." I bite onto my lower lip, shaking my head. "Lee said she found him."

Trudy gasps, covering her mouth. "I can't believe it. Are they sure it was suicide?"

"I think so...I haven't spoken to anyone official yet." I look to the door where the officer is positioned. There are two more standing outside, looking our way.

"I haven't had a chance." I look around us, realizing with a sigh that Herms has left. Something else occurs to me at that moment. Lee seemed to recognize him. Not only that, she was afraid of him. So much so that she ran away. *Ran. Away.* My heart is pounding.

It can't be. It doesn't make any kind of sense. Why would Lee know Sly Herms? How would their paths have ever crossed? Sly is rich. He's well-known in these parts. A celebrity of sorts. By contrast, my brother and Lee barely get by. They're drug addicts. The only reason they have this apartment is because of a monthly allowance my mother left for him in her will. I'm the executor. I use it to pay the rent and amenities. Otherwise, they'd be living on the street. I find myself thankful that my mother didn't live to see this. She died young. I'm convinced that worrying herself sick over Bruce is what caused her death. The lies. The cheating. The stealing. The using. More lies.

The last time I talked to Bruce was a few weeks ago. He said they were clean. Like I haven't heard that one before. I'm not being callous or uncaring but it's difficult to trust a drug addict. My mother took him back in on more than one occasion. The last time, he didn't just steal from her purse, he cleaned out her jewelry and electronics as well. So, when he told me they were clean, that he had a real job, I didn't believe him. From the look of Lee today, I would say I was right. I still can't fathom why Lee would know Sly Herms. Maybe she was still high today when she saw him. Maybe she saw a picture of him on a billboard or in the paper and she just thinks she knows him. *Yeah, that has to be it.*

Trudy squeezes my arm, bringing me back to the cold, hard reality. "I think we should go and find out what happened."

I'm fiddling with my ring, it's what I do when I'm stressed. I nod once and allow myself to be led.

CHAPTER 2

AVA

Eight days later

Tony touches me on the side of the arm, his smile is genuine. Lines wrinkle the sides of his eyes, which are filled with warmth. "Are you sure you're okay to start work today?" He is my direct manager and a great guy. "You can take another day or two—if you want?" Concern is evident in their depths.

I nod. "I'm sure." I was given three days' of compassionate leave and ended up taking some unpaid days as well. I literally can't afford any more time off. The funeral was… It was a tough day, to put it mildly. It was Trudy and me, and the priest. No one else bothered to turn up. Not even his girlfriend. There was no sign of Lee at all. She had gone MIA since Bruce died. Anger bubbles up inside me. Did she care so little for him? They'd been together for six years. It was Lee who had introduced him to hard drugs in the first place. I was sure he would have fallen down that rabbit hole without her, but she certainly helped him along. They were each other's downfall. Not a good combination, and yet the least she could have done was to turn up to say goodbye.

It turns out that everything Lee told me on that pavement was the truth. Bruce died from an overdose of heroin. He had enough in his system to kill a bull elephant. There was no way a seasoned junkie like him would have made such a grievous error in judgment by accident. More anger wells. *Why did he do it? Why?*

Then there was the note, in Bruce's handwriting, that led the authorities to call his death a suicide. The note didn't say much. A scribbled apology to me for everything. For being a burden. For causing so much trouble. It was a cop-out if I ever saw one. For all of Bruce's weaknesses, I never saw this coming. I never took him for a coward.

Why didn't he come to me? I had two hard and fast rules when it came to Bruce. Never lend him money, because that would be feeding the beast, and never let him stay over at my house. Again, that would be feeding the beast. He stole from our mother, but he'd also taken a fair share from me. Having said that, I would have cleared out my measly savings to pay for yet another stint in rehab, or to get him psychological help. I would have done anything to prevent this from happening. Guilt welled. I should have stayed in touch with him. I should have —

Tony squeezes my arm. "We'll manage without you for a few more days. I have Moira on standby, just in case."

It's my turn to smile warmly. Tony is the sweetest boss I have ever had. If you do your job and keep your nose clean, he'll do anything for you. I nod. "I'm fine. I'll cope."

He scrutinizes me for a few moments longer. "Okay, then." His forehead creases with a frown. "Mr Herms has asked to see you before you start your shift."

What?

A lump forms in my throat. "Why?"

Tony shakes his head. "I don't know. I'm sure he just wants to check up on you to make sure you're okay."

Why would he want to do that?

I can tell that he finds the request just as strange as I do. Herms should not have turned up outside my brother's apartment and he shouldn't be requesting a meeting with me now either. Tony is my direct superior. There are several levels of management between Herms and me. This makes no sense. I want to tell Tony that my shift is about to start. That there isn't any time left to make it to the executive offices and back before then. I don't want to meet with Herms. This whole thing is making me anxious.

"I don't think you have to worry," Tony tries to reassure me and fails.

I force a smile.

"I'm sure it's nothing." He misinterprets my frown. He probably thinks I'm worried about losing my job or getting into trouble, but that's not it at all. The opposite is true.

"You go on. I'm sure he's waiting for you. It will be an hour or two before traffic picks up. It's early yet."

I look over at the VIP section. I was recently promoted.

I serve the elite – high-rollers in the casino. Food and drinks are on the house. It's always busy and service is expected to be top-notch. Day and night all bleed together. There is no such thing as time when you're between these walls. Some of my regular clients will be asking for me. Some of them won't be happy I am gone. Tony is just being nice.

"I'll be as quick as I can," I say as I begin walking towards the elevators that will take me to the exec offices.

Tony nods once.

The security guard uses a card to summon the elevator. He was expecting me. *Of course he was.*

I smooth my blouse and pull down on the hem of my skirt. It's too short for my liking but since most of the clients frequenting the VIP section of the casino are men, this is what I have been given to wear. Low heels, stockings, a short black skirt, and a sheer, white blouse. Thankfully we're allowed to wear a camisole underneath, but my cleavage is still on display. It's the one downer when dealing with intoxicated patrons. They can be crude and even get handsy on occasion. We earn good money in the VIP section, tips too, so I will suck it up until I can find something better. I step into the elevator when it opens. I'm pale and I've lost weight. My big, hazel eyes are slightly sunken. My dark hair is lackluster. Probably from the lack of sleep and the stress of dealing with my brother's death.

I look back down at my frame. Notice that I've lost weight everywhere except for my chest. I have huge boobs. They seem even bigger now that the rest of me is slimmer. I've been big-busted since I was fifteen, and my breasts are not my favorite attribute. Men leer. It's what they see first when I walk into a room. I was teased relentlessly at school. Truth is, they're not as great as smaller-chested women think. I would have made them smaller by now if I'd had the money.

I don't.

I take one last look at my reflection. Why did I wear the red lipstick? I should have gone with something more subtle. Less 'out there.' I feel underdressed and exposed even though I'm not. This is how Herms makes me feel. I'm reminded of the looks my boss has given me in the not too distant past. The flirtatious remarks he's made. He's asked me out twice, which must be against a whole lot of company policies. I guess the owner of the casino is above red tape. I'm not interested. The knot in my stomach tightens. I pull in a deep breath as the elevator dings to alert me that we have reached the top floor.

It's beautiful. I've never been up here before. I stop and take in the stylish finishes. No expense was spared, that much is clear. The artwork is bold. I know nothing about any of this, but I know money when I see it. This must have cost a fortune. *Why am I here? What does Herms want with me?* I'm essentially a nobody. At least, that's what I am to him. The same questions roll around in my head over and over.

Why?

"Ahhh…Miss Jones," a clear voice chimes out. There is a woman sitting behind a large desk. She looks to be in her late thirties. Maybe even early forties. It's hard to tell. She is elegant, stylish and quite beautiful. I can't believe I didn't see her sitting there.

"Mr Herms is expecting you, you can head right in." She gestures towards a closed door.

I swallow a lump down. It doesn't budge. My hands feel sweaty and my mouth is dry. I knock once and enter when I don't hear anything…or in this instance…anyone. Herms is sitting behind his desk.

"Good morning," I manage to get out.

He leans back. It looks like he is taking me in, his eyes drifting down and then back up my body in a quiet perusal. His mouth turns up at the corners, not quite making a smile. His eyes glint. "Come in and close the door behind you."

I pull in a steadying breath and do what he asks, feeling anything but steady.

"Sit down, Miss Jones." He glances at one of the chairs across the desk from him.

Again, I do as he says. I don't lean back or make myself comfortable in any way. I fold my hands across my lap, keeping my eyes on the man in front of me.

"Would you like something to drink? A coffee? A water maybe?"

"No, thank you." I want to know why I am here. I don't like the way he is looking at me. I don't like this horrible feeling that keeps growing inside me. If I'm honest, it started on the pavement in front of Bruce's apartment. A disquiet. A turbulence. I told myself it was grief, frustration, and loss. Although I have felt all of these things, this feeling I have has nothing to do with any of them.

His eyes hold mine for what feels like the longest time. I have to force myself to hold my tongue. Force myself not to squirm.

Herms pushes out a breath and clasps his hands under his chin. His elbows are resting on the table. I am struck at how big he is. How imposing. It feels like my chair is lower than his. Like I'm sitting on the ground. My face feels warm. I lick my lips, wishing I'd accepted his offer of water.

"We have business to discuss, Ava."

Business? Why in the world would we discuss business? I frown. "What kind of business, Mr Herms? My shift started ten minutes ago. I need to get back." I try not to sound rude.

"Your colleagues will cover for you." He lowers his hands, leaning back once more. His eyes looking me over in a way that makes my skin crawl. They linger on my chest and then my lips; he seems to catch himself, lifting them to my eyes. Herms smiles. "Don't look so anxious. So ready to run away. I'm not going to bite."

Bite.

He's my boss. He shouldn't be saying things like that to me.

"Let me cut to the chase, Ava. Did you know that your brother worked for me?"

I suck in a deep breath. I'm shocked. "You own a courier company?"

Herms laughs. He shakes his head, still looking amused. "Bruce did courier work for me, but to answer your question, no, I don't own a courier company."

"He worked for the casino?" That makes even less sense. I would have known if Bruce was on the payroll, wouldn't I?

"No." His response is curt. "I run several operations. My father always taught me never to put all my eggs in one basket. He delivered packages and I paid him."

"What kind of packages?"

"Let's not get into that, shall we?" He winks at me. He's still smiling, only it's turned tight. A touch nasty.

"Why am I here? Why are you telling me all of this?" Anger and irritation lace my voice, but it can't be helped.

"About a week before his suicide..."

I wince. It's still hard to hear it. *Suicide.* My baby brother took his own life. It hurts to hear the word out loud. Hurts more than I thought possible.

"...Bruce lost one of those packages. He never turned up at the drop-off point."

"What was in the package? How did he lose it and what does any of this have to do with me?" I push my chair back, about to get up.

"I don't know exactly how, and I don't care." His voice has lowered about a hundred octaves. "Bruce owes me twenty-K."

My blood is running colder and colder with every rapid beat of my heart. "Twenty thousand dollars?" I gasp the words. "That's insane." I can hardly breathe.

"Insane but true. Now I'm left with a very real dilemma."

"What dilemma would that be?" I have to work to keep my voice even. Panic is creeping in.

"I need payback, Ava. I need something in return for what was lost. Like I said when you first came into my office, we have to talk business."

"Bruce is gone, Mr Herms. He's dead. Your money is gone." I shrug. "I'm not sure what there is to talk about. Your business was with him. This has nothing to do with me."

"You're his only living relative?" He raises his brows

to show that he's asking a question, even though it's clearly rhetorical.

I don't answer.

"You are his only living relative, am I right, Ava?" His voice turns hard.

"Yes," I push out.

He smiles for a second. "Then the debt has now landed solidly on your shoulders. We both know that his junkie girlfriend will be no use whatsoever. You are it. All he has."

I snort out a laugh, even though I am feeling absolutely no humor right now. At this moment it is difficult to comprehend that I will ever feel the emotion again. "This is a load of bullshit. Prove that he lost this package. Prove that the package was worth as much as you say it was. None of this will hold in court. You have nothing on me."

"I don't give a shit about the law...or the justice system, or any of that nonsense. Your brother lost twenty K. Debt like that doesn't just go away. My investors are out for blood. They want me to hand them your head on a silver tray. An example needs to be made."

I take a steadying breath, trying to calm my racing heart. What the hell did Bruce get himself into? What did he get *me* into? I believe the man in front of me. It's all making sense. The way Lee looked at Herms that day. The terror in her eyes. She *did* recognize him. She had met him before. "Investors?' I furrow my brow. "My head? What kind of an investor would want my head?" There's no doubt in my mind that he's talking about my actual head.

"The Russian mafia. I can't get more specific than that.

They want their product…package…or they want cold, hard cash. Failing those two things, they want your head on a—"

"I got that part!" I blurt out.

"Good girl. I was right about you…you're not just tits and ass. There's a brain in there as well."

I want to tell him to go to hell, but I force the words back down instead. "What now?" I'm wracking my brain. "I have about three, maybe four thousand in my savings account." I chew on my lip. "My mother left a trust for Bruce and me, but I can't take the money out. Maybe I can find a way to—"

"Stop right there."

"You said you needed money." I lick my lips, still trying to come up with a plan. "I might be able to get it for you." I sigh deeply. "I'll need a couple of months. Worst case scenario, if they won't let me withdraw my trust, it'll take a year or two. I'll have to pay you every month." Only if I live in a dive and eat noodles. I'll do it though. I'll do anything to sort this out. "But I'll pay you back every cent. We can agree on terms and interest and—"

He's laughing. The bastard has thrown his head back and is laughing…loudly. "You are funny, Ava." He turns deadpan. "You have three days."

My whole body goes numb. The air catches in my lungs. I want to say something… anything…but I can't. My mouth opens and closes a few times like a dying fish.

He holds up his fingers, just in case I can't count. "Three days or—"

"It's impossible!" I snap. I'm pissed. *What a dick. 'Talk business,' my ass.* "I will never have that much money in three days. I need longer. Give me two weeks."

"You don't have longer." His eyes are glinting. He's loving this. He's getting off on the whole thing. "You have three days. That's more than most people would get. You're lucky."

Lucky? Not hardly. "It's impossible," I shrug, stating the obvious. What else is there to say?

"Unless…" he smiles. It's a smile that turns heads. I've seen it firsthand. A smile that melts panties. Not mine. Not even close.

I fold my arms across my chest and narrow my eyes. "Unless what?" My voice is devoid of emotion.

"Unless you want to negotiate an arrangement." His eyes are glinting again. They're focused on me.

"What arrangement?" I practically spit the words out at him because I know exactly where this is going. *The bastard!*

"I'm sure we can come up with something." He winks.

"I don't think so," I answer immediately, shaking my head.

"I *do* think so, Ava. In fact, I don't think you have too much of a choice."

"What arrangement?" I ask again. I want him to spell it out for me. "I'm not agreeing to anything until I know exactly what it is you're referring to."

"One night, Ava. I want one night with you. I'll pay your debt the morning after."

And there it is. "By 'one night,' you mean…"

"I want to fuck you. A good couple of times…just so we're clear." He licks his lips.

It feels like I've been sucker-punched. I can't believe what I am hearing, even though I'd almost anticipated the proposal. "Why?" I splutter the word. "Why would you be remotely interested?" I'm not bad-looking but I'm nothing like the women he normally dates, and I use the term 'dates' loosely. "There is a whole line of eager women out there. Willing women." I was sure I'd seen a picture of him in one of the magazines with a movie star just the other day. I can't remember her name. Point being, this man can have any woman he wants... Almost any woman. "It doesn't make any kind of sense that you would be interested in a nobody like me."

"That's just it." He leans back and scrutinizes me all over again. "You're not affected by me like most other women. It's a strange concept to me. One I find oddly fascinating. You are an attractive girl. You interest me, Ava, and I want to fuck you. I also want to help you, so this would be a win-win. That's all there is to it."

Talk about being straightforward. *Win-win, my ass.* "Not going to happen."

"Are you sure about that? You have a pretty head, but it won't look so great once it's been hacked off your shoulders."

"I'll come up with a plan." I'm reeling at his words, but I don't let it show.

He raises his brows. "Do tell how you expect to get that right."

"None of your business. You told me I have three days and I plan to use them." I have absolutely no idea how to come up with that kind of money in such a short timeframe. I don't know anyone who will be able to help me. In short, I'm in trouble. Deep, deep trouble.

Oh, Bruce! What did you do? What were you thinking? No wonder my brother took his own life. His letter of apology is beginning to make sense now. Did he know they were going to come after me? Anger welled all over again. Anger and sorrow.

"You can take the three days. I don't have a problem with that, but know that when your time runs out, you will need to come up with the goods." He smiles, his gaze dropping back to my cleavage. "And unless you want to die, I expect you in my bed and willing. Do you understand me?"

"You mean with a pretense of willingness, Mr Herms?"

"You can call me Sly. If we're going to be fucking, we may as well get over the formalities, don't you think?" I hate how he has already dismissed the possibility of me ever finding my way out of this.

"Now I know how you earned the nickname 'Sly.' You have money enough to help me, but you choose to take this route."

"Sly is my actual name. It's English, inherited from my great-grandfather, Sylvester. I don't give handouts, Ava. It's not my style. In most instances, I wouldn't intervene, but I like you. Bottom line, you have something I want. I can help you, and in more ways than one. I'm a decent fuck. You would enjoy yourself, I assure you."

"I sincerely doubt it. The name suits you down to a T, by the way. Now if you'll excuse me, I have a job to do." I rise from my seat.

"Three days and not a second more."

"I'll have your money." I make sure I sound calm and assured. I'm freaking out inside.

"Twenty-two large, Ava."

"Twenty-two?" I gasp. *What the hell?*

"Interest, babes." He winks at me. "There's nothing I can do about it."

Like hell there's nothing he can do. *Like hell!* I pull my shoulders back and lift my chin. "I'll have the money." I walk out of his office wondering how I'm going to get through my shift. I will have to act like everything is hunky-dory when in reality it is the furthest thing from the truth.

There is no way I'm coming up with twenty-two thousand dollars, in cash, in three days. There is also no way I am ever going to whore myself to pay off the debt. I'm in a whole lot of hot water. I'd better figure something out fast or I'll be fish food.

CHAPTER 3

AVA

Three weeks later

This can't be happening.

I hit my hand against the steering wheel, feeling the rounded surface jam into my hand. How stupid to have lashed out so hard. Now my hand is going to be bruised, and my car still won't start. Although it's futile to try, I turn the key one more time.

Nothing.

Even the strange ticking noise from before is gone. The engine is dead. There's irony there that is not lost on me. I can't help the groan that is pulled from me as I slump forward, putting my forehead against my throbbing hand, which is still resting on the steering wheel. *What now?* The only saving grace is that I managed to pull over as this hunk of metal was dying, coughing and spluttering. Otherwise, I would have been stuck in the middle of the road, horns blaring behind me. My poor car. She's never let me down.

There is a crumpled fifty-dollar bill in my pocket…and that's it. It's done. I'm done. The chase is over. Maybe I should wait right here for Sly Herms to find me. He almost had me nine days ago, and then again two days back. I'm still not sure how I got away. He's close. Right behind me. Has been the whole time. I don't know how he does it. It's like he can read my mind.

I'm exhausted. Bone weary. There's a part of me that's happy this is finally over. It's the part of me that makes me want to close my eyes right here and right now. Sleep until he catches me. I stifle a yawn. Thankfully, there's a bigger part of me that refuses to give up. I need to get my car off the street. I need—

My eyes catch a sign across the road. *Dragon Customs.* Above the sign is a vehicle. I rub my eyes and look again. Yes, a car is on the roof of the building. It must have been hoisted there with a crane. It's an older model sedan. *A Cadillac, maybe?* I don't know cars, so I don't know the make or model. It's fancy. It's been resprayed in gorgeous royal blue paint with a fire-breathing dragon painted on the side. I don't know much about paintjobs either, but it's a masterpiece. A work of art, if ever I saw one. Whoever painted the metallic surface is talented. They've enhanced the raw strength and beauty of the beast in a way that is uncanny. The blue contrasts with the creature's iridescent scales. The rims are shiny silver. It looks like the leather interior is a bright red. *Wow!* Just wow. I gape for a few seconds.

Then I pull myself together. This is no time to sit and gawk. If they customize vehicles, perhaps they can fix mine. I'm sure some of the vintage models need repairs as well as pimping? Not that I would be able to pay them to help me. I doubt fifty bucks will go very far. I unbuckle my seatbelt and get out of my car. My mind is racing. I have to come up with a plan. I keep hitting blanks. I don't have any choice, I need to head over there and try my luck. There's nothing else to it. I push the button to lock the vehicle and walk the short distance across the road.

A part of me is afraid of hitting another dead-end, but I have to try. At the very least, maybe someone working there will be willing to help me get my car off the street. Maybe Sly will think I drove straight through this town. I didn't catch the name on the way in. Despite it being a fair size, I had actually planned to drive right on through, on account of that bastard being right on my tail. Hopefully, he won't know I'm stuck here. At least for a short while. I'll be able to figure something out. I can't give up. I refuse. It doesn't matter how tired I am. How sick I am of running. I *will* keep going. Sly will have to hack my head off himself. I am still shocked that he has come after me himself. I had expected him to send a bunch of his goons, but he hasn't. It's him. Just him. On his own.

Hunting me.

I shiver and pull in a deep breath, trying to calm my nerves. "Here goes nothing," I mutter as I open the front door to the shop. An old-fashioned bell tinkles as I enter. The receptionist is nothing like I expected, and yet she's perfect. She's wearing a pencil-skirt with a white tank top. Her heels have red polka dots on them. They match her lips, which are red as well. Her blond hair is in a bun at the back of her head. Her glasses are thick-rimmed tortoiseshell. Her left arm is covered in tattoos. An entire sleeve of swirling colors. I try not to stare but I can't help it. She's beautiful.

"Hi." She smiles, lifting her brows. "Can I help you?" She cocks her head, looking at me like I don't quite belong. Like I shouldn't be here. Not the normal clientele…and she's right.

I'm wearing daisy dukes and a pink t-shirt. Bright pink. They're the only items of clothing I have left that are clean. My flip-flops are red. My hair is in a messy ponytail. Emphasis on 'messy.' I washed it in a basin this morning. There was no time to brush it. I had to choose between my hair and my teeth, and you can tell which won out by looking at me. In short, I'm a hot mess.

"I need help," I blurt. "I'm stuck. Broken down…just across the road actually…" I giggle. It's what I do sometimes when I'm nervous. That and talk. Way too much. "My name is Ava and I'm…I need to move my car. Actually," I widen my eyes, "I need to *fix* my car, but I need to move it first. I need help with that and the fixing part too." I giggle again sounding like a complete idiot. I want to keep talking but I manage to shut my mouth and keep it that way.

The other woman smiles. It's not a condescending or an unkind smile. There is pity there. I can already tell that she's going to turn me down. "We're not a towing company," she shakes her head, "and although we do have a repairs division it's not our main focus. We're body repair specialists. I would be happy to sit down with you…" She gestures to a table and chairs to the side of the room. "We can discuss options for your ride. I'm talking interior and exterior from sound systems to —"

"No…" I shake my head and push out a heavy breath. "I'm not looking for anything like that. Actually, a paint job would be fantastic." I giggle…again. *What the hell is wrong with me?* "I drive a Hyundai Elantra." What's that you say? How is Sly able to spot me so easily if I'm in such a popular vehicle? One that should blend in. The answer to that question is easy. "It's mustard yellow," I mumble. "Like baby poop," I add unnecessarily. "I got the car for a steal. This couple bought it for their daughter who happened to love the color. That was, until she saw her new car. The little princess quickly changed her mind. Mustard color does not work for a car." I shake my head. "They put it on the market but—surprise, surprise – there were no takers. I don't think anyone wanted a baby poop-colored car." I giggle for the umpteenth time. "Anyway, I needed to get from A to B and didn't care about that…at the time." I care now. Boy, do I ever. A yellow car. May as well have a neon sign with an arrow pointing straight at me. "I wish I hadn't bought it." It hurts me to say, because I love my car.

The other woman cracks a smile. There is genuine humor there this time. "You've come to the right place. Let's sit down and—"

My shoulders slump and I shake my head. "I won't be able to afford a paint job. My car broke down. I need it fixed. Please help me. It's just outside." I point in the direction I just came from, and if you look out the window, you can see Miss Sunshine. Yes, I named my car Miss Sunshine. There's nothing wrong with trying to make the most out of things. "Please," I add, holding her stare.

She purses her lips, then sighs. "I'm going to take serious flack for agreeing to take this on." She chews the top of her pen. "I'll make an exception just this once. I'm Susan..." She holds out her hand.

I take it and shake. "Good to meet you." I pull my bottom lip between my teeth. "I don't have any money." I may as well get that part out of the way too. "That's not true, I have fifty bucks but I'm guessing that won't be enough. Also, if I give you my last fifty, I would have to sleep in my car tonight."

Susan's face falls and her eyes cloud. "Can't help you then." She looks at me with big blue eyes and they're filled with concern. "I'm really sorry, Ava...you did say your name was Ava, right? We don't take on charity cases."

"Yes, I'm Ava." I nod, "Please...I'm desperate. We can negotiate a deal." Now I'm sounding like Sly. "I can work for you guys or...I can pay you off or something. An 'I owe you.' I always pay my debts."

"I don't mean to be callous but what about that?" She looks down at my hand where I am fiddling with my ring.

On instinct, I snatch my hand behind my back. "No. That's not for sale."

"Pity." She licks her lips. "If that thing's real, you would have enough for repairs and a paint job, as well as a whole month, or more, in a great hotel—"

"Not happening. It's sentimental." I twist the ring around and around. It belonged to my mom. She left it to me when she passed. Said it was from my father. I never met him. It meant so much to my mom that she never took it off, which was lucky, since Bruce took everything in her jewelry box. This is it, all I have left of her, of my dad. My eyes prick and my throat clogs. I mustn't cry. *Don't damn well cry.* I'm don't want pity. I don't want handouts, but I need a lifeline here. "I'll work for you for the next few days. I'm strong and willing and—"

"Can you operate a spray gun?"

I shake my head.

She narrows her eyes. "You aren't a seamstress, by any chance? Can you work with leather?"

"No." I shake my head some more. "I'm afraid not," I mumble.

"Artist?" She raises her brows. "The kind that paints or does graffiti?"

"I can carry five plates of food all at once?" It's true. I might even be able to carry six.

She frowns and shakes her head.

"I can mix a mean martini?" I force a smile. "Three olives?"

She shakes her head again, still not caving.

"I can carry twelve Cosmopolitans on a round tray without spilling so much as a drop."

Susan looks impressed, she even nods her head. "That takes talent, but not the kind we're looking for here. I'm sorry—"

"I'm lucky! My clients call me their lucky charm." I'm reaching here. Reaching big time.

She looks at me like I've lost my mind. Considering my current circumstances, I doubt I look lucky at all. I certainly don't feel it.

"Call your boss," I push out, sounding desperate. "Please. I'll sweep. I'll cook. I'll... Just please call your boss."

She chokes out a laugh. "Not a good idea."

"Please," I beg. I'm not beyond begging. "Even if you just helped me move my car. Somewhere off the street. Maybe into the alley...or an underground parking lot. Please help me with that at least."

She cocks an eyebrow. "Husband or boyfriend?"

"I don't know what you're —"

"Who's after you? Is it the husband or the boyfriend? Let me guess, he laid into you one time too many and you finally left his ass. Good for you! I like guts. You have guts. It took guts coming in here."

"Will you help me then, please?" I'll take it. I'm winning her over, I can tell!

"I would help you..." She nods.

Yes!

I release a shuddery breath. I sense a 'but.' "You would help me...?"

"But...that's the problem. There's a 'but.'"

I knew it!

"I don't make the decisions around here. You would need to speak to Forge and, like I said, I wouldn't go there if I were you. You'd be better off taking your chances with your ex than heading into the workshop." She points at a door. It has a bright red stamped sign on it that reads 'No Entry! Try me! I will hurt you!.'

I feel my mouth twitch. "You can't be serious?"

"I am. He's not much of a 'people person.'" She grimaces. "I doubt he'll agree to tow your ride. As I said, we aren't into that."

"He can't be that bad." I shake my head.

She chuckles. "Not that bad? Going in there would be

like waking up a hibernating bear. You have guts, girl, but that would be plain stupid."

I square my shoulders. I have two choices – going back out on the street to face Sly, or waking a bear. I've always loved animals. We get along just fine. "I'll take my chances with the bear," I say, sounding more confident than I feel.

"I like you." Susan winks at me. "Good luck." She gestures to the door. "Don't tell me I didn't warn you."

It can't be that bad.

He can't be that bad.

Can he?

FORGE

Mmmmm! Something smells fucking delicious out front, which is weird since Susan doesn't have much of a sweet tooth. My receptionist-slash-assistant isn't much of a baker either. Butter cookies with…I sniff once or twice…with a hint of chocolate and syrup maybe. They smell fresh. Delicious. My stomach grumbles as I put down the spanner. My dick stirs as well, which is an odd reaction to have to food. Then again, I haven't fucked anyone in a while. It's been a good couple of weeks…make that months since I scratched that particular itch. Too long, apparently, because now my dick is hard for baked goods.

I shake my head and wipe my hands on a nearby towel. They leave grease smears on the cotton. The air-conditioning unit isn't working in the workshop. Susan has called the maintenance company responsible for my building. Until they get here, it's a fucking furnace. I growl low in irritation as I peel off my coveralls and tie the sleeves around my waist. The white tank underneath is plastered to my skin. With no coverall, it's bound to get dirty to the point of no return, but I don't care. It's better than the alternative, namely dying from heatstroke. Sweat drips from my brow. If it gets any worse, I'm going to have to lose the coveralls completely.

I can hear my guys in the workshop next to mine. There's the whir of a spray gun. The clanging of tools against metal. They're grumbling about the heat as well. We're all feeling it.

Why the separate workspaces, you ask? Simple, I do my best work alone. I take on the more difficult custom jobs. I take my time. I don't like banter. I detest small talk. I'm a grumpy motherfucker who would disrupt the good mood and camaraderie that most employees thrive on. So, here I am, alone…just the way I like it.

The door to my workshop opens. Interruption normally irritates the shit out of me but this time it's welcome. All I can think is 'thank fuck!' "The air conditioner is through here." I point up at the ceiling without looking at the repair guys. Several large fans span across both workspaces. My voice is deep and rasping. Probably from disuse. "Don't dawdle!" I snarl, grabbing a dead blow hammer. It's big. Bigger than most. I had it custom-made along with a couple of other tools in my shop. I'm large myself. Six and a half feet of raw muscle. I'm stronger than most so I need a hammer that's bigger than the norm.

I'm about to get to work on the body of a gorgeous — at least she will be when I'm done with her – '66

Mustang, when I hear the door click shut. Another whiff of cookies hits me deep in the snout. My cock twitches. *The fuck?*

I turn my gaze to the person who has just walked through the door. It's not a maintenance guy. Not even fucking close. It's a woman, and she's wearing a tiny pair of shorts. Her legs go on for miles. *What the hell is she doing here!?*

"Lost?" I grumble, frowning hard.

Her eyes widen. They're a hazel color and framed by thick lashes. "You *are* a bear… she was right." At least, I think that's what she said. On account of that's a weird thing to say. "A ginger bear…" she giggles. "That's one heck of a big hammer you have there." She looks at the tool in my hand. She giggles again and the sound shoots straight down my spinal cord and into my cock. My balls pull tight.

Big. Hammer.

Um… yes!

Irritation flares. "Get out! No customers are allowed through here!" I point at the door, using my dead blow.

"That's just it… I'm not a customer. I want to be but I… you see… I'm in a pickle…" She licks her lips. They're full and pink. Lush as fuck. More irritation rushes through me, along with a healthy dose of desire. Humans don't normally have this effect on me. I'm thankful my coveralls are tied over my front because my cock is rock hard. If she thinks the dead blow hammer in my hands is big, well, she ain't seen nothing yet.

"Susan!" I yell. This woman has to go, and she has to go right now!

She holds up both hands, like she's trying to placate

me. "Susan knows I'm here. She said I should chat with you." She advances. Her scent grows stronger. I can't help but pull in a lungful. I want to groan. My mouth waters for a taste.

She's more than likely ovulating. I am part beast after all. There is a large part of me that is governed by instincts. There is an underlying need to procreate. Most days I embrace the beast. Some days, though, it irritates the fuck out of me! Good thing I'm only part beast. Not the bigger part. I am able to resist. Having to push the urge aside pisses me off.

"You see, I..." she goes on, still advancing.

"Get! Out!" I all but snarl. "I'm trying to work. Susan... what the fuck!" I growl.

I expect the waif of a human to clamber back. To leave as quickly as possible. I half expect her to piss herself or to shriek, but that doesn't happen either. She frowns and takes another step towards me. *Towards* me. Does she have a death wish? Not that I would actually kill her, but she doesn't know that. I'm huge. I have a beard. I'm covered in tats. Then there's the hammer in my fist and the fact that my voice is sounding part beast right about now. Most humans sense danger and run. Not this one.

I don't seem to deter her in the least. Her frown deepens. "You're being rude. You shouldn't speak to a customer that way." She's berating me. Me! *Fuck!* My dick goes ballistic. People don't stand up to me. They cry. They run. They even beg. Not this tiny human. She holds my gaze. She looks angry. She even puts her hands on her hips.

I drop the hammer on my work table and the little human flinches when it clangs. Not completely unaffected then. I cross my arms, which I know will make my chest look huge in the white tank. My arms bulge with thick, corded muscle. "You just told me you weren't a customer. You have ten seconds to tell me who you are and what you want before I physically remove you from my premises." I take a step towards her, but she holds her ground.

"I need help. My car broke down just outside—"

"I can't help you!"

She blinks. "What? Please… it wouldn't take much of—"

"Susan will give you the numbers of several towing companies. One of them…"

She's shaking her head. Her eyes look huge and haunted. For just a second I'm tempted to help her. *What the fuck?*

No!

I won't do it!

This is probably just a ruse. Pretty lady. Short shorts. Tight T. Wide, innocent-looking eyes. No make-up and messy hair just to throw me off. Like she isn't trying. To make this whole ploy look authentic. *Nope!* I'm not buying it. There is a waiting list as long as both my arms and my dick combined – about a fucking mile long—of people hoping to get their vehicles under my nose. Hell, there's a guy from Germany and two from England on that waiting list. I have the luxury of being able to choose which jobs I take on. "Susan will help you," I insist.

"There's no time. I need my car off that street in the next ten minutes. It might even be too late already," she mutters more to herself. "I need it fixed but I don't have any money. I'm desperate. We can negotiate a deal."

A deal.

My cock likes the idea. My eyes drift down to her chest for half a second before I realize what I'm doing. Checking her out. *Fuck! No!* I don't work that way.

"Not that kind of deal." Her eyes blaze. I don't blame her for being angry. "What is it with you men? There's more to me than what's between my legs." Her chest is heaving. Her jaw is tight.

"I don't want to fuck you." My cock disagrees but he can go to hell. I don't fuck clients. Hell, I don't even meet them... ever. I also don't fuck women I know. Only strangers. Not that often either. They're nameless faces. Quick meaningless encounters. We get each other off. I leave. End of story. "We're not that kind of establishment," I add.

"I didn't mean it like that." She looks completely flabbergasted. "Look, forget about it. Susan was right, coming in here was like waking up a hibernating bear." She turns around before turning back to face him. "No... it was worse. It was like waking up a hibernating bear with a sore tooth and an attitude that stinks. I'm sorry I bothered you. I'll get out of your beard now so that you can get back to being an ornery asshole. Have a wonderful life being a dick to everyone. While I'm at it, have you ever heard of helping a person out? Helping a fellow human in need? Of being kind? What's that...?" She puts a hand up to her ear. "No! That's what I thought." She gives a cute little snort and walks out, leaving a cloud of cookie scent in her wake.

I choke out a laugh as soon as the door slams shut. It's filled with disbelief. No one has ever spoken to me like that and lived. No... make that, no one had ever spoken to me like that, period. The smile soon fades.

Susan sticks her head around the jamb. "I tried to warn her." She shakes her head.

"Don't you ever pull a stunt like—" I begin. The air conditioners spark back to life out of nowhere.

What the — ?

I look up and—yep—the fans are all turning again. How it happened I don't know.

"That's a bit of luck," Susan says. "Shall I cancel the callout?"

"Let them come and check just to be sure," I say. I shake my head. "Don't you ever send a—"

Susan looks sheepish. "Yeah, yeah, I won't... it's just that she seemed like she really needed a helping hand. I suspect she has a hothead boyfriend after her. She has guts and I don't know her, but I like her. Are you going to help?"

"What do you think?" I growl.

Her face falls. Susan and I have known each other our entire lives. She knows my answer. "I'll leave you to get back to work."

CHAPTER
4

AVA

Shit!

Shit!

Shit!

What now? What the hell am I going to do? I need to get out of here, that's what. I don't have money to buy a ticket, so I need to hitch a ride, which is crazy. Stark raving mad! Completely nuts! My mother taught me never to hitchhike. She said I might end up dead in a ditch. Guess what? If I stay anywhere near Miss Sunshine, I will be dead anyway. So, I decide to throw caution to the wind. After quickly packing the essentials into a bag, and with a sigh, leaving the rest locked in the trunk, I start walking. I have to stay on the main road if I want to catch a ride. The hairs on the back of my neck are standing on end. Sly could come by at any moment. Hopefully, someone will stop soon. It's my only hope. I hold my breath every time a car passes by. I'm worried they might stop *and* I'm worried that they won't.

I still can't believe that guy. What an asshat. Chivalry is not only dead but rotten and buried as well. *Unbelievable!* That guy could've towed my car in ten minutes flat. Heck, he could have picked up my Elantra and carried it into the alley himself. The big meanie is huge. His muscles have muscles. Pity he's all brawn. There's not a kind bone in his body.

I hear a car slowing. Yep, definitely about to stop. My heart is racing. I swallow hard, wanting to run for it. If it's Sly, I might be able to get away if I head back in the other direction.

My heart is pounding when I turn to see who it is. A pick-up. *Phew!* Sly wouldn't be seen dead in an old, rusty pick-up. I can't believe it when I see a little old lady behind the wheel. I can't help smiling at her open, friendly face.

"Hello, little Missy." She peers over at me.

"Hi." I wave, leaning down so that I can see her better.

"What's a lovely young lady like you doing hitching a ride? Didn't anyone ever tell you it's dangerous?" Her eyes are wide.

"I know, but my car broke down and I can't… I need to be somewhere," I finally say. I don't want to admit that I'm practically broke and can't afford repairs.

"Hop in." She gestures to the seat next to her.

My mood instantly brightens. "Are you headed out of town?"

She smiles and shakes her head. "Nope, but you look

like you could use a hot meal. I'll get my grandson, Jacob, to fetch your vehicle. You can point it out before we go. He and Samuel can tow it up to our place. We're on the edge of town. Those boys are mighty good at fixing things. I'll bet they have your car running again in no time."

I burn to accept her hospitality. I ache to... but I can't. It would mean putting this sweet old lady and her family in danger. I look up and then down the street. I see nothing out of the ordinary. A couple of hours, what could it hurt? I need this. A break. One little break.

Arghhhh!

I can't do it.

I smile. It hurts to do it because all I want to do is cry. I smile anyway because I have to. Anything less would be rude. It would mean I'm giving into self-pity and I refuse. "Thank you so very much for the offer. I can't tell you how much it means to me, but I can't. I need to keep moving. Like I said, I have somewhere I need to be."

She frowns. "Are you sure? A few hours won't make too much of a difference." My thoughts exactly. "Besides, you'll have your car back."

I pull in a deep breath. I have to stick to my guns. "I can't. I can't tell you how much I appreciate it, but I just can't." My eyes well with tears.

She looks at me for a few long moments before finally nodding once. "All the best, darlin.' Trust your gut. If it feels wrong," she narrows her eyes, "it probably is." Someone blows their horn behind us. "Oh, hang onto your hat!" she yells, flapping her hand at whoever it is making a fuss.

"Thank you. I will." My smile widens. I feel a little

better. She waves as she pulls off. I'm grateful to know that there are good people in this world.

I get going. That eerie feeling of being watched hits me all over again. Goosebumps rise and the hairs on the back of my neck stand up once more. I realize that there more than likely isn't anyone there. It's my overactive imagination. I hope. I put out my thumb to indicate I need a ride and keep walking. The bag on my shoulder is already feeling heavy. I'm hungry and thirsty but the need to get out of town is more important than stopping for supplies. Besides, I need to watch my limited resources. Maybe ditching Miss Sunshine wasn't a bad idea. I just wish I'd had enough time to sell her rather than leaving her out there in the road. I feel a pang.

I hear a vehicle slowing. I pray that this person is actually leaving town and not about to offer me a meal. I smile as I turn—

Fuck!

My heart slams in my chest. *Fuuuuck!!* I may have actually screamed that out loud. Sly grins at me. "Get in, babe," he says, as if meeting me in the street like this was part of the plan. I'm shocked all over again at how normal he looks... for a cold-blooded killer.

I drop my bag on the sidewalk, turn and run. The street is fairly busy. It will take him half a minute to turn and come after me. I'm about to duck down a side alley when I see him. The asshole Grizzly bear. He has my car on a flat-bed. I've been gone for all of five minutes and he's got Miss Sunshine. I should head in the other direction, get the hell out of Dodge, but I don't. There is a good chance Sly will find me regardless of where I go and what I do. I'm beginning to see that. I won't stand a chance if I'm on my own. I might just live for one more day if I'm with Grizzly bear over there. The big meanie owes me for trying to steal my car. Because that's what he's doing. He's taking her. I pick up speed and arrive just as he's giving the side of my Elantra a double-tap with his fist, showing that she's secured and ready to go.

"What do you think you're doing?" I blurt, sounding annoyed. I hadn't meant to say that. I need him to help me. Not antagonize him.

"What does it look like?' he barks, eyes narrowed on me.

It looks like he's stealing my car. *The bastard.* I can't say any of that. "I'm not entirely sure," I answer. It's not the most intelligent of comebacks. In fact, it isn't much of a comeback at all, but a killer is literally right behind me, so cut a girl a break.

As if on cue, I hear the soft purr of a sports car. *Sly!* My hackles go up. Without giving it any thought, I sidle up to the Grizzly bear. I get close, putting my back to him so that I can watch Sly. He grins at us. *Asshole!* And parks his fancy car.

"Is this the bozo who's been giving you trouble?" the bear asks.

"Yes," I squeak, since my throat is closing. My hands are shaking. This wasn't a good idea. I'm putting this hulk of a man in danger. It doesn't matter how big and scary he is, he won't be able to stand up to the likes of Sly. Not if the casino owner and shady business dealer is carrying a gun, which I suspect he is. He deals with the Russian mob, for god's sake. Not that I know much about the Russian mob, mind you, but I'm sure they're bad people.

"I… I… should go…" I stammer as Sly gets out of the car. He's taking his sweet time, like he knows my number is up. He doesn't seem to have a care in the world and isn't worried about the massive man at my side. This isn't going to end well for either of us.

I start to turn to run but the Grizzly takes my arm. "Stay put! I've got this." His voice is still a deep rasp but it's also reassuring. "Susan told me about your boyfriend troubles. You don't mind if I hurt him?" His voice turns… it turns… chilling.

I can tell it isn't really a question, but I shake my head anyway. "He's bad news," I whisper, since Sly is almost here. "Careful," I add.

The bear gives a soft snort, which tells me he is underestimating Sly. *Shit!*

"Hey, babe." Sly smiles at me. "It's time to go." He winks. The nerve of this man.

"She isn't going anywhere with you."

Sly looks up at the Grizzly. I can't believe he has to look up, since he's one of the tallest guys I know.

I realize that Mean Beard… *Why do I keep making up nicknames for him? I need to stop.* Anyway, I realize that he still has his hand wrapped around my wrist. He is pushing gently, trying to get me to move behind him. I do what he recommends. It would be a bad idea to get between these two.

"Should I call the cops?" Someone leans out of the tow truck. I hadn't even noticed him until now.

"No, I've got this," the Grizzly says, cool as a cucumber. "Stay in the truck." His voice holds a warning.

"Rather call an ambulance," Sly smirks, not taking his eyes off Grizzly. "For him…" He nods at Mean Beard.

"The girl is mine," he adds, his face becoming serious.

"Not according to her," Grizzly states. "You should get back into your car and head back to whatever hole you crawled out of."

"I'm not leaving without her. She. Is. Mine."

"I'm not yours," I interject. My voice is laced with frustration. Sly ignores me flat, keeping his stare on the Grizzly. "I'm giving you one last chance to walk away and to keep out of business that has nothing to do with you." He looks down at himself. "I happen to like this shirt. I wouldn't want to ruin it by getting your blood all over it."

The Grizzly laughs. It's a scary sound. Deep. Harsh. Resonating. "Do you want to go with him?" he asks me.

"No way." My voice is hard and filled with false bravado. Truth is, I'm quaking in my boots for what is about to come. The air is thick with pending violence.

"You heard the lady."

Sly's jaw tightens.

It is astonishing how quickly all hell breaks loose. One second they're talking in an almost cordial fashion and then fists start flying. Sly throws the first punch. Grizzly ducks to the side but Sly's fist still connects with the side of his face. I hear a meaty thud. The Grizzly doesn't make a sound. He doesn't even seem to notice he was just hit. Hard.

Grizzly is quick to retaliate with a punch of his own. Sly dodges and all Grizzly hits is air. Sly is quick with an uppercut that gets Grizzly solidly in the gut. He makes a noise that seems laced with confusion, like maybe he can't believe that he's taken two hits and has yet to land one himself. He's a big guy who fights like he's been in more than a few brawls and yet he's taking blows. I tried to warn him about Sly.

I can see where this is headed. It's not looking good for the Grizzly. Just as I suspected… and yet I'm disappointed. I should take the opportunity to run. Maybe I can still get away. Let Grizzly act as a distraction, even if it just ends up being a minute. It's something. Maybe enough to escape. I should take it.

I can't!

Just like I couldn't put that elderly lady and her family in danger, I can't leave Grizzly to deal with this by himself. A fight that's not even his. Even if he is a dick and a car thief… maybe a car thief. I guess he could have changed his mind about helping me. It looks that way. He is fighting on my behalf. Bleeding for me, so I have to stay.

I move further away because I'll be of no use if I get caught in the crossfire and end up injured… or worse. I look around to see if I can find something to use as a weapon. Anything.

There is another meaty thud and Sly grunts loudly. I look up just in time to see his face. It's filled with shock and confusion, like he can't believe he just took a punch. It sounded hard too. He spits out a mouthful of blood. His eyes narrow with rage and he goes at the Grizzly, using his head as a battering ram.

The Grizzly is pushed back a couple of feet. His face pinches with what looks like pain, but he quickly recovers, kneeing Sly on the side of his torso. There's a sickening crack. Did Grizzly just break my ex-boss's ribs?

Sly makes an 'oomph' noise and his eyes widen. He staggers backward. The Grizzly advances, his muscles are bunched. He looks huge. Even bigger than before, which seems impossible but clearly isn't. His muscles must just be pumped from the adrenaline and exertion. I take a few steps back when I see the rage in Grizzly's eyes. Sly rushes to meet him. Despite having broken ribs, he still looks surprisingly fast.

Grizzly takes an uppercut to the chin but doesn't flinch. He retaliates and headbutts Sly… hard. I shudder at the sound of something else cracking. I am also oddly thrilled at the sound. Sly is getting his butt kicked. Holy crap, but Grizzly is strong. Maybe he'll win after all. Maybe I was wrong to dismiss Mean Beard. I feel bad calling him that right now. Even if it is just in my own head.

Sly has a cut on his forehead. It's bleeding into one eye. He's staggering all over the place, looking dazed. His shirt is getting bloodied up alright, just as Sly predicted, but it's not Grizzly's blood. It's his own.

Then my darkest fear becomes a reality. Grizzly is about to go at him again when Sly pulls a gun from the back-waistband of his pants. Sly looks scared. He also looks… shocked. Yep, definitely shocked. I don't think he's used to losing.

I cover my mouth with my hand. I knew it. Men like Sly don't play by the rules. They don't play fair. He's going to make me get in the car with him now. I'll do what he says so that no one gets hurt. It's over for me. After a long hard run, I've lost.

It's the worst thing that could have happened.

The worst.

Sly narrows his eyes on the Grizzly. The noise is deafening as the gun discharges. Blood blossoms on

Grizzly's white tank. He's been hit. Sly shot him! I'm screaming. I can't help it. My hand is still clamped over my mouth.

Shit!

Shit!

Oh, god!

I can't believe it. The circle of blood gets wider and wider, spreading out on the front of his tank. He's going to die and it's all my fault. "No!" I shout, running at Sly. I pummel him with my fists, and he lets me. It's that, or he doesn't notice me.

Suddenly the impossible happens. A fist comes out of nowhere and catches Sly upside the head. A second one lands as I reel back to get out of the way. Sly goes down and the gun clatters across the pavement as he lets it go. Grizzly might be wounded but he doesn't look it. Not at all. He doesn't let up an inch and kicks Sly in the belly. Sly grunts and rolls himself into a ball. Grizzly kicks him again, aiming for his head.

This is where things get weird. I'm still screaming. I'm panicking for sure, but I know what I see. Instead of Grizzly's foot connecting, it keeps on going. The momentum puts Grizzly off-balance and he lands on his ass. Sly is gone. As in *gone!* He's gone. Not there. It sounds insane but he's disappeared into thin air. One second he was there and the next he is gone.

"What the hell!" I yell. "What in...? What?"

I look around us. He can't just be gone. He can't! People don't just disappear.

"The fuck?" Grizzly exclaims as he gets up.

"What just happened?" I ask.

The Grizzly ignores me.

"Speak to me!" I try again, freaking out. "Where did he go? He disappeared."

Still nothing.

"Hey!" I yell, "Bear!" He looks my way. "What just happened?"

He finally seems to see me, looking as shocked as I feel. He's frowning heavily, his eyes darting around the ground and vicinity. "No damned way." He crunches over his middle, looking like he's trying to catch his breath. I know better. He's about to double over. He must be weak from blood loss.

"You're injured." I'm breathing too fast. Still panicking a little. Okay, a lot. Adrenaline is buzzing through my system.

"I'm fine," Grizzly pushes out as he stands to his full height. He turns to the tow truck. "Jarrod." That must be the driver's name. "Call Trident," he commands.

"I already did. Can I get out of the truck now?" he asks, in a mocking voice. "Would that be okay with you, sir?" he adds.

"Don't be a wiseass," Grizzly grunts.

A younger-looking guy gets out of the truck. He's pretty. That's the only way I can describe him. Still baby-faced and very beautiful. It's not often you can say that about a man, especially one that's big and built like Jarrod over here. "Tri should be here in five," he remarks. He doesn't seem the least bit worried about Grizzly, considering he was just shot.

"You need to call an ambulance," I say, sounding normal for a person who just witnessed... *What the hell was that?* "And the cops."

"What just happened?" Jarrod is confused. "Did that guy…?"

"That fucker was fast," Grizzly interrupts, his voice so deep it gives me goosebumps. His eyes are narrowed on Jarrod.

"I'll say." Jarrod shakes his head. It looks like there's a hint of humor in his eyes.

"He wasn't just fast, he disappeared," I add, sounding cynical.

"People don't just disappear." Grizzly looks at me like I've just grown an extra arm.

"I know what I saw." I point at the ground where Sly had been lying just a few minutes ago.

"Nope." Grizzly shakes his head.

"You need to sit down." I'm speaking too quickly. "You've been shot." I stare at the blood on his tank. There's a lot of it. Red on white. Hard to miss.

Grizzly shakes his head. "He missed me."

"He did not miss." I'm yelling a little at this point. "You have a ton of blood on your shirt." I point.

Grizzly shakes his head. "Not my blood."

Am I going mad? "There's a hole in your shirt where the bullet penetrated. Why are you lying about something like that? You need medical help."

"I didn't get shot. Would I be talking to you right now if I had a bullet lodged in my torso?"

"I… I…" I frown. "I guess not." I keep staring at what looks like a bullet hole. I watched the bloodstain grow. "I know what I saw," I mumble, more to myself.

"Jarrod. Get rid of the piece." Grizzly points at the gun on the floor. "I'm sure the cops have been called. I need to get cleaned up." He looks down at himself. "Nothing happened." He looks my way when he says it. "If anyone asks, a vehicle backfired. We'll take care of this internally." He looks back at Jarrod, who nods.

Internally?

What does that even mean?

Crap! Have I just jumped out of the frying pan and landed in the fire? He looks my way, holding my gaze. I nod even though I want to argue. This isn't the time and besides, I'm still in shock. I couldn't call the cops before. I certainly can't go to them now. So, keeping quiet seems like the logical thing to do. No one got hurt. At least, I don't think so. *Where the heck is Sly?*

"Hey…" Grizzly is trying to get my attention. By the look on his face, he's tried a couple of times already. "Good to have you back with us, Oreo. You listening?" he asks me.

"What?" *Did he just call me Oreo?*

"You need to come with me." He points at his shop. "Jarrod, tow the car into my workshop. You will need to hustle," he adds.

Jarrod nods and jumps back into the truck, slamming the door. He starts the engine.

"What did you call me?" I narrow my eyes. The adrenaline must be affecting my hearing.

"Oreo… because you smell like baked goods. I'm thinking cookies." He makes a face like he doesn't care for them.

I look down at myself, uncertain. I even sniff at myself. I don't smell like baked anything. "Don't call me that. My name is Ava."

"Ginger Bear?" He raises his brows. "Don't think I missed that earlier."

My cheeks heat. At least I didn't call him Mean Beard out loud. I fold my arms. "I don't remember your name." I finally admit. "You are a bit like a bear. A grizzly if we're going to be specific. You also happen to have red hair. More coppery than outright red but I guess it's a matter of semantics." I play with my ring trying to stop my mouth from going off.

"And you smell like cookies, Oreos if we're going to get specific." He is scowling darkly. I wonder to myself if he always looks this angry. "It's Forge, by the way." He lifts his head, like he's listening to something. "They're coming."

"Who?"

"The cops."

"I don't hear anything."

"I have good hearing."

I listen hard for a few seconds. I normally have better hearing than most. His must be freaky good. I shake my head.

"Trust me on this. We need to get off the street right now." He begins to walk. I look up and down the road. It's quieter than it was before. I finally decide to follow him. *What choice do I have?*

CHAPTER 5

FORGE

What the fuck was that?

I don't turn back. I can hear that the woman is following. *Ava.* I prefer Oreo since she smells just like them and is tiny as well. Oreos are one of my favorite cookies. The biscuit itself isn't too sweet. The creamy center... don't even fucking get me started. I need to pull my head from the gutter. Her name is Ava. This situation is a fuck up.

There is only one thing I am sure of; her boyfriend isn't human. I'm not sure what he is, since he smells human. He can't be though. Too strong, too fast and... um... humans can't disappear into thin air. That was the big decider. She seems oblivious to what he is but that could be a big act. I don't know what to make of her. I should kick her to the curb, but I need to find out what the fuck is going on.

We go inside.

"Are you okay?" Susan looks pale. "Do I need to contact anyone?"

"I'm fine," I say. "Tri is on his way."

She nods. "I swear to god!" She clutches her chest, her eyes wide. "Don't scare me like that again. I almost called the cops." Speak of the devil. They're close enough for Ava to hear them now. She sucks in a breath, her eyes darting back outside. They're about a half a minute away.

Susan looks down at his shirt. "You okay?"

"Perfect." I turn back towards my workshop. "This way, Oreo."

"Don't," she warns, there's a whole lot of irritation crammed into that one word. She should be afraid of me, but she isn't. She wasn't affected by Jarrod either, which is also interesting to me. Wait until Tri gets here. I've seen grown women drool. As in literally having to mop up their mouths. They sometimes even beg. Their panties fall round their ankles as soon as they catch sight of him. It's pathetic. I find myself reluctant to watch that happen to her. It's normally comical to see. In this instance, I don't think I'll like it.

I pull the ruined tank over my head and stuff it into the bottom of one of my many toolboxes. I was in a fight. I won't be able to lie my way out of that. There are sure to be witnesses and I'm not hard to describe. They don't need to see how much blood there is on my tank, or the bullet-hole. Ava was right to question that. I don't think she quite buys my story about not being hit. Panic is a strange thing though, it makes you second-guess yourself. Once she's calmed down, I'll bet she's going to start asking a whole lot of questions.

My coveralls are navy, the blood smears look like grease. I turn and walk to the closet. The human is staring. She's staring hard. I'm big. I may not be as good-looking as the rest of my kind, but I can still turn heads. I find I like the interest burning in her eyes. I tamp down this emotion. I don't trust her. It would be stupid to do so. Besides, Trident will be here any second. Her burning stare will soon be averted. I find I'm jealous of the fucker for the first time since making him my best friend when we were what…? Three. I don't like it.

Her gaze moves down to my stomach, which is smeared with blood. Beneath the flaking, congealed mess is a puckering scar. A healing bullet wound. She won't be able to see it. I can't believe that fucker actually got a punch in, let alone shot me. I can still feel the bullet lodged inside me. My flesh has knitted around the foreign object. If left, the missile will slowly work its way out of me. It would mean weeks of discomfort. I sigh, thinking about the pain I'll be in later when Trident removes it. Better that than a week, or more, of irritation.

"You need to go and wait in there." I point at a door.

Her big brown eyes flare in question. "Why?"

"I don't want the cops to see you. They'll want to take you downtown for questioning."

"Why are you helping me?" Her eyes narrow, I can see the barely contained panic just below the surface.

The sirens are still blaring. They're just outside. It suddenly goes silent. It won't take them long to make their way here.

"We'll get into that later. Right now, you need to accept my help and get your ass in there." I point at the door again.

"What's in there?" she asks but is already walking.

"It's a closet."

Her eyes widen. "And through there?" She points to the door a couple of feet to the left.

"Bathroom, but I can't guarantee you won't be found out. Cops need to piss too."

She nods and exhales. "Okay," she sets her shoulders, "the closet it is."

I open the door and turn on the light. "Holy shit!" she exhales sharply. "How many coveralls do you need?" She's looking at the racks of clothing. Mostly work gear. I have coveralls in various colors depending on my mood. Most of them are dark. There's also a section for everyday wear. I often work late, and it helps to clean up and dress before I head out.

"Lots," I finally say as I grab a shirt off a nearby pile. I pull it over my head.

"You have tons of clothes, period." She looks around.

"It's a dirty job. The cops are here. They're talking to Susan." I lower my voice and zip up my coveralls. I have blood on my right hand. *Oh well!* I was in a fight. It'll mesh in with my story.

"You can hear them talking?" She frowns. "I don't hear anything."

I nod. "I told you I have good hearing."

"Freakish hearing," she whispers.

I turn out the light, not wanting to discuss it.

"Hey!" she whispers louder. Her eyes are wide.

"You're not afraid of the dark, are you?"

"No." Her jaw tightens.

"Good. It would be strange if I left the light on in a closed closet. You need to stay put. I'll tell you when you can come out."

"Fine," she huffs, not sounding pleased.

I close the door and head over to the Mustang in the middle of my workshop. I put my hands into the engine, locating the bearings. They're slick with grease, which I smear onto my hands. Partly to cover the blood and partly because I want to make it look like I've been busy instead of hiding a woman. I hear the door to my shop open. I ignore whoever has just entered. There are several of them. I count three... make that four.

"Causing shit again, Forge?" Detective Ross Coleman walks over to me. The rest of his team hangs back.

"It's my favorite detective," I say, sounding bored. "I didn't cause any shit before and certainly didn't cause any now." I get out from under the hood.

"There was a reported altercation outside. Punches were thrown and a shot was fired. One of the parties was dressed in coveralls and built like a brick shithouse. Two witnesses stated that he was covered in tats and had a beard. Oh, and... he was reported to be a ginger."

A ginger bear.

A grizzly.

That's what the human called me. To my face as well. I find her interesting. Far too interesting for my own good. Maybe it's better that Tri will be here soon. I push the thoughts aside.

"Sound familiar?" Coleman doesn't wait for me to answer. "Let's cut the crap. It was you."

"It was nothing. Less than nothing, and definitely no shots were fired." I shake my head.

"The person who called in said that there was also a woman reported to be at the scene. A looker with long, dark hair. She was wearing cut-off shorts and a pink t-shirt." He's reading from a notebook in his hand. He looks up. "Sound familiar?" Detective Coleman scrutinizes me. He's good at his job. A few months ago, we ended up crossing paths soon after I agreed to work on a rare vintage Pontiac. It wasn't a job I could turn down. I even offered to buy the car. Nearly concluded the deal when Coleman here intervened. Turns out the car was stolen. Coleman got the guy. I might have helped him. So what? I believe in right and wrong. I'm wired that way.

I need to answer Coleman, so I pull myself back into the conversation. I know to stick to the truth as much as possible. I nod. "She tried to bring in her ride. Wanted me to customize the car. I declined. Her boyfriend arrived as she was leaving the reception. They fought and he got aggressive. Susan called me and…"

"You intervened?" Coleman raises his brows.

"I don't like it when fuckers beat on women. We had a few words. He wouldn't listen to reason. He hit me first. I hit him back. Then he disappeared."

The detective frowns. "What do you mean he disappeared?"

I shrug. "He left… quickly."

"There were several accounts of a single shot being fired. The person who called it in said that you were the victim."

"Do I look like a victim? Do I look like I was just shot?"

If only he could stick me under an x-ray machine right now.

Coleman shakes his head. "Who's the woman? You got a name?"

"Nope. I didn't ask."

"Funny that, Susan didn't ask either. What about her car?"

"What about it?" I wipe my hands on a nearby cloth.

"Don't give me shit, Forge." He sighs. "I can bring you in."

"You won't."

"Don't be so damned cocky." His eyes blaze.

"I have no idea what she drives. I don't care either. I was never going to take the job. What would have been the point?"

"You don't know anything?" He's giving up. I can tell.

I shake my head. "Only what I've told you. The guy high-tailed it out of here and so did the woman. I'm sure I'll never see either of them again."

"You'll call if you do?" He looks down at my hand for a good few seconds before he lifts his gaze.

I look down as well. Beneath the grease is red flaking blood. I shrug again. "I did admit to hitting him after he hit me." I quickly add. "He might have bled some." My mouth twitches.

"I'm sure he did." Coleman smiles. "You'd better hope he doesn't try to lay charges."

"He hit me first," I reiterate. "I'll call if I see or hear from either of them," I falsely promise. "I still have your number, Detective."

Coleman nods and starts to walk towards the reception. One of his crew opens the door for us.

I follow until we're out front. "I do have something for you," I say.

He hesitates. "Tell me."

"The Porsche on the other side of the street… it's his… the boyfriend's." I wouldn't mind if the scumbag got taken in for questioning.

Coleman turns and steps to the window. "What Porsche?" He's perplexed.

I step up beside him. True as shit, there is an open space where the red sports car had stood just seconds earlier. Pussy wheels for a pussy. Tells me one thing, the fucker didn't disappear after all. I catch a flash of royal blue as a familiar SUV rolls past. Tri is here. He is more than likely going to park further up the street. He'll wait until the action dies down.

CHAPTER 6

AVA

I should have told the police I was here. I should have spoken up. I didn't. Now I'm at his mercy.

Him.

Forge.

I shiver, recalling how his chest looked naked. Not just his chest, his back too. Jesus H. I've never seen anything like it. I couldn't stop looking, even after he caught me staring. I bite my lip.

So big. So strong. So sexy. Back to the big part. I should be petrified. I'm not. I don't feel vulnerable anymore, either. I feel safe. I feel relief. It's weird. I don't know Forge or Susan or Jarrod or this Trident guy. They're strangers and yet... I won't say I trust any of them, but I think I'm safe here. I'm safe with him. With Forge. My gut is telling me so.

Then again, I keep going over what happened in my head. Forge was shot. He *was*. It couldn't have happened though, since he seems fine. Another thing that's boggling my mind is how Sly disappeared like that. One second he was there and the next... poof... gone. Forge was just as shocked. He can say what he wants but I saw it on his face. *Am I losing my mind?* It feels like it.

I'm missing something. I'm being kept in the dark here... literally. I'm in a dark closet. I stifle a laugh. It's mostly born of nervous tension. From — I don't know — being closed up in a dark closet. I'm also being kept in the dark about other things. Things that make no sense.

The door opens and I am momentarily blinded. I put a hand in front of my face and squint.

"You didn't tell me she was hot," someone says. "Smoking," he adds.

I hear a grunt of annoyance. It's a voice I recognize. *His.* It takes a few more seconds for my eyes to adjust.

There's a guy standing grinning in the doorway. He's almost as big as Forge. Are they gym buddies? Must be. Forge is behind him looking pissed off, for whatever reason. I have no idea what that reason might be, other than he's a generally a grumpy bastard.

I turn my attention back to the other guy. Smiley over here has the most amazing blue eyes I have ever seen. They're piercing and seem to look right into me. He's older than Jarrod and a ton better-looking than anyone I've ever seen. He sniffs and frowns. "I smell something baking. Something good. Do you have a stash of cookies in your closet?"

What's with the cookie nonsense?

"It's her," Forge says; his voice is a deep vibration.

"You're kidding." Smiley sniffs again and then grins. "You look good, sweetheart, you smell heavenly. I can only imagine how fantastic you must taste." He licks his lips.

Really?

Is this guy for real?

"Yeah, you'll have to keep on doing that… imagining." I keep my voice deadpan. "Would you mind stepping back so that I can get out of here."

Forge chuckles. He actually smiles while he does it. *Wow!* He's pretty good-looking when he shows some emotion other than brooding asshole.

Smiley looks completely shocked. He opens and closes his mouth a few times. Then finally steps back. "Um… what's happening?"

"You just got red-lighted."

"I don't get red-lighted… ever." He sniffs. "You really do smell like a batch of… I don't know… choc-chip cookies."

"I. Do. Not." This is getting weirder by the second.

"Nah." Forge shakes his head. "Not chocolate chip. Chocolate chips are too sweet. Ava over here smells like Oreos. Good old-fashioned Oreos." He looks at me, daring me to argue. I don't, even though I don't like this line of conversation.

Smiley looks like he's thinking it through. His nostrils are flaring as he continues to sniff the air. It's bizarre. "I'm getting butter. That and some chocolate…" He turns to Forge. "You're right, not too much on the chocolate front. Then…" he sniffs and cocks his head in thought, "… maybe… just maybe a creamy center." Smiley grins. "You might be right. Oreo it is." He nods, "I'm Trident." He holds out his hand.

I take it. "Nice to meet you, Smiley."

He looks taken aback.

"That's what I'll call you if you even think of calling me Oreo. I'm Ava." I let go of his hand.

Trident is laughing… hard. "I like this human."

It's an odd thing to say. *Why did he say that?*

"I quite like the nickname myself," Forge says. "Oreo has a certain ring to it."

"Don't you dare, Grizzly. I swear…" I point at him.

Trident laughs some more.

Forge shrugs but doesn't say anything. He's gone back to looking all mean and brooding.

"Can we please cut the crap. What the hell is going on?" I finally ask.

"We were just about to ask you the same. Who is this boyfriend of yours?" Trident asks.

I set my jaw. "You first." I lock eyes with Forge. "What happened out there?"

"You saw what happened," Forge counters.

"You're right. I did! I want answers. How is it that you got shot and yet you're fine? I watched you bleed. I saw the hole in your shirt. I'm not an idiot."

He shakes his head… hard. "I didn't get shot. We've been through this." He gives an exasperated sigh. "I don't like repeating myself."

"You talk a whole lot of bullshit. I'm not buying it."

He holds my gaze but doesn't say anything.

"How is it that Sly disappeared into thin air?" I ask, taking a step towards him. "Your boot was about to make contact with his head, and he disappeared. Otherwise, you would never have landed on your ass like you did."

"You landed on your ass?" Trident chuckles.

Forge gives Trident a look that could slay an orc – I've read *Lord of the Rings,* so sue me. "Sly. That's his name then. Your boyfriend?" His jaw tightens as he says it.

"Yes, Sly Herms."

Trident's eyes widen right up. "Weird name," he snorts.

"You're one to talk, *Trident*," I say. "Sly is short for Sylvester. It's English apparently. Anyway, let's get something clear. Sly is not my boyfriend. He's my boss."

"Where do you work?" Trident asks.

I tell them all about the casino and my position.

Trident takes a step back, looking at me like I did something wrong. "A casino? Interesting. Did you steal from him or something?"

"Or something."

"Tell us, Ava. I can't help you unless you come clean." Forge looks sincere and for a moment I'm tempted to tell them everything. One thing holds me back – they're not being honest with me, so how can I be honest with them? I can't. Not completely.

"We're all that stands between you and him," Forge says. "I can't help you if you don't tell us."

I.

He said 'I' and not 'we.' I don't know why but it

means something to me. Like he's personally taking responsibility for this. For me and my problems. It warms me up from the inside.

"My brother got involved with Sly. A 'courier' position. I don't know what he was running but it can't have been anything good. Bruce lost a package. Something worth a whole lot of money. Money belonging to some bad people."

"What does that have to do with you?" Trident asks.

Forge folds his arms.

My eyes sting and my throat suddenly hurts. I still get emotional when I think about Bruce. I sometimes feel anger, but I mostly still feel the pain of his loss. "Bruce knew he was in real trouble. He…" I pull in a deep breath and my voice wavers. "He killed himself some weeks back. Now Sly is after me."

"I'm sorry about your brother." Trident pauses. "Why not pay him off?" he says it so nonchalantly.

"Because I don't have twenty-two thousand lying around."

Forge nods his head, looking far more understanding. "What kind of a deal is he trying to broker?"

"Deal?" I shake my head, acting stupid.

"You heard me, Ava. He wants something in exchange for the money. What is that something?"

"Sly said he'll pay my debt for me if I…" I feel my whole body bristle at the idea. At even saying the words. "For one night with me. He wants me to whore myself out. It's that or he's handing me over to the Russian mafia, who will have to make an example out of me. Something about my head being removed from my shoulders."

Trident whistles low.

Forge looks so angry his face has turned red.

"It doesn't make sense." I shake my head. "A guy like Sly has women falling over themselves to be with him. He's rich and attractive – if you like tall, dark and slimy."

Trident chokes out a laugh and Forge cracks a hint of a smile.

"I really like her," Trident says to Forge, "but you found her first, so you get first dibs."

"Excuse me, asshole!" I narrow my eyes at Trident. "I'm standing right here. I'm a human being with feelings, opinions and I am quite capable of speaking and thinking for myself. The two of you don't get to talk about me like I'm a thing to fight over."

"This is a novelty." Trident's eyes are wide with shock. "I'm not sure I like it."

"What?" Forge still has a hint of a smile playing with the edges of his mouth. "You can't say what you want and get away with it?" He turns to me. "You'll have to excuse Tri, women are normally blinded by his good looks and charm. He's not used to being snubbed."

"Charm, my ass," I say since Smiley has zero charm. He's a big lug. Pretty but still a lug.

"I *am* charming." Trident looks put out.

I shake my head.

Forge softens his stance. "I respect how you stood up for yourself against this Sly. How long have you been on the run?"

"Three weeks."

Forge looks taken aback. He and Trident exchange

looks. Whatever it is they're thinking, they're not sharing with me.

Just then, the back roll-up door of the workshop slowly lifts and Jarrod drives in with the tow truck. Miss Sunshine is still on the flatbed. "What should I do with this?" he asks, looking back at my car.

"You can leave her with me," Forge says, pointing to an open section in his shop.

Her.

I like that. Then he turns to me. "It's getting late." He looks at the clock on the wall. "I'll take care of it in the morning. You need to come with us, Ava. You can sleep at my place. I have a spare bedroom. You're not safe and you're broke, by the sounds of things."

"Why are you helping me?"

Forge shakes his head. "I'm not entirely sure."

It's a cryptic, shitty answer but I nod anyway. I'm too desperate to look a gift horse in the mouth, or in this instance, a gift grizzly bear.

CHAPTER 7

FORGE

Tri pushes the box away and rubs his stomach. "That was good."

"Two pizzas." The human looks baffled. "You polished off two whole pizzas..." She looks from Trident to me and back again. "Each!"

"We're big guys," Tri remarks.

"I'll say!" She looks my way as she says it, her eyes drifting to my chest and biceps for a moment before she looks away.

I'm floored. No woman has ever looked at me for even half a second after Tri has stepped into the picture. Not just Tri, any of... my kind would have had the same effect. Trident just happens to be the prettiest of the bunch. No woman has ever turned him down before, let alone called him an asshole. I love it. I find myself liking the human. She has guts and grit. She could have given that dickhead boss of hers what he wanted and watched all her problems disappear, instead, she stood up for herself. I respect that. I still have to be careful, though. This could still be a ploy. A way to infiltrate our organization. It has never happened before but there is always a first time.

Ava yawns. "I'm beat."

Three weeks of running will do that to a person. I can't believe she managed to elude Sly for that long. I literally can't believe it because I'm sure it didn't happen like that. Either she's lying or he was fucking her around. I'm going with the latter on this one. "I can imagine," I say. "You're welcome to head to bed." I showed Ava her room earlier. It has a small en suite bathroom.

Ava nods.

"I put that shirt you asked for on your bed," I say.

"Thank you and thanks for letting me do my laundry, as well as for letting me stay here." She looks around.

For once I wish I had a bigger place. I can afford it. I just never felt the need. "No sweat." I nod. Even her dirty clothes smelled delicious. I have a female under my roof for the first time in my life and I'm already turning into a pussy.

"Good night then," she says.

"Night, Oreo," Tri smirks.

"Night, Smiley," she quips over her shoulder as she disappears down the short hall that leads to the bedrooms. The spare bedroom comes up first. The door clicks shut behind her.

"Don't call Ava that." I'm bristling. I don't know why but I am.

Tri chuckles. "Only *you're* allowed to call her that."

"No." *Yes!* I shake my head. "She doesn't like it."

"You should tap that," Tri remarks, still smirking. He takes a swig of his beer.

"What?" I frown. "Are you crazy?"

"Oreo likes you and I know how much you love cookies." Trident winks. "Especially Oreos."

"Not a fuck!" I growl. "It would be like pissing on my own porch." I shake my head. "We don't know her. She's definitely trouble."

"I'd go there."

"You're a slut," I snort. "Besides, she wouldn't let you." I hear the shower splutter to life.

"You're loving it. The human has a thing for you."

"Nah." I *have* caught her looking at me a couple of times but that doesn't mean much. All humans look. "She doesn't even know me."

"I'd bet money she'd like to. Get to know you, that is. Particularly a certain part of your anatomy." He bobs his brows.

I take a sip of my beer and shake my head. "Not happening. There's something off about her. I can't put my finger on it. That guy, Sly, if that's even his real name, he's not human."

Trident's jaw tightens. "Tell me more."

"I was shot. Bullet's still inside me."

Tri winces. "That sucks."

"It does indeed. It's also why you're still here."

He makes a face and then grins. "I thought it was my company."

"Not a chance." I take another sip of my beer.

"Good thing I brought my knife then."

"Good thing." I nod. The shower stops running.

"So, Oreo was right when she said she saw you get shot?"

I nod.

"Was she right about this Sly character disappearing like that?"

"Yep." I sip my beer, holding onto the fizzy liquid for a few seconds before swallowing. "One second he was there and the next..." I think back on earlier today, "he was gone."

"That's fucking nuts." Trident rubs his chin. I hear his stubble catching. "He teleported like Night can?"

"Yes, so not so nuts." I pause. "I mean, you can control water. Jarrod can see someone's past."

"Did he read anything from her then?" Tri interrupts.

I shake my head. "Not a thing." It does happen sometimes that Jarrod gets nothing. So not such a big deal but it would have been handy. "Back to what we were saying. We won't even get into Rage's and Bolt's powers. I'm pretty sure he teleported."

"Sounds that way." Tri picks at the label on his beer, which is nearly empty. "Maybe Hades fucked around with more than just Night's mother." He raises his brows. "Maybe Night has a half-brother he never met?"

"Thing is, he didn't scent like one of us."

"What does that make him then?" It's a good question.

"Fucked if I know." I finish my beer and stand. I throw

the empty pizza boxes into the trash along with my bottle. There are a few dishes in the sink which I start to wash.

"What are you going to do with the girl?" Tri asks, taking a final swig of his beer. "Besides the obvious." I can hear he's smiling.

"I'm not fucking her, so you can get that particular thought right out of your head."

"Can I have her then?"

I turn to glare at him.

Tri laughs. "What then?"

I shrug. "I have no idea. If she's innocent, I'll continue to help her. We need to find out who this Sly motherfucker is. More importantly, *what* he is and what he really wants with Ava."

"I don't buy that it took him three weeks to find her. The fucker can teleport."

"I don't buy it either. I'm not sure what his deal is. I'm not letting him have Ava." There is a steely edge to my voice.

"Looks like a certain Oreo already has you dying to get your fingers in the cookie jar. I don't blame you, buddy." He snickers.

I don't say anything.

"Be careful, bro. That's all I'm saying."

I turn back. "I'm always careful."

Trident just laughs; there's this look in his eyes that I can't quite decipher.

AVA

I can't sleep.

I've tried for what feels like hours, but has, in reality, only been just over two. Feels so much longer that I'm becoming wired. My head feels like it's filled with cotton wool. It's frustrating because I'm completely exhausted. I feel it in every part of myself but can't seem to drift off.

My mind won't stop working. It won't stop playing through the events of the last few weeks. The last few hours are burned into my head. *What the hell is going on? Why is Forge lying to me? What is he keeping from me?* Not just Forge but his friend as well. Both of them are hiding something. I could see it in the looks they gave one another.

I strain to hear what's going on out there. Nothing has changed over the last hour and a half. Initially, I heard the soft murmur of talking. Then the light drone of the television. The thing is still on. I don't think I heard Trident leave, but I can't be sure. It's just turned ten, so it's not all that late yet.

I'd love something to drink. Something hot like chamomile tea. I get the feeling a guy like Forge won't have herbal tea. It would help me sleep. I don't want to venture out there though. My clothes are still in the dryer. All I have is Forge's shirt. No underwear. Nope, I'm staying put.

I hear a strange noise. It makes me hold my breath for a second or two so that I can listen more acutely. I'm just starting to breathe out when I hear it again. It makes me sit up in the bed.

It sounded like a soft groan. Like someone is in pain but they're trying to hold it in. Is it the television?

There.

I hear it again, followed by a whisper. I'm shocked to find myself at the door to my room. I'm listening hard. I carefully open the door. The hinges must be oiled because it doesn't make a sound. Yep, there is whispering alright. Two voices. It isn't the television. I hear the noise again. Like someone is groaning internally, between clenched teeth, but they're unable to stay completely quiet. The drone of the television doesn't quite cover it.

They're up to something. I know it like I know my own name. Time to find out about that tea. I head out, walking as quietly as I can. I'm not sure why I'm sneaking around. Only that I feel I have to if I want to find out what's going on around here. The living room is dim. The television is causing the light to flicker. It takes me a good few seconds to comprehend what I am seeing, and even then, I'm not entirely sure. My mind can't quite believe it because it's… it's stupid-crazy!

Trident is holding a big-ass knife above Forge's stomach. The blade glints. Not as much as it should. I soon realize why when the blade disappears into Forge's belly. The knife is covered in blood. Forge's blood. Trident proceeds to dig around in his gut. Forge does that groan thing. His face is pinched with pain. His eyes are scrunched shut.

"Pussy!" Trident whispers.

"I can't believe you can't find it," Forge whispers back. They speak so softly I can only just make out what they are saying. "Should I call Jarrod?" He groans. "You're fucking around." He groans again.

"Jarrod has fuck all experience with these types of things." Trident digs around some more.

Forge shudders, his teeth clenched tighter. He does a good job of keeping fairly quiet, considering that there's a knife in his belly. The blade is buried halfway into him. Halfway! *Good lord! How is he putting up with this?* My eyes are bugging out. I'm barely breathing because I'm afraid they'll hear me. If I wasn't holding back, I'd be hyperventilating.

Then Trident gives a quietly triumphant exclamation as he replaces the blade with his fingers and roots around in Forge's belly. He holds something up. It glints.

"I knew it!" I announce, walking into the living room. "That's a bullet."

Trident pulls this, 'I've just been busted' face. He closes the bullet in his fist, which he puts behind his back. "You're sleepwalking," he tries. "Seeing things," he adds.

Forge gives a half-groan, half-sigh. He scrubs a hand over his face which, even in this light, looks pale and sweaty. *No wonder!* I look down at his blood-smeared belly. There's a sizable hole in the middle of his six-pack, which should not be impressive in this situation and yet somehow is. I gasp. "Holy shit! What the heck? Shouldn't we be calling an ambulance? Is that knife sterile? Are you a doctor?" I ask Trident. "You'd better be a doctor." I point at him.

They both gape at me.

"Is someone going to tell me what the hell is going on?" I yell.

"You look great in that shirt." Trident is looking at my chest. More to the point, my boobs. I'm not wearing a bra. I'm in one of Forge's shirts. A white t-shirt with some sort of muscle car on the front. It comes to my knees. My boobs are out there. They're always out there.

I fold my arms across myself and try to cover up as much as I can.

"Hand me the towel," Forge grunts.

Trident does as he asks.

Forge holds the towel to his belly and sits up. He winces.

"What now?" Trident asks. "We need permission to say anything. Humans aren't allowed to know."

"Why do you keep referring to me like that?" I swallow thickly, not liking where this is going. Like they're not human. What would they be? They *look* human. "What's going on? How did you heal so quickly? Why did Sly disappear?"

"You can't repeat any of what I'm about to tell you," Forge says.

"No!" Trident pushes out forcefully. He shakes his head. His name has changed from Smiley to Frowny. "You can't! You'll get into huge shit."

Forge presses the towel more firmly against his belly. "The human knows enough to be able to put some of the pieces together. She knows too much, Tri."

"What are you saying?" Trident runs his hand through his sandy blond hair. "She doesn't know much of anything. Are you sure you can trust her?"

He lifts his head and looks into my eyes. His jaw is tight. His gaze is intense. Even in the low light, I can see how green his irises are. Something softens in their depths. "Yes, we can trust her."

"That's your dick talking." Trident shakes his head.

"It's not," Forge growls.

"It is," Trident insists. "Oreo cookie over there is gorgeous. She's —"

"Stop calling her that!" Forge sounds pissed. He *looks* pissed, even gets to his feet. The towel is still clamped to his wound. If he's in pain he's not showing it.

"See. You're defending her. Getting all irritated."

"I'm not all irritated," Forge growls. "No more than normal." He shrugs.

Trident makes a face. "Point taken," he concedes.

"Are the two of you done?" I ask.

Forge's jaw tightens and Trident nods.

I pull in a deep breath. "Please tell me. You're not entirely human, I'm assuming." I bite my lip for a second. "I can't believe I even said that. Not human… what else would you be? You have to be human." I giggle. "Surely?" I don't sound sure at all. I play with my ring. I try not to say anything more.

"We're quarter human," Forge says.

"Although that's debatable," Trident chimes in. "There are those who believe that it's more than that. Although, it wouldn't be by much."

"Let's not confuse things," Forge growls.

"Quarter." I nod. "Okay… alright. Got it!" I'm freaking out a little. "And the other three quarters?" Okay, I'm freaking out a lot! Not being entirely human would explain a lot of what I saw today.

"That's where things get complicated," Forge admits.

"Oh, god!" Trident scrubs a hand over his face. "We're going to be in so much shit. I'm blaming this all on you."

"Go right ahead." Forge keeps his eyes on me.

Trident hangs his head. "You know I won't leave you out to dry," he groans, sounding more pained than when Forge was having a bullet dug out of his stomach.

Dug out.

I breathe in and out... slowly.

"Don't freak out." Forge puts a hand up.

Too late. "I won't." I nod once.

"We're half dragon-shifter."

I laugh. I laugh so hard I have to bend over to stop myself from getting a stitch. "I'm sorry."

Dragon.

Shifter.

"You're freaking out," Forge says, it's not a question.

"Yes." I stop laughing. The blood is draining from my body. I sit down on a nearby sofa. More like drop down. "I am, but just a little." My mouth is dry. My eyes are wide. "You can't really blame me."

"Dragon shifters are half-dragon and half-human. That's where the quarter human comes from. Our mothers are dragon shifters."

"Okay." My voice is high-pitched. "There are more of you, from the sounds of things?"

He nods.

"What about your dads?"

"My father—I've never met him—is a god." He is watching me intently.

"God? God as in...?" I'm wracking my brain.

"As in Poseidon, Hades, Zeus… we're demigods," Trident says.

"Like Percy Jackson?" I name the famous character.

"What?" Forge is unimpressed. "No! Nothing like that."

"We call ourselves dragon demigods," Trident chimes in. "There are a few of us. Dragon shifters too, although there are quite a few more of those. The human population doesn't know about any of us, even though most of us live among you."

"Demigods." That's utter craziness. Straitjackets are in order. Maybe I need one. That and drugs. Of course, it would explain what happened.

"My father is Poseidon," Trident continues. "I never met him. None of us have met our fathers except for Night but that's a long story best left for another day. I don't want to freak you out."

Too late. "Poseidon, as in the god of the sea?" My voice is shrill. "*That* Poseidon?" *Can't be.*

"One and the same." Trident nods his head.

My mouth gapes.

"My name kind of speaks for itself." He shrugs like it's a no-brainer.

"And what about you?" I raise my brows. "Forge?" I frown.

"Forge's father is less known," Trident smirks.

"My father is Hephaestus. God of fire. It's the reason I'm good with my hands. I can fix anything." He lifts his arms and I can't help gaping at his large hands.

I'm listening to his every word, but he doesn't continue. Trident picks up where Forge left off. "Not as good with people. Great with cars. 'Fix anything' is an understatement. You're an artist, don't forget that part."

"The dragon... did you paint that?" I'm reminded of the car on top of Forge's shop. The one painted on the side of the vehicle.

Forge nods once.

"Wow. That is talent." I'm still freaking out, but not as much as I should be. Not human. Half dragon shifter. Half god. *Sheesh!* It's a ton to take in.

"You *do* believe us, don't you?" Forge asks. He seems... vulnerable, but it's hard to think of Forge that way.

"I do." I nod. "I mean, you took a bullet," I shake my head, "and sat around and ate pizza like nothing happened."

His shoulders relax.

"Can dragon shifters actually shift into dragon form?" There is so much I want to know.

Trident laughs.

"Don't!" Forge warns.

"Oh, my god!" I feel my eyes widen. "Can you shift? You can, can't you?""

"Don't you fucking dare," Forge warns. His eyes are on Trident, who has gone back to being Smiley.

"We can." Trident nods. "We're a whole lot slower than full-blown dragon shifters at doing it. It can take a minute or two to complete a shift. Turn on the light and I'll show you."

"Tri... I swear to fucking god!" Forge's voice has gone down about a thousand octaves.

"Calm down. I won't do a full shift. I wouldn't want

to break anything." He looks around the room. "We get big." He winks at me. "Besides, I'd have to get naked and then you would fall in love with me."

"Like hell," I snort.

"Then again, maybe I *will* get naked." Tri bobbed his brows at me.

Forge makes a growling noise that reminds me of a wild animal. One that is about to attack.

"I'm teasing," Trident says to Forge.

I do as Trident says and flick on the light switch. When I turn back, he has his shirt lifted. He also has tattoos, although not as many as Forge. He's built too, although, not nearly as much as—

I cover my mouth when scales pop up on his chest. They're green with flecks of blue. I look up and Trident's pupils are slitted, like a reptile's. His blue eyes look even bluer. Like ice-shards.

"You can stop now," Forge growls the words. He sits back down and winces as he does.

"Oh. I'm sorry." I go to Forge. "I completely forgot about your injury. Does it hurt badly?" I widen my eyes, feeling like an idiot. "Of course it does, what a stupid thing to ask. Where do you keep your first aid kit? I'm going to assume you don't want medical help or—"

"I'm okay." I notice that his coloring is better, but his face is pinched. Like he's in pain.

I go down on my haunches in front of him. "Let me take a look. We should probably disinfect the wound. If you have a bandage..."

I lean forward. He's wearing a pair of grey sweatpants. I can see a clear outline of his... of his... junk.

My face turns red.

My mouth may have fallen open.

Okay, it *has* fallen open and I can't close it. I can't stop looking. It's huge. The outline is massive… like the rest of him. Forge is in proportion. Very much so.

"You two should get a room." Trident sounds like he's grinning.

I snap out of it and clear my throat. "Let me see it." I turn my gaze to where he is holding the towel. Where it should be… namely, not on his… man-part.

"You definitely need to examine Forge. He needs some serious doctoring." Trident laughs. "Yep… you should definitely head on down the hallway and find yourselves a room. Would this be a good time for me to go?" He chuckles.

I say 'no.' Forge says 'yes.' He also pulls the towel away and I almost fall on my ass. I reach out and grab onto something. That something happens to be Forge's thigh. *Good lord.* He's carved from stone or something. His muscles are thick and corded.

"Your wound has closed already." It's still an angry red and raised but it's well on its way to being healed. "I can't believe it." I sound like I'm in awe. I *am* in awe.

"There won't even be a scar come morning," Forge says. "I don't need disinfectant or a bandage. I definitely don't need doctoring." He sends Trident a dirty look and I am oddly disappointed. Stupid, I know.

I realize I'm still holding onto his leg. I let go and stand up. I rake my hand through my hair, then tuck a strand behind my ear. "This is insane."

"You can't tell anyone. You understand that, don't you?" Forge emphasizes.

I nod. "Yeah, I understand. I won't."

"We shouldn't have told you without permission from the others," Trident says. "The world is not ready to know about us." For once, he is very serious.

"They're not! Not at all!" The world is definitely not ready. I'm not sure how ready *I* am. "What about Sly?" The question has been playing on my mind. "He's not human, is he? He *did* pull a disappearing act? I'm not going crazy." I shake my head.

"You're not crazy," Forge reassures me.

Trident laughs. "I still can't believe you fell on your ass. I would pay hard cash to have seen that. I don't think I've ever seen anyone take you down."

"The fucker didn't take me down," Forge says. He's completely calm. "I was about to break him, and he knew it. There is no way he's human. I'm not sure what that was. He didn't just turn invisible, he was there one second and then gone."

"How is that even possible?" I ask.

"Most dragon demigods have powers. Some of us have better powers than others." Trident puffs out his chest.

I roll my eyes.

"I really do nothing for you?" Trident narrows his eyes. "Like when I lifted my shirt..." He does it again, showing his washboard abs.

"Nothing." I shake my head. "You're a good-looking guy and I'm sure women look."

"Look?" He says it like he can't believe what he is hearing. "They don't just look, sweetheart. They beg. They plead. I can have any woman. Anywhere. Anytime—"

"No, you can't." I shake my head.

Trident looks put out. "It's weird. Just plain weird."

"I agree," Forge says.

"It's not weird," I say. "I'm not into you. It's not —"

"Trident is right. Women love us. Even me." He says it like there's something wrong with him. "You seem immune."

"Mostly." Trident winks at Forge who glowers at him. "Then there's the way you smell."

"It's… interesting," Forge muses.

"Interesting?" Trident snorts. "Fucking delicious, if you ask me."

"Human, though," Forge points out.

"But not." Trident shakes his head. "Humans don't smell like that."

"What about Sly? Did he smell… different in any way?" I ask.

"No." Forge shakes his head. "But he's not human. You say he owns a casino?"

I nod. "He told me he inherited his name from his dad's side. I assumed it was a nickname. I noticed that you guys have unique names too… Forge and Trident. You also mentioned someone called Night?"

"We'll investigate this Sly asshole in the morning. I also want to take a look at your car." Forge's expression shifts. Like he's thinking things through.

"We'll have to have a little chat with the rest of the boys," Trident says. "They will want to meet you," he says to me.

Forge nods, frowning darkly.

"I'd better get going. You two go straight to bed

now… long day tomorrow." He throws out a laugh. *Is that another innuendo?* Maybe Trident can sense some tension between Forge and me. More from my side than his, though.

Forge ignores the comment. I struggle to do the same. I have checked Forge out a couple of times. Who wouldn't? He's massive. Not just big but imposing too. His eyes are beautiful and so intense. Everything about him radiates power. I haven't come onto him in any way. There hasn't been any flirting. Forge hasn't been inappropriate to me in any way. I don't know why Trident is being a dick. Two adults can share a house without sleeping together. It's more than possible. Things are complicated right now. Sex with Forge would complicate them even more. My core tightens when I think of sex with Forge. I get the feeling it would be just as intense as he is.

Stop!

I clear my throat. "Good night," I say as Trident heads for the door.

"Here…" He turns and tosses something at Forge.

Forge catches the object, snatches it right out the air. Then he opens his hand and the bloody bullet glints in his palm.

"A souvenir. I'll see you both in the morning." Trident opens and closes the door behind him. Just like that, he's gone. The air seems to thicken.

Forge turns back towards me. I notice that he doesn't lock the door. He still has smears of blood on his belly. The wound is a puckered-up mess but considering it was open and bleeding not so long ago, I'd call that a miracle. Seeing it is a reminder of what Sly is capable of. I shiver.

"What is it?" Forge asks. "What's on your mind?"

I go to the door and turn the lock. "I'm worried." I hug myself again. "You may have won the first round, but I don't think this is over. Sly is the kind of guy who's used to getting what he wants. I don't think he's going to give up so easily."

"Let him try," Forge says. Those green eyes of his seem to be looking right through me.

"It's not your fight. I can't expect—"

"Don't say that." Forge shakes his head. "You were right when you told me my attitude stinks and that I'm an ornery asshole."

Crap! I did call him that. It seems like forever ago. "I didn't mean it when…" I stop there. "Okay, I *did* mean it when I said those things, but you've proven me wrong. I'll even admit, when I first saw you loading my car onto the tow-truck, I thought you were stealing it. Pulling a fast one."

"You weren't wrong about me acting like an asshole, but I wasn't trying to steal your ride. I would never pull a move like that."

I snort. "I know that now. I told you I changed my mind and may have been a bit harsh in my judgments."

"You called me out and I decided to help you. This really became my beef when that prick treated you like a piece of his property. When he punched me." He rubs his chin. "Then he disappeared like a coward." His eyes blaze. "Besides, we may not know what he is yet, but like I said, he most definitely isn't human. You aren't equipped to deal with him."

That just makes me shiver again. I can't help it. It's both fear and loathing. I've come to hate Sly. I hate that he has this hold on me.

"Also, he's using his powers for evil, which means someone has to step in. I'm that someone." His jaw clenches as he says it.

I feel warm inside. "Thank you." It's a lame thing to say but I mean it. "Thanks for helping me. For letting me stay here and… for the shirt," I blurt the last.

"Looks better on you." Forge almost smiles. I notice that he doesn't look down. He sucks in a breath. "We'd better get to bed." His voice has grown steely again. He looks angry. "Tomorrow is going to be a big day. Also," he looks rueful, "excuse Tri. He's used to getting away with murder. He doesn't normally have to mind his Ps and Qs around humans. Particularly around the females of the species."

I nod. "He's rude and arrogant but he's not a bad guy." I like Trident. He has this way about him.

Forge's mouth twitches.

"What's so funny?"

"Nothing. Nothing at all." Just like that, he's gone back to looking serious. Bristling is probably a better word. His brow is furrowed, and his eyes are brooding. Yep, Grizzly bear is accurate. At least he's not being an asshole anymore. That's something.

I say goodnight and Forge grunts, disappearing down the hall. I want to watch him go but force myself to head into the bedroom instead. I turn the key, locking myself in. Next, I make sure that the window is latched. *I'm fine. I'm safe.*

I'm wrong. I'm none of those things. I try to convince myself anyway. Otherwise, I won't be able to sleep.

CHAPTER 8

AVA

The next day

I close the book, putting it on the table. It's a political thriller. I grabbed it from Forge's place. It was in-between a bunch of car magazines on a shelf in the living room. It doesn't look like it's ever been read. I'm struggling to concentrate and so I give up. My attention deficit seemed to coincide with the moment when Forge started working on my car.

I watch him, he has his head under the hood. He's been under there for the last ten minutes. He looks good in coveralls. Despite the air conditioner whirring along, he has them tied around his waist again. This time he's wearing a royal blue tank top. *Holy hotness!* I have to stop myself from drooling. I never thought I would find red hair attractive, but I do. It's a rich, deep coppery color. His beard as well. It's sexy and well-groomed. I'm betting he washes it in the shower when he does his hair.

His skin is tanned even though he works indoors. If he has freckles, I haven't seen them. *A hot ginger… who would have thought?* My mind flashes back to a half-naked Jamie from the *Outlander* and shake my head. *Forge is hotter!*

I'm tempted to get up and to go over there. Forge instructed me to sit quietly in the corner of his workshop. He didn't want me out front, didn't deem it safe. He's been a bit grumpy all morning. Grumpy is the wrong word. It makes me think of one of the seven dwarves and there is nothing dwarf-like about this man. Brooding is probably a better word. I'm glad I'm here, with him. I feel safe when I'm around Forge. Sly wouldn't dare try to take me now.

I lean back on the sofa. He's set up a chill area complete with a coffee station and a kitchenette. I'm all set. Pity I can't seem to get comfortable or focused. I can't sit here any longer. I put the book onto the table and head over to Forge. He's still fiddling with my car. I can't see exactly what he's doing.

"How's Miss Sunshine?" I ask when I'm a few feet away.

Forge lifts his head, hitting it against the hood. There is a loud thunk. He groans, funnily enough, louder than when Trident had the knife inside his stomach. He grabs the top of his head as he comes out from under the hood. His eyes are stormy. "How the hell did you sneak up on me?"

I shrug. "I didn't… I didn't mean to."

"It's the second time. Last night you snuck up on both of us." He's still rubbing his head.

"I'm sorry. Is your head bad? You hit it pretty hard. Also, I didn't sneak up on you last night. You didn't notice because you had a knife in your stomach. How's the head?" I notice he's still holding it.

"It's nothing. I'm fine." Then he looks at me funny. "What did you just call your car?"

"Miss Sunshine." I smile. "It's her color."

He almost smiles and once again I'm astounded at how good-looking he is when he lets all of that broodiness fall away. Don't get me wrong, he's quite gorgeous when he's brooding as well. *Oops!* I need to stop this. Focus on the fact that I could… get caught… and end up dead.

Dead.

Murdered.

I need to pull myself together.

"I got that," he says. "Miss Sunshine." He kind of chuckles. Half and half. Like he wants to, but he can't quite get it out.

"What? You strike me as the kind of guy who would give his car a name."

"Me?" He makes a face of disgust. "Not a chance." He nods twice. "It does work though… Miss Sunshine. The color is terrible. If I were to customize this ride, its color would be the first thing I would change, amongst other things." He's looking at her like he's planning a whole custom job. I guess he can't help himself. It is what he does for a living.

Technically, I agree. I would never have chosen this color and yet, I can't concede defeat. "There is nothing wrong with yellow. It's a happy color. It's the only reason I could afford a car like this. I love Miss Sunshine. She's never let me down."

Forge folds his arms across his chest and cocks his head at me.

"Okay, okay… she let me down once… just the once. Yesterday was the first time."

"At a point in your life when you needed her the most."

"No! It wasn't like that." I shake my head.

"Really, now?" He keeps his eyes on me.

"Maybe it was meant to break down. In a way, breaking down saved me. Miss Sunshine saved me by failing me."

He frowns.

"She did! My car brought me here. It brought me to you and you're helping me. Miss Sunshine helped me by breaking down."

He pulls in a deep breath. "I guess I can't argue with that." He gets back under the hood.

"Do you have any brothers or sisters?" It's a lame question. When I'm around Forge, I seem to say stupid things. I don't know why. Sure, I'm attracted to him, but I've been attracted to people before. I've never been this bad.

"Only a half-brother. The gods came down for a short time and have never been back since… not to our knowledge at any rate."

"So, you never met your dad?"

He shakes his head as he reaches for a spanner. "Nope. Only what my mom told me about him. The gods arrived one day, swept a whole bunch of unmated dragon shifter women off their feet and left weeks later. Every single woman found out she was pregnant. Only males were born." He shrugs. "It must be a genetic issue with the gods, since our dragon women are quite capable of producing females when paired with other dragon shifters."

"Interesting." I nod. "Was it tough growing up without a father?"

I see him visibly stiffen. He breathes out. "I have my brothers. We're not brothers in blood but brothers in how we were bred. We have always been there for one another." He puts down the spanner and picks up another tool I can't identify. It's not really much of an answer. He's skirting around giving a direct reply.

"I never met my father either," I blurt. It's not something I speak about often.

Forge stops working and looks at me, his eyes locking with mine for a few seconds. An understanding passes between us. At least, that's what it feels like. "Not many people know that Sam wasn't my father. I called him dad. By all accounts, he was my father. He and my mom met soon after I was born. He raised me." I shrug once. "They were always open about it. Told me as soon as I could understand. Sam always maintained that it didn't change how he felt about me, and I always believed him. I had a great childhood. I still struggled with it—not knowing my birth father. I felt guilty about my feelings. My mom met a guy and they spent a month or two together..." I feel the familiar pain rise up in me. "Then he just up and left." I'm playing with my ring. "I sometimes wish I knew him. That I had met him or seen a picture of him. Something. All I have is a first name,

Forde. That, and this ring, that's it. It didn't matter how happy my home life was, I always craved that."

"I used to feel that way, but I got over it," Forge says. "I was angry growing up. This bozo created me on a whim and then left. My mother was nothing but passing fun for him. The gods were bored." He snorts. It doesn't look like he's gotten over anything. I understand where he's coming from. "At least I know *who* he is," Forge goes on. "Even if I don't actually know *him*. I can't imagine being completely in the dark. It must be tough." He holds my gaze for a few moments longer. Something definitely passes between us.

I nod once. "Now it's just me," I swallow thickly, "now that Bruce is gone."

"Your brother?"

"Yep." I lick my lips. "It's weird, I always envied him. I was jealous. Sam was his actual dad and yet, Bruce was…" I shrug. "He always had issues. I remembered how much he cried as a baby. He struggled at school, even failed one of his grades and eventually dropped out. He could never hold down a job. Bruce was a troubled soul."

"Who got involved with the wrong people."

"That's for sure."

Forge turns, he wipes his hands on a nearby towel. "Looks like your car may have been tampered with."

It takes my brain a few seconds to comprehend what he is saying. "Tampered with? How do you mean tampered with?"

"I mean… this doesn't look right. When did you last service…" there is this glint in his eyes and his mouth twitches, "Miss Sunshine?"

I can't help my broad smile, despite the situation. "It was a couple of months ago."

"Have you had any engine troubles since then?"

"Up until yesterday," I shake my head, "none whatsoever."

"Tell me about these engine troubles." He leans back against my car.

"I struggled to start her up, which was strange since she's normally no problem. Then my engine light kept coming on."

"What did you do about that?"

"I was fleeing from a guy who threatened to hand me over to the Russian mob so that they can cut my head off." I swipe my finger across my neck. "What do you think I did?" *Way to go, Ava!* I remind myself that Forge is trying to help me. I suck in a breath. "I didn't do anything. I don't know anything about cars. I kept going in the hopes that the light would stay off."

"It didn't, though." A statement, not a question since he knows exactly what happened next.

"No, it didn't. My car started to make these clicking noises which turned into splutters. Once I hit town it got way worse. I think it was the stops and starts. I stopped at a red light. Miss Sunshine jerked and spluttered a whole lot more when I tried to pull off. It got so bad I had to pull over to the side. Then she died completely. When I tried to restart the engine, there was this clicking sound. Then nothing at all."

"I want to show you something." He lifts off the car and turns around, glancing back at me, telling me to follow using his eyes.

I scoot next to him and lean in. I'm close enough to feel

his heat. My left arm brushes against his right one.

"These are the valves," he says, pointing at the parts in question. "Those are sparkplugs."

I'm confused. "Why is that one different from the others?" I ask.

"It's old. The other three are new. Someone replaced one of your perfectly good sparkplugs with an old faulty one. That's why you had car troubles. It turns out you were right about Miss Sunshine being reliable."

It warms me when he calls my car by her name. Like my quirks don't bug him. "It had to have been Sly," I say.

Forge nods. "Good chance."

"But that makes no sense, why tamper with my car instead of capturing me?" I shudder at the thought. It means that Sly was there, more than likely at the motel where I caught a few hours' sleep the night before last. "He would have been there, while I stopped for a rest." My mind is spinning. "Why sabotage my car? Why not come after me? Why waste time?" I'm thinking out loud.

"I think he's been playing with you. Enjoying the chase."

"That's sick!" I push out, feeling nauseated. "Loving every minute, no doubt," I mumble to myself.

He looks at me with concern in his eyes, which have softened. "There's more."

"More." *What else could there be?*

"I found it when I first started my inspection of your car."

"Found what? I'm not going to like this am I?" My stomach feels tied up in knots.

He shakes his head. "No. You're not." He gestures to

a board on the ground. The one he lay on earlier when taking a look at the underside of Miss Sunshine. "I think it would be better if you took a look for yourself."

"You want me to lie on that?"

He smiles at me. It lasts all of three seconds but my stomach clenches. I'm not just attracted to Forge, I like him as well. I'm thrilled he smiled because of me. I want to make him smile again. It's not a good idea to give in to this in any way, so I push the thought aside.

"Yes, I want you to lie on the board. I want you to see this for yourself. It's not so bad."

"I'm in a dress." It comes to about midthigh. I probably shouldn't have worn it to a workshop, but I wanted to look pretty and feel normal after so many weeks of chaos. A girl sometimes needs a break.

"There's no one else here and I won't look." He holds up his hand and crosses two fingers. "I swear."

"Okay."

He moves behind me. "I'll keep my eyes averted."

I nod. I trust him not to look. I start to go down, putting a hand on one side of the board so that I can sit. I yelp when the thing slides out. I'm about to fall on my face when he grips my hips with his huge warm hands. My heart goes nuts. I assure myself that it's not because he is touching me, it's because I came close to losing half the skin on my face. That's all!

"You okay?' he asks.

"I thought you weren't going to look!" I blurt.

"You yelped. I looked. Good thing I'm fast."

I heave out a breath. "Good thing." I'm thankful my dress is still covering my girl parts.

"I'll lower you down. I'll keep my eyes on the ceiling. You're good."

"Okay." I sound breathless. I need to get a grip.

He chuckles. It's warm and throaty and sends goosebumps popping up on my body. "You have to let go of me for this to work."

"Oh. Crap!" I giggle. I realize I'm holding onto his biceps for dear life. Both of them. What biceps they are. No wonder my hands won't loosen their grip. "Of course." I force myself to let him go.

He lowers me down until my ass is on the board. I position myself until I'm lying down in the center of the board.

"I'm going to spin you to the right and then push you under the car. You ready?"

"Yep." I'm not sure where to put my arms, so I cross them over my chest. I move my legs, stepping as we go. Then I'm under my car. It's cool to see her from this angle.

"It's on the side. If you—"

I gasp.

"Do you see it?"

"Yes. The bastard!" I growl the words, feeling pissed to my core. I can't believe it.

"I'm pulling you out now."

I'm too angry to say anything. I just nod, even though he can't see me. I see his face as he pulls me out and it's filled with sympathy.

I stay lying down on the board, even though I can get up now if I want to. "Is it what I think it is?"

He nods. "It's exactly what you think it is."

"A tracking device." I want to curse, I'm so angry. "You were right when you said he's been playing games. It's been cat-and-mouse for three weeks. All this time he's been tracking me. He knew exactly where I was at all times. He could have had me ten times over. He's sick!" I sit up. "When he decided he was done playing, he put that faulty part in my car?"

"He orchestrated the whole thing. Good thing you broke down in front of my shop."

"Good thing." I feel cold all over. Sick to my stomach.

"We just need to find out why."

I frown. Not sure what he means. "I told you why."

"The real reason." Forge keeps his eyes on mine. "We need to find out the real reason, Ava. I'm not saying he doesn't want sex from you, but it isn't the only thing he wants."

He's right. Forge is absolutely right. I've been thinking it all along. There's more to this. I'm not sure how we're going to find out. I'm not sure I even want to. It will mean seeing Sly again.

CHAPTER 9

AVA

Later that day

"What the fuck, Trident?" A big guy with black hair and very dark eyes answers the door as the three of us arrive. His eyes are so dark they're almost black like his hair. They're framed with long, thick lashes. His skin is milky white. There's a scar that cuts across his right eyebrow slashing onto his forehead. I force myself to look away from it. It's jagged. Must have hurt when it happened. He doesn't have a single tattoo that I can see. He's big and built and very good-looking, so I'm assuming he's one of them.

A dragon demigod.

I still can't believe they exist. His eyes seem to darken as they narrow in on me, reminding me of lumps of coal.

Just as cold too. I have to fight not to step backward. Not to run away and fast.

"She's with me," Forge says.

The guy does a double-take. "You have to be fucking kidding me," he says as soon as he recovers. "I thought you would have known better. You're not bringing her in here." He tries to smash the door shut but Forge puts his foot out, slamming his hand against the wood.

"Move it or lose it!" the angry guy snarls.

"Stop your shit, Rage." Forge's face is red. His jaw is tight, but otherwise he seems completely calm.

"You called a meeting and you brought *her*?" His eyes widen. "I honestly thought you knew better. This is against every rule. Please tell me she doesn't know anything." His voice drops to something just shy of a whisper.

"She knows," Forge says.

"Fuck!" the guy snarls. He turns and walks into the building. Rage... what a name. It suits him perfectly.

I jump when Forge puts his hand to my back. "It's okay," he says. "I've got you."

I instantly relax.

"Let's do this." Trident looks worried, even though he sounds upbeat.

I glance at Forge. He still has his hand on my back. He looks like he always does... brooding. His bold presence reassures me. I take a deep breath, square my shoulders and head inside.

Trident walks ahead of us. I follow him. Forge stays one step behind me. We walk down a long hallway and then through a set of double doors into a large room. In the middle of the room is a long table. There are several men seated around the table. Rage is one of them. He just sits there and glowers at us.

Jarrod waves and is given several dirty looks by some of the other guys. He clears his throat and pulls his chair closer to the table, his eyes are downcast.

"So, this human knows about us?" The guy who speaks looks at me like I'm a piece of shit under his shoe. He has bleached blond hair and a tan to match. His eyes are a deep, dark blue. His whole body is tense with raw energy. He has tattoos but only on the left side of his body. His left arm is covered. From his fingers, his palm, all the way up his arm. He even has tattoos creeping up his t-shirt on that side. And on his neck. Only on the left. A skull... I think.

"Yes, she knows." Forge nods.

The blonde guy shakes his head like he can't believe what he's hearing. "We have rules for a reason." He shakes his head some more. His eyes are blazing. "You should have requested permission first. You know the rules. You both do." He gives Trident a scathing look.

"I made the call," Forge says.

"We both did," Trident adds.

"Unacceptable!" Blondie shouts, hitting the table with an open hand. It creaks but holds. Any harder and the wood may have split.

It's as if Forge can sense my trepidation, because he touches the side of my arm, brushing my skin with his fingers. His touch lingers for a fraction longer than it should. I know he's just trying to reassure me. It works.

"You have a lot of explaining to do," the same guy says.

"You can start with who she is." Another guy speaks this time. He's in a three-piece suit. He has dark hair and a five o'clock shadow that works. His eyes are silver-grey. He leans back and folds his arms.

We're still standing at the head of the table, barely inside the door. It feels like there's a spotlight on us. All eyes are on me. Although Forge is about to speak, I step forward. I'm not letting him speak for me. I can introduce myself. I have nothing to feel guilty about. I did nothing wrong. "I'm Ava Jones." I tell them where I'm from and a couple of basic facts, like my age and where I used to work before my life imploded.

They don't show any emotion. "Explain," the bleached blonde says, eyes on Forge now. He's dismissed me outright.

I pull in a breath to tell them what happened, but Forge bumps his arm against mine. He gives the smallest shake of the head. "Where are Lyre and Samuel?" he asks.

"Lyre's in the middle of some surgical procedure he couldn't get out of and Samuel is —"

"Asleep," Forge finishes for Blondie. "I forgot... it's still daytime." A weird thing to say since most people sleep at night. "Ava's car broke down across the road from my shop," he begins.

Blondie snorts. "How convenient." He looks over at Silver Eyes and they exchange a knowing look that irritates the crap out of me.

I see Forge's jaw tighten. His whole body bristles. "She saw my sign and tried to talk me into towing and fixing her car."

"I thought you had better sense than to fall for bullshit like that," Blondie sneers, getting on my last nerve.

"He turned me down flat," I say. "And it wasn't bullshit. My car really did break down."

I am, again, ignored. They all keep their attention on Forge. "Ava asked for help and I turned her down. She called me a couple of names, and I changed my mind."

"I'm sure you did." Blondie gives me the once-over. I don't like it and neither does Forge because he growls low. "A sweet little thing like this," he goes on. "I must say, though, I would've expected as much from Tri but not from you. Allowing yourself to be swayed by a piece of ass."

I clench my fists and a strange squeak leaves my throat. "How dare you!" I push out.

Forge clasps my elbow and squeezes lightly. "I'll deal with this." His eyes are pleading with me to keep quiet. He lets go, taking a small step forward, putting himself slightly in front of me and yet not blocking me off from the conversation. "Although her car was still there, I couldn't find Ava. I didn't know that she was trying to hitch a ride out of town. I had Jarrod load her car onto the tow truck anyway. Susan was convinced Ava had an ex after her. That he would be out looking for her wheels, which are quite distinctive…" Forge tells them the rest of the story without any more interruptions. The fight, Sly not being human. Ending with how I caught Trident removing the bullet from Forge's stomach.

When Forge is done, they all just sit there looking at us for a while. "You were both played," Blondie tells Forge and Trident; he's completely deadpan. "I think this human," he looks at me with disdain, "is in cahoots with this Sly asshole. They were looking to infiltrate our organization and they succeeded. Way to go."

"That's a bunch of bull," Forge barks. "Not many people know about us."

"With good reason," the guy with the grey eyes says. "It just takes one slip up to have knowledge of our existence in the wrong hands. You messed up. You should have left well enough alone."

"What choice did I have?" Forge asks.

"Stay out of shit that has nothing to do with you," Blondie snaps.

"I hear you, Night," Forge counters. "But I don't agree. Not this time. Ava was in real trouble. I couldn't just turn my back on her. You would have done the same."

"Not a chance," Night chuckles. "I'm definitely not as gullible as you were in this instance." He has gone back to being serious. "I maintain, you were played by this human. Start talking." Blondie... Night... whatever his name is, looks at me. If his name is Night, it works. It's a true reflection of his personality. Dark. Like the inside of a hole... an asshole, perhaps.

"I don't have to explain myself to you. Everything Forge just told you is the truth," I say, trying to stay calm.

"Start talking," Night repeats.

"I think I'll go," I say. I've had just about enough of this. I don't have to explain anything to this jerk.

"Good idea," Night sneers.

"Don't," Forge says.

"I won't stand around listening to them... him... the blond surfer dude speaking like that about me." I add the surfer dude reference because I know it will piss this Night person off, and it does.

His jaw tightens and his eyes narrow.

Trident chokes out a laugh which he quickly stifles. Jarrod's lip twitches and his eyes glint but he doesn't say or do anything. The rest of them look at me like I just kicked a puppy.

"I need to discuss this with my brothers," Night says. "You are not invited to listen in. Besides, I have a feeling I'll hurt your feelings, human."

"My name is Ava."

"Is it?" Definitely a question. He doesn't believe anything I say, including who I am. He keeps his eyes narrowed on me. "I don't trust you one bit," he adds unnecessarily.

"Gee, I hadn't noticed." I shouldn't rise to what he is saying but I can't help it. He's such a jerk.

Forge sighs and pinches the bridge of his nose for a second before looking my way. His eyes soften. "Would you mind waiting outside while I finish this discussion? We need to hash this out and maybe it is better if you're not here when that happens." His whole disposition grows gentler. "I would appreciate it."

I nod once and head out. Forge follows me. He closes the door behind us. "Look, I'm sorry about this," he says.

"No, it's I who should be apologizing. I'm sorry I got you into trouble. I'll leave altogether if it will help. I've said it before and I'll say it again, this isn't your problem." I've told him this several times. I mean it. It's the last thing I want, but I don't want Forge to get into any more trouble. I turn and start to walk away.

CHAPTER 10

FORGE

Ava is right but she's also wrong. She *did* get me into serious shit, but I made choices for myself. One of those choices was a commitment I made to her. One I intend to keep. I will protect her from Sly and keep her safe. I will get to the bottom of this.

"It *is* my problem!" I try not to growl as I take her arm, stopping her. "I told you I would help you and I will." I turn her around. "I trust you." I release her, realizing that I mean every word. You can't fake the surprise and the shock I saw written in her eyes this morning. I saw both when she realized her car had been tampered with. I heard the shock in her gasp when she found the tracking device. I've seen her fear. It's real. Ava is telling the truth. She's terrified of this Sly motherfucker. "Night, Rage and the others will come around. Trident and even Jarrod are with us… I know they are. Give me five minutes to talk this through with the rest of them and maybe I can convince them too."

She chews on her lower lip for a second. "I somehow doubt you'll convince them. Night seems sure that I'm out to get you. That I'm working with Sly." I see her shiver. She tries to cover it up, but she can't.

"Give me five minutes?" I ask again. "I grew up with them. I'll bring them around."

She licks her lips, looking like she's thinking it through. Ava finally nods. *Thank fuck!* "Don't go anywhere," I warn. "Stay right here."

"Okay." She pulls in a lungful of air and leans up against the wall.

Ava looks fucking amazing in that dress. It's bright and floral. It's not showing too much skin. It isn't tight or anything… but fuck! She looks gorgeous. She has curves for days. She could wear a black bag and you wouldn't be able to miss them. Her skin is tanned. It's her eyes that floor me. They're big and expressive. It's easy to read her emotions just by looking into their hazel depths. I might be attracted to her. Night is right on that note but he's wrong about everything else. I need to convince him of that. "I'll see you in a few minutes."

She nods, clutching her purse strap. Even though she's a strong woman, she exudes so much vulnerability that for a moment I'm tempted to say 'fuck it' and leave, but I can't. I would die for my brothers and they would do the same for me. There is no way a woman is coming between us. Not ever! If I left with her now, that might happen. I'm going to help Ava and then I'm sending her on her way. I first have to get her out of this situation. She's so far out of her depth.

I head back into the boardroom. They stop talking as soon as I do. It's clear that I was the main topic of conversation.

Night leans back in his chair. "You're putting us all in danger over pussy."

I launch myself over the table and grip his throat as my feet hit the floor. "Don't!" I warn.

"Must be *some* pussy if you're this riled up." His voice is strained.

"I haven't fucked her. You know that as well as everyone in this room."

"It's just a matter of time." The words are choked, and I realize I am closing my fingers around his windpipe.

I let him go with a snarl. "She needed my help. Still does. I trust her. That's all that should matter."

"The problem is," Night rubs his throat, it's red beneath his hand, "I don't know if I can trust your judgment. There is something not right with that human."

"Her name is Ava," I say, holding his stare.

Night shrugs like he doesn't give a shit.

"Both Trident and Jarrod believe her as well," Bolt says, playing with one of his cufflinks. "Maybe we should cut Forge some slack."

Night looks like he is thinking it through. "Did you pick up on anything?" he asks Jarrod, who shakes his head.

"Not a thing."

"What about you, Stephan?" Night asks Stephanus, Jarrod's twin brother.

"Nothing whatsoever. Not even a thread... nothing."

The twins are psychic. Jarrod can see what has already been and Stephanus can predict the future.

"Like I was saying," Night shakes his head, "that's not normal. The twins normally read humans easily. Not this one. Why? I don't trust her for shit."

"Jarrod and Stephan can't always read humans," I throw back.

"It's rare though." Night says. "Especially for both of them not to get anything. I don't care what you do, as long as she never talks about us… ever."

"What are you saying?" I narrow my eyes. I don't like what he's hinting at.

"Scare her, fuck her. I don't care which. Just make sure she keeps her pretty little mouth shut about our existence. And don't go getting any ideas."

"What ideas would those be?" I struggle to keep the venom out of my voice.

"You can't keep her." He shakes his head. "We can't take mates. We can't have young. We made an oath that our bloodlines stop with us. Have you forgotten, Forge?"

"I haven't forgotten anything. I'm helping her out of a mess and at the same time, trying to figure out who and what this Sly asshole is. It's not like that."

"Are you sure about that?" Bolt asks. "You do seem… attached, and quite quickly, considering you just met her yesterday."

"Attached?" I snort. "It's not like that. I don't plan on keeping her." I can feel myself grimacing.

"In that case, I suggest you don't settle yourself between those thighs… as lush as they may be. You might just forget yourself. Forget us."

I'm starting to see red. Night's talking about Ava like she's a piece of meat. I also think he has forgotten that we are equals around this table. "Who died and made you the boss?"

"It's a suggestion. You seem infatuated enough with the human as it is. I wouldn't throw sex into the equation. Her pussy might just be tight enough to—"

That's it. My fist connects with his face before I have a chance to think it through. It makes a satisfying crunching noise. Night is still on his chair as it flies back. It clatters as it hits the ground. Apparently, it's not satisfying enough because I still want to hit him some more. I straddle him and punch down with all my might.

My fist hits the floor... hard... as Night disappears out from under me. White, hot pain explodes. There is another crunching noise as bones break. My bones. That fucker has just used his powers to teleport away. The scent of ozone fills my nostrils. I am fucking livid.

AVA

I play with my purse strap. I'm angry but I'm also trying to see things from their perspective. Dragon demigods. I wipe a hand over my face. They have superhuman strength and healing powers and yet they are vulnerable. If the human race were to hear about them, they'd be locked away, experimented on... and worse.

Humans are not the most tolerant of species. We generally look to exploit and destroy. Just take a look at our planet and the many animals and plants that are already extinct. That's on us. The dragon demigods would end up extinct too. I don't think they would be easy to kill, but they bleed and therefore they can die. I understand their fears. That Night asshole doesn't have to be quite so rude about it, though. He made it personal, which pisses me off. I don't like that Forge is getting into trouble over me. He's taken me under his wing and that fact has made me protective of him as well. I meant it when I said I would leave to make things easier for him, but I won't lie, I was very thankful when he insisted I stay.

I pace up the hallway and then back down again. I can hear them inside. It sounds like things are getting heated. I can't hear what they are saying, only that voices are raised. They might even be yelling. For a moment I am tempted to go inside there again. I want to defend Forge. This is all my fault. I know I'll just make things worse, so I pace back up the hallway instead.

The air freezes in my lungs. Everything in me goes cold. My throat closes. Sly has just materialized out of nowhere. That's the best word I can think of for what just happened. He materialized. One second he wasn't there and the next, he is.

"Hey, babe." He winks at me.

I can't move. Can't speak. I'm frozen.

"Miss me?" he smirks.

I pull in a breath to scream and he grabs me. My stomach lurches. I get that feeling you get when the rollercoaster drops on a particularly hectic ride. My stomach feels like it has twisted inside of me. I struggle to breathe and see white dots. It feels like I'm going to throw up.

Everything stops. It's so sudden I fall. The ground is

soft. Thankfully it's a thick pile rug or I might have bruised my hip when I landed. *Wait a minute.* That isn't right. It takes my mind a few moments to process my thoughts. The hallway had slate tiles. I am lying on a rug. *What? How?*

Sly.

He's here. He has me. I sit up and the room spins. I hold my head and groan, feeling the nausea return.

"You'll feel better in a minute. The first few times are always a little rough."

I turn to the voice. It *is* Sly. He *is* here. The bastard smiles. "I'm glad you're finally with me. Glad we're together," he says as he pulls the foil off the top of a bottle of champagne. Then he pops the cork.

My head is spinning. My mouth is dry. I feel dizzy. At least the nausea is passing. "Whath...? Whath are yoou...?" I try but my words are slurred. I shake my head to try to clear it. It doesn't work.

"It's time," he says, pouring two glasses of the bubbly liquid. "This little adventure has gone on for too long. It's time we sealed our little deal. I'm not normally a patient man."

He hands me a glass and I throw it back at him. I'm weak and still feeling woozy, so the glass goes wide of him, landing on the rug. It doesn't break. I watch as the champagne soaks into the rug.

"Tsk, tsk," he tuts like I'm a little child. "That's not very nice." He refills the glass while I struggle to my feet. I stagger like I'm drunk.

"What shall we toast to?" he asks.

I stand there, swaying. I'm still out of it.

"Oh, I know." He smiles brightly. "To us!" He clinks

the glasses together and then proceeds to drink the contents of both. "There. It's done. Now, let's put all this nastiness behind us and move on, shall we?"

"Fthuck you!" I stagger, only just staying up. My limbs feel heavy.

"I lied when I said I only wanted you for one night, Ava. I need you for a little longer than that." He winks and the nausea is back.

I don't say anything. I'm hoping that my strength will return soon. I don't like the look I see in his eyes.

"I didn't lie when I said I wanted to fuck you. Nope." He shakes his head, his eyes drifting down my body. They turn greedy. "I've wanted you for a while now. A long while. I'd been searching for you, or for someone unique and special like you. Imagine my surprise when I walked into The Winged Palace one day and there you were. I'd searched for years and you fell right into my lap." He laughs and pours himself another glass. "You refused all of my advances. I discovered I hate being rejected. I tried to do this the nice way. I asked you out. I made it clear I was interested." He points at the bed. "Take the dress off and go and lie down."

I shake my head.

He clenches his jaw. "Last chance, babe. We can do this the nice way. Have some fun," he sneers. "Or we can do it the hard way."

"Don't!" I shake my head, feeling panic well. I look around. We're in what looks like the penthouse suite of a hotel. "Don't come near me." No more slurring, but my limbs feel heavy. Too heavy. What the hell am I going to do? He's too strong.

"I lied about one other little thing." Sly grins. "I said I

wanted you willing. That I'm not into forcing women. That's not true, babes. I don't give a fuck either way. You are mine!"

"No," I try. Tears are rolling down my cheeks. I'm helpless. "I'll scream. I'll…"

I watch as Sly picks up a remote and turns the music volume up. "You go right ahead, babe. I'll work on turning your cries into moans."

No!

I am readying myself to fight Sly when the surfer dude demigod appears about five feet to the right of us. For a split second, I'm sure I'm seeing things. His lip is cut and bleeding. Drops of crimson roll down his chin. If I were to conjure Night up, he'd be hurt and bleeding because he's an A-hole, so maybe I'm dreaming. Then he launches himself at Sly, fists flying and I realize that he isn't a figment of my imagination. One, two, three blows connect before Sly falls back onto the bed. He kicks out as he's falling, in a double-barrel that hits Night in the midriff. Sly doesn't land, he disappears before the bedsheets even rustle.

Night is bent over the middle. He's breathing heavily, holding his stomach. A second later, he's pulling himself up to his full height and grabbing me by both my arms.

It happens again. My stomach lurches. It's worse this time. My stomach heaves and then everything goes dark.

CHAPTER 11

AVA

Oh god!

Sly!

Run.

I have to run. I have to hide.

Away.

I have to get away. I sit up and drag in a breath. I'm already moving. My eyes are wide, and I can't catch my breath.

"It's okay." Strong arms hold me. "You're okay."

I try to pull away. I have to go. Run. Flee…

"It's me… it's Forge." He's speaking softly and carefully, using a soothing tone. "You're safe." His hands are firm but not rough.

Forge.

Thank god.

I collapse against his chest. He puts his arms around me. I can't help it, but I cry. I feel like a baby as heavy tears course down my cheeks. He rubs my back in slow circles. He doesn't say anything to try to make me feel better or to soothe me. He just waits it out. It takes a couple of minutes before I am able to pull myself together. I rub my face and hiccup once.

Forge gets up and goes into the bathroom, returning within seconds with a wad of toilet paper, which he hands to me.

I wipe my face and nose. "He took me." I shudder. "That bastard." After the tears come anger. "He... he..." I grit my teeth for a moment. "He was going to rape me." If I had a gun and he was in the room right now, I wouldn't hesitate to kill him. That's how pissed off I am.

"I know." Forge nods once. "Night told me. He heard the ass-end of your conversation, he heard what that motherfucker said to you. That's how teleporting works. The good news is that Night believes you now." He reaches out and touches my knee.

"Oh my god! What happened to your hand?" I say, looking down. It's purple and green across the knuckles but also spilling over onto the top and his fingers.

"Night and I got into a spat. It's almost healed. You should have seen it before. It was triple the size."

I heard yelling just before I was taken. Must have happened then. I frown. "How did he know I was in trouble?"

"Night can teleport too. Apparently, he can sense if someone else teleports close by and can follow the path-signal. He didn't know it before but there you go." He rubs his forehead, easing the furrows there. "I don't know how it works exactly. But yes, Night can do it. Only, it takes a lot out of him to move within this realm."

"This realm? What do you mean by that?"

"Night's father is Hades. God of the Underworld. Night finds it easier to teleport in and out of hell than what he does up here."

I can't say anything. My mouth is gaping. "Surfer Dude is the son of Hades? I can't believe that. He has a tan. How can he have a tan?"

Forge smiles. Oh, good lord, but he's cute when he smiles. After all that's happened, I should not find him cute right now. I should not be looking at his lips. Or at how well he fills out a white shirt. "Night AKA Surfer Dude – I love how you called him that by the way – is the son of Hades. He isn't a bad guy. He's the only one of us who has met his father. They have an estranged relationship. I think he would have been better off not knowing him. It's fucked him up." He pushes out a heavy breath. "Like I said, he's not a bad guy. Believe it or not, Night volunteers at our local shelter. He walks a couple of the dogs every day. He owns a gym and sponsors several youths who are less fortunate. He does it to keep them off the streets and out of gangs. As the son of Hades, he worries about turning evil, so he overcompensates."

"Not with me he didn't."

Forge rubs his jaw. "I know! He's also very protective of us… of me. You guys got off to a bad start but—"

"You don't have to defend him. He saved me from Sly." Crap, I feel tears well. "I'm infinitely grateful. I'll tell him next time I see him."

"About that…" He makes a face. "Maybe lay low for a while." He narrows his eyes, which are glinting. He looks like he's holding back a smile. "I'd stay away from Night if I was you." He winces. I can see he's teasing me. What I don't know is why.

"What happened?" I ask. "Tell me," I add when he just sits there, his mouth turned up at the corners.

"You kind of puked all over him when he teleported you out of there."

"Oh shit." I cover my mouth. "I did, didn't I?" I finally say as I take my hand away. "Just before I blacked out." My stomach lurched and… *Oh no!*

Forge nods. "All over him. He was covered in it. It did not smell of cookies, Oreo. Not even a little bit."

My cheeks turn hot. I'm mortified. I fall back on the bed and realize that I've never been here before. This isn't Forge's apartment. It's bigger, fancier. "Um…" I say as I sit up, "where are we and how long was I out for?"

Forge looks at his watch. "Two and a half hours. We're at Tri's place and he's at mine in case Sly pops in." I watch as his eyes turn stormy and his muscles bunch. "You had a tracker in your purse. I'm sorry but we had to look, and I couldn't ask for permission since you were out cold. Two teleport trips in a row will do that to a person."

"It's fine about looking in my purse." I don't mind. There are a couple of girly things in there—not those things – but for the most part, it's a standard purse with your standard things inside. "Where was the tracker?" I still feel hot all over; this time it's anger.

"We found a tracker sewn into the lining. We figured

he had to have something on you because he found us. He should not have found us so easily. There was one in your car, so, it was the obvious explanation."

It feels like the floor drops out from under me. I'm reeling. I can't believe what I'm hearing. "He must have had someone put it in while I was working. He planned this whole thing." For a moment I'm speechless, then I choke out, "Bruce! Maybe my brother's death was orchestrated as well."

"It's possible." Forge nods. "I'm sorry. We're dealing with one sick bastard. You need to tell me everything that happened. Everything he said. We need to try to get to the bottom of this."

I nod and tell him everything I remember. Forge is frowning. "Sly said he had been looking for you. Or for someone like you."

"Yes."

"That's an odd thing to say."

"It didn't sound like he was talking specifically about me, but I could be wrong. I think he might have used the word 'special'… someone special like me. That he had been searching until I fell into his lap when I started working at the casino."

"He planned on keeping you for longer than just one night." Forge's voice has grown deep and menacing.

I swallow hard. "Yes, and… he… he…" We both know what Sly wanted.

Forge's muscles bulge and lines appear on his forehead. He takes my hand and squeezes once before letting go. "I won't let him get to you again. I doubt he knows where you are now. I doubt that he will be able to find you, but just as a precaution, I don't plan on letting you out of my sight… not for a second. Tri is at my place. Night, Rage and Bolt are trying to find intel on him. Night will teleport to the casino as soon as he gets his strength back. They will find him and make him pay, I promise you that. That prick dared come into our house… onto our territory." Forge is bristling. His whole stance is tense. He looks at me strangely, like he is sorry about something.

"What is it?"

"Tri has your phone. He'll keep it with him just in case he's using it to trace you somehow."

"It's a burner."

"Still." He shakes his head. "You can't contact anyone. No friends or family."

I only have Trudy and we sometimes go weeks without chatting. Bruce and I may have been estranged but he was my brother. It was always good to know I had family. *Someone.* Trudy is still very much someone but still, not family… I feel sad all over again knowing that I am all alone. For a moment, I'm overwhelmed… I've been through a lot. I feel like I need to be alone. I need to decompress.

"Okay, but the first order of business is to take a shower." I make a face. I'm sure I stink of nervous sweat and possibly vomit. "I can do that on my own," I add.

His stare doesn't waver. His eyes stay locked with mine. "Um… you can't shower without me."

Is it just my imagination or have his cheeks turned slightly pink? "That fucker abducted you a few feet away from a room full of us. You were just through a door. When I say I'm with you, I mean it. I can't teleport, Ava. I don't have a power like the rest of the team does. I'm strong but that's it. If he gets you, he'll teleport and then he'll have you. You understand that, right?"

I nod once. "What if I need the bathroom or…" I'm freaking out a little.

"We'll figure it out."

"You can't watch me pee… or," my eyes widen, "the other thing. No way! Just no!" I shake my head.

He pushes out a breath. "Maybe we keep the door open when you go to the toilet. You would need to be really quick. We talk the whole time."

"The whole time?" My eyes are wide.

"I don't know what else to say." He rakes his hand through his hair. "Ideally you don't go out of my sight. You're not showering alone."

"You're not watching me shower. How would you like it if I watched you shower?" I realize that I sound ungrateful but… this is too much.

"You can watch me shower." He shrugs. "I wouldn't mind."

"I'm not watching you shower!" It comes out sounding harsh. Like it would be the worst thing in the world to watch him take a shower. Only because the opposite is true. My body tingles with awareness. I wouldn't mind showering with Forge. I reckon we'd do more than just wash each other's backs. That's a problem right there. I shouldn't even have these thoughts after what just happened, which makes me feel like there's something wrong with me.

"Wear a bikini or take a bubble bath." He looks uncomfortable, his Adam's apple works. "I'll try not to look. I'll work even harder to keep my thoughts… pure."

I raise my brows. "You'll try?" I want to laugh at his

serious face. He's so kind and sweet. I can't believe I ever thought badly of him. I'm beginning to realize that it's just a façade. Forge is a nice guy. His complete discomfort is making me feel better. Lighter.

"I will. I swear." I can see he means it. See what I mean, so sweet.

"I don't have a bikini. I threw some stuff in a bag and ran. A bikini was not on my packing list."

"Your underwear then. We can check if Trident has some foam bath. I wouldn't put it past him." He grins for a second. "We have to hole up for a couple of days. We can't go anywhere. We have to be really careful. I have to insist, Ava. I'm sorry."

I nod. Adrenaline is pumping through me at the thought of Sly getting his hands on me again. He'll rape me, use me for as long as he wants. "I still don't get why he wants me. Why he's become so obsessed."

"The guys will find out. It might just be that he's a sick bastard. He wants you because he can't have you. It's driving him insane." I can see by the way he's looking at me that he doesn't quite buy it. There's more to it. We both know it.

I want to forget about Sly for a little while. "Shall we see if Trident has any bubble bath? I need to get clean and I desperately need to eat something."

"Yes, of course." Forge doesn't look eager at the prospect. The opposite is true. I should feel happy about that, but I don't. It's confusing me right now.

FORGE

I promised to keep my thoughts pure. Or at least to try. It's going to be tough when I'm already failing, and Ava hasn't taken a stitch of clothing off yet.

I'm a bastard.

I wish I could turn off my attraction for this woman. It would make things so much easier. I can't. It's just not possible.

When Night offered to watch her instead of me, I reacted badly. I may have snarled at him. Ava is my responsibility. *Mine!* It doesn't matter that Night is the obvious choice to guard her – he can teleport, and I can't. The human is mine to protect and as long as I stay close, that fucker won't be able to take her. I'm fully invested. I'm not handing over this responsibility to anyone else. Even with his teleporting powers, Night would still have to be near her every moment to protect her and that is not going to fucking happen.

If it means having a hard-on half the time and working on 'pure thoughts' the other half, then that's what I will do.

If it means that Ava has to be a little uncomfortable at times, then so be it. I don't like the fact, but if it keeps her safe, then that's how it has to be.

I watch her fish her toiletry bag out of her luggage and follow her into the bathroom. Ava gasps as she walks into the large space. "*This* is Trident's bathroom?" She sounds completely shocked. I don't blame her.

"He likes water." I can't smiling at her sheer joy. "He also likes fish."

"I can see that." Her eyes are wide as she follows one of the colorful creatures as it dances between the coral.

"I have strict feeding instructions for these guys," I say.

She smiles, which makes me feel good. *What the fuck is happening to me?*

The tub is huge, it takes up a whole corner of the bathroom. One entire wall is a fish tank.

"It's quite something," Ava remarks.

"It is." I lean against the doorjamb, feeling like an intruder. I wait a little longer for her to take in more of the large room. Things like the two-person shower and the mosaic on the floor. It's of Poseidon. Trident's father.

It makes my place look like a hovel. Somehow, despite Ava's reaction, I don't think she is swayed by money. If she was, she'd be all over Sly. As it stands, she's more interested in the fish than in the marble tops and gleaming finishes. Aside from my vintage rides—I have seven—I'm not much of a materialistic person. Things don't interest me. They never have.

I walk over to the vanity. It's a large double unit. I can't help noticing that everything is built for two people. Then again, the tub could fit at least six. I can just picture Trident lounging in it with a glass of some or other fancy wine in his hand. I start to smile and then bite it back as I picture some female bouncing on his dick. That would be more realistic. I don't want to think about that, so I continue my search.

I open the cupboard doors. I find the usual. Things like shaving cream and mouthwash. There is a bottle of foam bath but it's almost finished. There's a jar of bath salts but it won't help protect Ava's modesty.

"I take it there's nothing in there?" Ava asks.

I shake my head. "Not enough." I hold up the almost finished bottle, watching her face drop. I'm tempted to tell her I can give her five minutes but that's exactly what happened earlier today. I left for a few minutes and Sly almost got what he wanted. It won't happen on my watch.

I'm also cursing my lack of powers. Why wasn't I given a power like every other demigod? I'm grateful for my talents. Engines... parts that move in general, have always come easy to me. I just know how to take things apart and how to put them back together. I definitely know how to fix something if it isn't working. I always have. I didn't need to study. I'm also a gifted artist. I have had to work hard at honing my painting skills but they're there in spades. I'm not complaining about my talents, but right now, they're useless to me.

"You're sure you have to be here?" she tries. Not very hard, even though her big hazel eyes are pleading. *Fucking killing me!*

"Yes, I'm sure," I say simply. What else is there to say?

"Then I guess we'd better do this thing thing." Her face drops and her eyes well with tears. "I feel dirty after what happened. Sly touched me... he—"

"That fucker touched you?" I snarl the words as I take a step towards her. "You didn't say anything about—"

"Not like that. He didn't have time to get that far." She licks her lips.

"Thank fuck!"

She smiles. Her face is pure sunshine. Like the clouds

clearing after the rain. Like a bird taking flight after the cage has been opened. "You're so sweet to be helping me like this."

"Not really. I'm a guy, so, in this instance... I'm not sweet." I rake a hand through my hair, holding the back of my neck.

"You are, Forge. You're incredibly sweet and nothing at all like Sly. You're one of the good guys. I believe that wholeheartedly."

That's the thing about Ava, she makes me want to be a good guy. She makes me want to be a better person. She has from the moment I met her.

She swallows and I watch the column of her throat work. "We're both adults." I can see she's putting on a brave face. "It's no big deal. You've seen plenty of women naked before. I've been naked in front of a guy once or twice."

Why does hearing her say that make my gut churn?

"I'll stay in my underwear. It will be fine." She pulls in a deep breath and pulls her dress over her head. I have to work really hard to keep my eyes on hers.

Pure thoughts.

Pure.

I think of my mother. My niece, Becky. I even think of my cousin, Susan. Yep, Susan is a dragon shifter. She's family. She's worked with me for several years now. Runs the front end of the shop like nobody's business. Those are the women in my life. I respect and cherish each of them. I need to respect and cherish Ava in the same way.

I can't.

Pure thoughts.

Pure, for fuck's sakes!

I manage to somehow keep my eyes on Ava's face. I can sort of see her body but I'm trying hard not to. She's fucking perfect. Her bra is strapless. It's hard not to miss that. It's hard not to miss the slope of her breasts, or the fact that they're so fucking full. Her hips are lush too. I don't have to look down to know that. Her ass will be tight and yet have substance. This woman is gorgeous. My balls hurt and my dick is trying to fill.

Pure thoughts.

I remind myself that it's her eyes that are her best quality. I keep mine firmly on hers. I'm glad to see that she doesn't look frightened, or uneasy in any way. She pulls her bottom lip between her teeth for a moment and then turns. I want to bite on that lip of hers. I want—

Pure!

The water splatters to life. I lean back and cross my arms. I have to stay vigilant. I can't let my guard down, even for a second.

I feel my blood boil at the thought of that cocksucker, Sly. I want to kill him with my bare hands. I want to watch the light fade from his eyes. I want him dead. For a moment I am sorry I insisted on being the one to keep Ava safe. I should have been the one tracking that fucker. The one taking him down. But then Night would be here now instead of me.

Fuck that!

I picked the right assignment. Ava lathers up her hair and then rinses it. She is working quickly and efficiently. She throws a glance at me every so often. My balls feel heavy but my cock is behaving... for the most part.

Pure thoughts.

A minute later and she's turning off the shower. I grab a towel off the rack and hand it to her. I will feel a whole lot better when she's covered up. "Thanks." She uses the towel to wrap her hair.

Fuck!

I hand her another one. This time she wraps it around her body. I am able to breathe again.

"That wasn't so bad," I say.

"No." She shakes her head. "I appreciate you helping me."

I nod once.

"You said you don't have a power?"

"No. I don't." I push out a breath.

"I wonder why," she muses, taking the toothbrush and toothpaste out of her toiletry bag on the vanity.

"I've wondered my whole life. It used to bug me almost as much as not having a father in my life but just like with that, I got over it. I'm bigger and stronger than all of my brothers."

"The dragon demigods?"

I nod. "Yes. We're more powerful than the dragon shifters, even though we have some drawbacks."

"Such as? Are you allowed to tell me?"

I shrug. "Like Tri mentioned, it takes us much longer to complete a shift and we can't stay in dragon form for extended periods."

"I would love to see you shift." Her eyes light up.

I half-smile. "Maybe." *Not a fuck!* Once I've been in my animal form, I become base for a while after shifting back. I'm more prone to act on impulse. To allow emotions to control me. Urges too.

I'd have Ava on her knees. I'd take her. I know I would. My cock is now throbbing and fully erect. *Way to go!*

Fuck!

I grab a towel and hold it in front of me. I like wearing sweatpants around the house. It's comfortable. It's a habit that has to stop. Right now, they're tented.

"Oh, thanks." Ava sees the towel and wants to take it.

"Brush your teeth first," I growl. I sound angry and see her flinch. I clear my throat. "I'll hold it for you until you're ready," I say, more calmly this time.

Ava has been through so much. I have vowed to protect her. To look after her. Not to take advantage of her. Fucking her would be doing just that. Taking advantage. I refuse to do that to her.

Pure thoughts.

Night was right. He was a dick when he gave me the advice, but he was ultimately right. Sex would be stupid. It would be wrong. It isn't going to happen. My cock listens. Thank fuck, because Ava has finished brushing her teeth and is taking the towel from me. We go back into the bedroom.

It's instantly awkward. Ava takes the towel off her hair. It's still damp. Dark strands cascade down her back. She smiles. I want to smile back but I'm afraid that I might grimace instead. Holding onto pure thoughts isn't easy.

Then she heads over to her bag and takes out a pair of jeans, a t-shirt and another set of underwear. White. *Fuck!* I try not to look too closely. I don't want to know if they're lace or cotton. Quite frankly, she could wear anything and look amazing. "Are you going to watch me get dressed now?" I can see by her smile that she's teasing. She laughs. "Your face! You look like you think that's the worst idea you've ever heard."

I'm trying to think pure thoughts here. It's not working. It's making me grimace and lock my jaw. I have to work hard, or my dick will quite literally grow its way out of my pants and scare the crap out of her. "No, I don't think that." My voice is deep and thick.

She narrows her eyes and tilts her head. "I think you do," she says in a singsong voice. She's still joking but I sense an underlying… something. I'm not sure what that something is. I've fucked a lot of women. I have, I'll admit it. I've never spent enough time with them outside of having sex, which means I don't understand them. Not really. It's bad. I'll admit to that too, but there it is. I don't know what's going on here right now. I don't know where she's going with this.

I know she's worried about me watching. Maybe that's it. I need to ease her mind. "I'll pull out the large set of drawers. You can stand behind those. We're good."

"Okay." She's still smiling, it's tense. She doesn't look happy. Why not? I move the furniture and she puts the clothing on top of the set of drawers. Then she heads behind them.

I saw them. Cotton. Her underwear is cotton. Not lace. There is something about that I like. A lot! I force my cock to behave. I beg my balls to stop aching.

Pure thoughts.

"Trust me. You're not missing out on all that much," she says, licking her lips. "I'm not sure why Sly is so hell-bent on this whole thing." She shakes her head. "I don't get it," she mutters to herself.

What the hell is she talking about? Then it dawns on me. *Holy fuck!* Ava lacks confidence. At least, she does right now. She has body image issues. It seems strange that someone so gorgeous, so smart, so amazing, might have that problem. Then again, most of us have some hang-ups. It's normal.

I watch as she slips the towel off. I can't see anything except the tops of her shoulders. Then she disappears as she bends to take off her panties. She doesn't look my way at all.

"I'm the son of Hephaestus," I say.

"God of fire." She pops back up.

"God of fire and blacksmiths," I elaborate. "The ugliest of the gods. So ugly, it is said that his own parents threw him off Mount Olympus when he was a baby."

Ava has just taken off her wet bra and is toweling herself dry. She stops. "That's harsh."

I shrug. "It is also said that the fall turned him into a cripple but according to my mother, that part isn't true. She said that she was attracted to his power. That she's never been hung up on outward appearances. My dad isn't a looker. Not like the other gods. She also told me that he has an amazing singing voice." I chuckle at the idea.

Ava smiles.

"I'm massive. Big enough to make most humans shit their pants. It's actually happened a few times." I hold up my arms and look down. I'm packed with muscle. I'm intimidating and mean-looking.

Ava giggles. "You have a great body." Her cheeks turn pink.

I fucking love that she just said that. This isn't about

me, so I go on. "A scowl comes easier than a smile. Makes me look mean."

She shrugs. "You're intense. A serious person. There's nothing wrong with that."

I lift both brows. "I'm a ginger."

"More copper than outright red. It's unique and quite…" Her cheeks turn even pinker. "It's nice."

"I'm not fishing for compliments, but thanks. I appreciate it." She was going to say something other than 'nice.' I want to know what that something was. I don't push it though. Again, this isn't about me. "What I'm trying to get at is that I'm an ugly fuck as far as being a demigod goes. Or even a dragon shifter for that matter."

"You are not!" Her eyes are blazing. "Don't say that about yourself. It just isn't true."

"Actually, it really is. I've had to grow up with fucking Trident as a best friend. Trust me when I tell you that I had to learn really quickly that if I wanted to bag a woman, I needed to go out alone."

Ava frowns. She frowns hard. "That must have been really tough on you." She fake-sniffs, looking put out.

Why would she be put out?

Shit! I can't believe it. I think she might be jealous. I'm a sick fuck because I like the idea of Ava being jealous over me. "I know all about confidence issues. I'm not sure why you're feeling the way you are right now, but I want you to know that I understand. I—"

Her cheeks turn blood-red while I talk. She busies herself with getting dressed. "You misunderstood me," she cuts in. "That's not how I meant it."

"Fair enough." I'm pretty sure I hit the nail on the head. I still can't believe a woman like Ava would have issues like that. It makes no sense. I drop it. I'm sure she's feeling sensitive after her ordeal. It affects people differently. That must be it.

"All done." She steps out from behind the dresser.

The shirt fits her snugly. She turns around to dig in her bag. The jeans mold her butt 'just so.'

Pure thoughts my ass. The next couple of days are going to be rough… but I'll cope.

CHAPTER 12

AVA

That evening

"How are we going to do this?" I ask as I come out from behind the dresser for a second time that day. I've just changed for bed, I'm in my pajamas. A pair of shorts and a shirt. There is a picture of a moon and stars on the front. The shorts are a loose fit, but the top is tight around my chest. Who am I kidding? Everything is tight around my chest. I contemplate leaving my bra on but decide against it in the end. It's not so that I'll be more comfortable; my intentions are less innocent.

I'm an idiot. That's why.

I want to see if Forge will look at me. He doesn't. I glance down, pretending to adjust my hem. My nipples are all over the place. My boobs still look okay under clothing. They're fairly perky for their size. Men look. They always damn well look. Forge is immune. He doesn't so much as glance. Not for half a second. Nothing. I should be happy about that fact.

I'm not.

It was the same when I was in the shower. He didn't look. He ended up lounging against the wall looking bored half the time and pissed off the other half. He's been grouchy. Like the last place he wants to be is here.

I snapped and acted all needy and mopey. Some of my insecurities surfaced. Guys just love it when girls get needy... not! Forge was sweet about it. He told me about his dad. He told me it's okay to have confidence issues. I'm mortified.

It's abundantly clear that all the jokes Trident made last night were aimed at me. Because of my attraction to Forge. It's obviously that clear that I'm attracted to him. I'm even more mortified. Especially since it isn't reciprocated. It can't be. I'd be able to tell.

As if to prove it, he throws a couple of blankets and a pillow on the ground next to the bed. "I'll sleep here," he announces.

For whatever reason, it pisses me off. Stupid, I know. You can't always help how you feel. "Sly could appear and take me without you ever being the wiser." I was being a bit of a wise-ass when I said it, but I suddenly realize that my words are true. Fear clogs my throat. My eyes sting. My chest feels tight. I sit down on the edge of the bed, trying not to have a panic attack.

"Fuck!" Forge growls. "You're right." His Adam's apple bobs. "I guess I'll have to sleep with you."

Forge looks like he hates the idea. Like he'd rather

sleep in a bed with poisonous vipers than with me. I forget my fear. I put a hand on my hip. "Sleeping with me won't be that bad. I might steal the covers and I can sometimes be restless, but... Look, forget about it. You really don't have to—"

"It's fine." He locks his jaw and his eyes blaze. He looks angry at the prospect of being in the same bed with me. Is he worried I'll jump him? "I'll do it," he adds with a sigh. You would swear he was agreeing to jump off a cliff.

"No, forget it." I shake my head. "I can see you hate the idea. I'm not about to force you to sleep with me... in the same bed as me." *Way to go, Ava, for insinuating sex.* "We'll be in the same room. Sly doesn't know where I am... I hope. No, I'm sure he doesn't know where I am. All of this is just a precaution. He wouldn't dare try to teleport me if you're here, even if you are on the floor – which, by the way, is insane. You can't sleep on the floor." I shake my head. "I'm the one putting you out. I'll sleep on the floor. You take the bed."

"That's not happening." His voice is a deep rasp. "If you're okay with it, I'll sleep in the bed... with you. You said it earlier, we're both adults. I won't try to do anything inappropriate."

Of course, you won't.

He narrows his eyes on me and I realize I just said that out loud.

"I mean, I know... of course not. I trust you completely. You're a good guy. A decent guy." I'm babbling. I need to stop. Right now. I close my mouth and push my lips together to stop myself from saying anything more.

"Then it's settled." He holds my gaze for a moment or two before turning around. Forge heads for a duffle bag on the far side of the room. He pulls off his shirt and my mouth goes dry.

Forge has a great back. Broad shoulders that taper down to a narrow waist. He's taking something out of the bag but I'm too busy admiring him while his back is turned. He steps out of his sweats and I have to stifle a noise that wants to break free. I swallow it down. I think it would be desperate-sounding. He's naked.

Naked.

His ass is meaty. He works on his glutes at the gym, that much is evident. He also has fantastic thighs. Thick and muscular.

Wow!

Holy freaking moly!

I'm trying to look away, but I can't. I can't move. I can hardly breathe. He steps into a pair of shorts and turns.

Busted. He stands there frozen, watching me watch him.

I swallow and pull in a much-needed breath. "Um… well… we… we should get to bed. To sleep… we should sleep." I sound like such an idiot.

"I should have warned you," he says, rubbing his beard. "I… you probably shouldn't look at me like that." He has narrowed his eyes. They're such a gorgeous green. So unique. I realize I'm gushing but… I can't help it.

Oh, crap! He just told me not to look at him 'like that.' I know exactly what he means. At least, I think I do. I shouldn't say anything, but my mouth goes off before I can stop it. "Like how?" My voice is squeaky. "I'm…

it's…" I can't think of anything to say. My mind has gone blank. I *was* looking at him like that. I have no excuse.

"Like… you're enjoying what you're seeing."

My face heats up like a light. I'm sure I'm bright red. I feel hot all over, embarrassed to my core. "I've never seen someone as big as you before and… and I… it's…" I'm a mess.

"You're attracted to me."

I squeeze my eyes shut and turn around. I don't want him to read on my face that he is right. *Nailed it on the head!* "You know what, let's just go to bed." I pretend to yawn and do a bad job of it. "I'm tired and it's been a long day."

Shit! I hear him approach. "It's okay if you are. It's—"

"You probably think there's something seriously wrong with me!" I blurt. It's no use trying to get out of this. Forge can see I'm crushing on him… a little… okay, a lot. There, it's out. "After everything with Sly, you would think I'd be a crying, hollow mess. That I wouldn't be able to look at a man, let alone…" *Have indecent thoughts about him.* I keep my mouth shut at this point.

He sends me a half-smile that does things to my belly. "I don't think that at all. I think you're a strong woman. I think it's great that you're not letting that bastard drag you down. It's commendable. This attraction you're feeling…" He pauses.

I want the floor to open up and to swallow me whole. I want to beg him to stop right there. To forget about it. I'm pulling in a breath to tell him just that when he goes on. "I'm attracted to you too. You're not alone in any of this… least of all in that." He smiles, properly this time and my stomach does this flip-flop thing. "Don't look so shocked." His voice is gruff. I can feel my nipples tighten.

"It's just that you gave no indication that... You've barely looked at me."

I watch his throat work. "It hasn't been easy, believe me. I wanted to look. Not looking has nearly fucking killed me. The thing is, Ava, there's nothing we can do about it. You know that, right?"

"Yes, I do." Disappointment hits, but he's right. Of course, he is. "It would complicate things."

He pushes out a breath. "That too. You've also been through a lot. I happen to be the guy who's watching over you." He shrugs. "You might be feeling this way because of the situation. It might not be genuine attraction."

"You can't be serious?" I feel a touch irritated. "My attraction to you has nothing to do with this situation. Not at all! You're wrong about that."

"It might not be." He shakes his head. "But you ultimately can't be sure. You're vulnerable right now. Not in the best place and —"

"I *am* sure! I'll say it again, my attraction to you has nothing to do with this situation. I happen to like that you're tall, I like all of your muscles. The tattoos are hot. Your hair and beard too. You have the most amazing green eyes. I like that you're brooding and intense. I love how deep your voice can go."

"Okay, okay." He chuckles softly. "Now I know how Tri feels."

"I could go on," I tease. "But if you turned into Tri we'd have a problem."

"You wouldn't want to give me a big head." He turns

serious. "It's not just the situation. I—"

"There's more?" *No! Why is there more?* I'm secretly hoping something comes of this. That this awful situation might have a silver lining. It doesn't look like I'm going to catch a break.

"I'm afraid so." He makes a face, like this whole thing sucks, which it does. "I think there's more than just an attraction... I like you, Ava."

I want to tell him that I like him too, but I don't, this isn't the right time. It probably won't ever be the right time. I keep quiet instead.

"If we had sex it would complicate things and on more than one level. It wouldn't be just a quick fuck to get rid of this tension we're feeling. I wish that was the case because if it was, I'd be all over you right now. All fucking over." His eyes drop to my mouth for a second before returning to my eyes. They're darker somehow. Even more beautiful.

My clit actually throbs when he says 'fuck.' I want to squeeze my legs together to try to relieve the building sensation. I don't think it will help. My breathing has become elevated. I think my nipples are trying to poke holes through my shirt. It's been two years since my ex and I broke up. That long since I last had sex. I'm feeling my dry spell. Feeling it so acutely I can hardly stand it. I shake my head. "I guess it wouldn't just be sex." I sound as disappointed as I feel.

"I can't get involved. Not with you. Not with anyone." He shakes his head. "My boys and I made a pact never to settle down or to take mates." He looks like he regrets it. "I don't date. I've never had a girlfriend. You're about to become the first woman I've ever slept with. As in, closed my eyes and slept."

I'm thrilled he's alluding to actual feelings for me. I'm jealous of all those women he's slept with, as in, hasn't closed his eyes with. I push all that aside. "I guess that makes me special. Yay me." I laugh. It isn't funny. I wish we could explore this. I have a feeling we could have something real. I know it.

"It does make you special, Oreo. It most certainly does." He looks at me with what I can only call longing. I have a feeling I'm looking at him in much the same way.

He's first to look away. "Let's hit the sack."

"I hope you don't snore like a grizzly bear." I smile.

"I have a feeling I'm not going to be able to get much sleep." He glances over his shoulder at me. "Not next to you, so don't worry about snoring."

The feeling is mutual. I feel wound up and tied up in knots. Why does life have to be so complicated?

CHAPTER 13

AVA

Two days later

I put down the novel. I've only read the first two chapters. It's the same political thriller from before. I find myself reading and then rereading the pages. I just can't seem to get into it, even though the book seems like it could be pretty good. I'm tired. Exhausted in fact. I yawn. I see Forge follow suit.

His phone beeps with another incoming message. He texts back and pushes 'send.' Then he puts his phone back down on the table. I can't help wondering who he's texting. I know he said that he doesn't get involved, that I'm the first woman he's actually slept with all night in the same bed. Not that we sleep much. It's difficult to sleep next to someone you're attracted to. I'm hyperaware of him and I get the feeling he's just as aware of me. I can hear from his breathing that he's often awake, just like I am.

I haven't had a boyfriend in over two years, so when I'm feeling… like this, I normally take the edge off. I help myself out. It's normal. I even have this little vibrator. I need my vibrator now. I need it really badly. All it would take is thirty seconds of alone time and I'd go off like a rocket.

I can't imagine how Forge must be feeling. He's a guy after all, and guys have a higher libido than most women. I have noticed that he hasn't been wearing sweatpants for the last few days. He puts jeans on the second he gets out of bed. It takes him a while to tuck himself in — he's really big down there. He showers in his boxers and I try not to look. I really do. I fail though. I don't have his willpower. I'm only human.

Another beep sounds on his phone, bringing me back from my musing. Forge types back, a hint of a smile playing at the one corner of his mouth.

I feel jealous. I think it might be a woman. He can't get involved with anyone, but he must surely have a booty call. Or two. Maybe he is chatting with her. Setting something up for as soon as I am out of his hair.

Forge looks up and sees me staring. He must pick up something in the look I'm giving him because his gaze softens. "I'm just letting Tri know that we're running low on certain supplies." He turns his phone towards me even though I'm too far to see what the messages say. "He's giving me a whole lot of shit. Just like he always does." He shakes his head.

Not a woman then. Why am I so relieved? I need to get

over myself. "You said you've been best friends since you guys were three?"

He nods. "For my sins." Then he smiles for a second. "We work well as best buds. I'm dark and Tri is light. I'm fire and he's water."

"You're the silent type," I say when Forge doesn't say anything more.

"And he doesn't stop," he acknowledges, grinning. "He's a pretty boy ladies' man and —"

I give him what I hope is a dirty look. "You don't give yourself enough credit. I happen to think you're way better looking than Trident."

He chuckles. "Careful now, Oreo."

I've grown to love it when he calls me that. Especially since he doesn't like it if anyone else does it. He also doesn't do it often. I definitely see it as an endearment. It's stupid, I know! "Careful or what? You'll get a big head?" I throw back, grinning.

"A big head?" He looks like he's pondering it. "Something like that." He throws me this incredibly sexy but naughty grin.

Why do I get the feeling he's not talking about the head on his shoulders? *Oh boy!* Now I'm starting to feel all hot. That achy feeling is back. *Thirty seconds...* Forget the vibrator....my hand would do just fine. I need half a minute of alone time.

I see his nostrils flare and he gets this look. It's dark... deadly even. He's talked about how women's panties fall off when Trident is near. *Forget Trident!* I think it just might happen now if I stand up. They'll fall right off. I need to change the subject and fast. I can't think of anything. I wrack my brain and mention the first thing I see. "Why all the tattoos?" I blurt. "I mean, I really like them. I like them a lot. I was just wondering what they mean?" Forge doesn't have his shirt on. Just his jeans. He often leaves the shirt off. *Lucky me!* I've had a chance to get a long, hard look at most of them. "Also, you heal so quickly," I shrug, "how did you get them to stay?" I giggle, fiddling with my ring. "I'm sorry if I'm bombarding you."

Forge's phone beeps but he ignores it. "Dragons are allergic to silver and titanium, which means we are too, to some degree. As long as the needle is made from one of those metals, the tattoos remain in our skin, although they do fade quicker than human's tattoos do, or so I am told. I'm not sure on the human front." He turns his back to me and runs a hand over the dragon tattoo on his side. "You can see it happening with this one. I need to go for regular touch-ups." He faces me again. "They all have special meaning."

I'm letting my eyes travel across his skin. "That's the same car from your roof."

Forge nods. "My first car. A '52 Cadillac Coupe DeVille." He gets a faraway look. "She was a real mess when I bought her. Found her rusting away in a scrapyard. It took me five years to get the parts to fix her up." He touches the tattoo almost lovingly.

"What about that one?" He has flames with a symbol inside them on his left pec. "The fire reminds me a little of Miss Sunshine," I say. "If she was pretty, she'd look more like that... I think." Then I realize how nosey I'm being. "You don't have to tell me any of this, by the way... I'm just curious."

"You can ask me anything," Forge assures me, touching the symbol. "It's my father's mark. It's part of who I am. I'm Forge... hence the fire." He turns sideways again and shows me his arm. I already know what's there. A hammer and anvil. "This too," he adds.

"They're beautiful," I try not to gush.

"If that's the case," he laughs, "I might need to have a word with my tattoo artist. They're meant to be tough, not beautiful." He frowns.

"They're works of art. I like them." *'I like you,'* I think to myself, picking the book back up.

"Thanks." His cheeks infuse with pink.

I like him far more than I should. I wonder if we will be able to remain friends once all of this is said and done. I don't think so. There is too much there between us to ever be just friends. It makes me feel sad.

CHAPTER 14

FORGE

The next day

There is a knock at the door. We're both instantly on high alert. I signal to Ava to get behind me. I can't be too careful. I doubt that prick would knock on the door, but stranger things have happened. It could also be one of Tri's many female followers. He has taken the odd woman home with him. They sometimes stalk him afterward. It isn't smart to bring anyone you don't intend keeping back to your pad. I pray to god I don't have to deal with one of them. I can't discount Sly or one of his men, though. Right now, I'm not sure which would be worse.

I gesture to Ava to keep quiet. She nods once. Her eyes are fearful. Her mouth a tight white line. I touch the side of her arm. *'I have you,'* I tell her with my eyes. I hope she can see it. I'd fucking die for her. I realize that sounds dramatic – I've only known this woman for a couple of days – and yet it's true.

She moves in behind me, even puts her hand on my back. It feels good when she touches me. It doesn't happen often. When it does, it's not in that way. Not in the way I want it to be and yet… I still like it. I'm turning into a pussy, but it is what it is.

I yank the door open, preparing for battle.

Night takes a step back. "Don't shoot." He puts up both hands. "Don't hit me either… and I happen to like my heart right where it is." He touches his chest.

I roll my eyes and smile. "You could have texted me first."

"Are you going to let me in?" Night lifts a brow, leaning against the jamb.

I nod and step to the side.

I watch as Night spots Ava. I feel my hackles rise just a little. I'm not sure what he's going to say or do.

Night cocks his head. "Well, if it isn't the little spewer." He chokes out a laugh. "I've never seen anyone vomit that much in my entire life, especially such a little human. I found peas and carrots in places you wouldn't believe."

Ava laughs and scrunches up her face. *She's so fucking cute.* "I'm so sorry!" She cracks open an eye. "I can't believe that happened."

Night shrugs. "Don't worry about it, it's normal." Just like that, most of the tension from the other day dissipates. He walks inside and I close the door.

"I see you came bearing gifts," I say.

"I did indeed." He holds up a couple of loaded shopping bags. "Tri mentioned that you might be running low on a couple of essentials."

"Bread, milk and greens." Ava rubs her hands together.

Night snorts. "More like beer, ice cream and Oreos." He looks bemused. "Trident specifically told me to bring you five boxes of them. Said you had a terrible craving." Night is frowning, giving Forge this look of confusion. "Do you know anything about that?"

"Trident can be a real dick," Forge says, laughing. "He is right though, for once. I hope you brought the cookies."

Night laughs. "Yes, I brought all of the above, including Oreos. I even brought peas and carrots." Night winks at Ava and deposits the bags on the kitchen counter. He helps himself to a beer, twisting the lid off. "I came with some news."

Ava hangs back, looking unsure.

"Isn't there something you need to say to Ava first?" I fold my arms and give Night a stern look. It's clear he's gotten over himself and is working hard at showing Ava that, but it isn't enough. Not fucking nearly.

"No," Night shakes his head, "I was wary of the human and with good cause. I won't apologize for that."

I take a step back and clench my fists. I can't help it. "You were fucking rude about it."

"It's okay—" Ava starts to say.

"It isn't," I interject.

"I was being frank." He shrugs like it's no big deal.

It *is* a big deal. A huge fucking deal. "You were being a dick."

Night looks from me to Ava and back again. He narrows his eyes. "I'm *not* sorry for being distrusting of the whole thing. I don't normally believe in coincidences but..." He looks like he's carefully considering what he's going to say next. *Good!* Best he watch his step. "I *did* act like a royal prick. I said some things I shouldn't have and for that... I *am* sorry."

Ava smiles sweetly. Her eyes are filled with warmth. "I understand. We did ambush you and you were only looking out for Forge's best interest. I can't fault that."

"See, the human gets it."

"Ava... dickhead, her name is Ava. Try using it for a change." My voice has a growl to it. I don't give a fuck. For the first time, I realize how arrogant and rude we are. It needs to stop. Especially where Ava is concerned.

"Ava." Night holds up his hands. "Here," he hands me a beer, "drink this and calm the fuck down. Ava, would you like a beer as well?"

"That would be nice." She nods once.

Night opens a bottle for her. "Shall I pour it into a glass, or are you happy with the bottle?"

"The bottle is good." She takes the beer.

This is much better. I lean against the counter and feel some of the tension drain.

Night holds up the bottle to both of us and we do the same back.

"Are we toasting something good?" I ask. "Do you know where that fucker is? Is he dead?"

"Slow down," Night says. "We agreed to try to negotiate first."

I see Ava frown.

"Let me guess, no deal? I didn't like the idea of negotiating with a rapist bastard anyway." I'm angry. A blind man would be able to tell.

"You planned on negotiating with Sly?" Ava sounds upset. "You should have told me."

"We planned on doing whatever it took to get him off your back. At getting his guard down. It was never going to be long-term," I speak softly. "I didn't tell you because I didn't want you getting upset and because… he is going to pay regardless."

She nods. "What happened?" I can see that her mind is racing.

"I told you that some of the guys headed to the casino," I elaborate. "Night was one of them. He tried to get a meeting with Sly. He left messages for him as well."

"We offered the sick fuck fifty large to back off," Night continues. "To leave you alone."

"He didn't take it?" Ava whispers.

"No." Night shakes his head. "He turned us down flat and sent a message demanding that we give you to him immediately."

"I hope you told him where to get off!" I practically yell.

"Absolutely." Night takes a sip of his beer. "I told him that he needed to back the fuck off. That we wouldn't hesitate to end him if he came for you again." Night turns to Ava. "He's not getting away with this."

"What did he say?" she asks, eyes wide. I hate how scared she is. I fucking hate it.

Night's gaze softens. "We got radio silence."

"He's still coming, isn't he?" Her voice is fearful.

"We don't know that," Night says.

Ava chugs a good deal of her beer. "I know it." She wipes her mouth and then shakes her head. "He won't stop until he has me. I wish I knew why."

"He won't get you," I say. "I swear to you." I take her hand. She's shaking. "You're safe with me."

I see some of the fear drain. She's still breathing fast. I hate seeing her like this.

"I'm bigger and faster than he is. I'll fucking kill him if he comes anywhere near you," I promise and mean it. That fucker needs to die.

She nods once.

"You can't let Sly touch you, Ava," Night warns. "If he touches you, he can teleport with you."

Ava nods.

"Also, we looked into the man's history. Did a whole lot of digging. There's a lot of stuff about him on the internet. I'm not going to get into it. I'll tell you the relevant information. Sly is thirty-two. There is only one parent on the birth certificate. His mother. She named him Charles, and his surname is Carter. He changed his name to Sylvester AKA Sly Herms when he turned twenty-one and started the casino in the same year. He called it The Winged Palace. It has an emblem – golden wings."

"What are you getting at?" I ask, even though I can guess.

"I suspect that Sly Herms is a demigod," Night says.

"What?" Ava's eyes are wide.

Night lifts his brows. "I think his father is Hermes."

"God of roadways, travelers and thieves," I murmur, almost to myself. "It would explain his ability to teleport."

"The golden wings are straight off the Caduceus."

"The what?" Ava asks.

"It's Hermes's symbol. Golden wings form a part of it. There are too many factors all pointing in this direction. At this point, I'm quite sure that Sly is a demigod." Night takes a sip of his beer. "We did some digging on his mother and she's human."

"So, he's a straight demigod then?" I ask.

Night nods. "Yep."

We'd always wondered if there might be more demigods running around. Sons and maybe even daughters of the gods, born to humans. Up until now, we've never found proof of it, but we always suspected. If the gods impregnated some dragon shifter women, why not human women as well? Mythology is rife with stories of gods romancing humans. "So straight demigods do exist," I push out, my eyes wide, my mind racing.

"Looks like they might," Night says. "That makes him strong."

"Not as strong as us," I growl.

"His power is to teleport. Moving from place to place is what he does. He's also naturally devious. Hermes is known to be a serious asshole." Night turns to me. "Are you sure you don't want to swap places?" he asks me.

"No," Ava and I say in unison.

"I'm the better person for this job. I—" he tries to change my mind.

"No!" I say, more firmly. "I have you on speed dial.

We have a plan. I don't intend on letting Ava out of my sight until this is over. If he takes her, he takes us both. If he gets her, I call you. Don't let your phone out of your sight," I warn Night. "If he tries anything, I'll crack open his chest and—"

"Can you give Forge and me a minute, please?" Night asks Ava. "I'm close enough that I will be able to sense if Sly uses his power. I'll be able to follow if I'm quick. And I am... quick, that is."

Ava looks at me.

"I'm sure there's something you want to do without this asshole watching?" Night says, trying to sound convincing.

Ava keeps her eyes on me. I am her protector right now. She trusts me with everything. It's a huge responsibility. I nod once and she nods back. Only then does she head to the bedroom. *Our* bedroom. I shouldn't think of it like that, but I do.

"If I didn't have a sense of smell, I'd swear the two of you were a couple," Night throws out as soon as Ava is gone.

"We're not fucking," I snap back.

"Duh... that's what I mean by sense of smell." He scrutinizes me. "You are getting mighty cozy, though, even if you aren't going there. You're taking this fierce protector role too far. It's moving into dangerous waters."

"Bullshit!" *He's right!*

"It's only a matter of time before you—"

"Don't say it." I shake my head. "We discussed it and it's not going to happen. We both agreed not to cross that line."

"You discussed it?" Night runs a hand through his hair. He snorts out a laugh. "What else are you discussing? It's going to happen. You're both kidding yourselves."

I don't answer. I've said my piece.

"We took that oath because…" He lets the sentence die. "Mark my words—once you're in a relationship, you'll end up deciding that you want to make it more permanent, so you'll mate." His eyes blaze.

I fold my arms and look at him like he's lost his mind.

"That's still not the end of the world. Mating would be fine. Except, then you'll forget why we decided not to ever procreate, and you'll have a kid or two or fucking five." He growls the last.

"They wouldn't grow up like us," I say.

"Holy shit!" he yells, looking at me like I just turned purple. "This is worse than I thought. It's fucking worse." He paces away. "You've been thinking about it. You've been considering mating and having offspring with this woman. Forge, think about it, we have no idea what kind of children we would have. They might have powers, they might not. They might be able to shift or semi-fucking-shift… or not. The best they could hope for is to be mostly human, but I doubt that would happen. They would belong even less than we do. They would end up outcasts."

"They wouldn't grow up like us… like me… because they'd have their father. They would have me." I hit my chest.

"They wouldn't belong. Not with the humans. Not with the shifters. Certainly not with the gods. Trust me, not knowing your father isn't a bad thing." Night looks hurt. Hades hasn't been the best example.

"I'm not Hades!" I have to work to keep my voice down. "I'm sorry you have such a fucked-up father, but I would be nothing like that. They would belong to a family. We would be okay."

"No," Night growls. "*You* would be okay. Your kids, not so fucking much. I urge you to reconsider."

"I haven't touched Ava and I won't," I bite out. I have been considering a relationship. It was wrong.

"If you mean that..." Night narrows his eyes. "You leave and I'll stay. You go catch that fucker and destroy him. I'll look after—"

"No." I shake my head. "I promised her I would keep her safe and I will. Me!" I slap a hand on my chest again. "You will have more chance of finding that teleporting prick."

Night puts a finger in my face. "Just remember that you made promises to more than just to her. You made promises to us long before you met her. Don't you fucking forget it."

"I won't!" I snarl.

There is another knock at the door. Someone is here.

CHAPTER 15

AVA

I hear a woman's voice. *A woman.* Why would a woman be here? I frown as I walk back into the living room. A beautiful blond lady is hugging Forge and he is hugging her back. He looks happy to see her. He's smiling, which doesn't happen often.

She is rubbing her hand up and down his back. "It's been too long," she says.

I can't believe the feelings of jealousy that well up inside me. This is bad. I'm not just physically attracted to Forge, I have, definitely and without a doubt, developed feelings for him. It doesn't matter that we haven't slept together. They're there anyway.

"I need to get going," Night says. He sees me and waves. "Remember what I said," he warns. "Good to see you, Sophia," he turns to the newcomer.

"You too, honey," the woman says. She knows Night too, then, but not as well as Forge. The ugly green monster is still hanging around.

I can't take my eyes off Forge and this woman. She's smiling at me now. She's tall and slim and athletic. Her hair is a golden blond. It's curly and long. Her eyes are a gorgeous bright blue. She's drop-dead freaking gorgeous.

I have to force myself to smile back. Her face is so open and inviting. She looks kind, and yet I have this intense dislike for her. It's born of jealousy. Plain and simple. I need to stop this. I am not this person.

"Aren't you going to introduce me to your friend, Forge?"

Forge glances back and his face falls, like he's sorry to see me. Why would he be sorry? He sighs. I wish I could leave. This feels awkward. "Of course." He nods. "Ava, meet Sophia. Mom, this is Ava."

Wait.

What?

Mom?

Sophia is his mother. *Oh. My. Word!* I'm astonished. "Mother... You're Forge's mom? Forgive me but you're young and gorgeous. I would never have said that you were a mother to a grown man."

"Young? Huh! If only, hun." She beams at me. "I'm sixty this year. The big six zero." She smiles broadly. If I look closely, I can see some fine lines around her eyes and her mouth. There might be a couple of strands of grey in amongst her golden locks. She looks amazing though. Must be those dragon shifter genes.

"Now," she puts her hands on her hips, looking at Forge, "a little birdy whispered that you found yourself a girlfriend. I had to come and see it for myself."

"Mom…" Forge warns.

"I'm shocked and pleased to see it's true." To my amazement, she comes over and hugs me. "You are quite lovely," she says.

"Mom!" Forge tries but Sophia ignores him.

"My boy has made me wait a long time for this day."

"Mom," Forge says, yet again, sounding frustrated, "Ava is a friend. Just a friend," he tries to set the record straight. "We're helping her out with a situation. I'm—"

"I went to go and visit you and imagine my shock when Trident was at the apartment instead of you. Tri explained everything," Sophia says, like she's completely in the know. "I heard all about Ava." She winks at me.

Forge groans. "I'm sure Tri told you everything."

"I always thought this whole oath nonsense was silly. Did you hear about the oath, Ava?" Sophia asks me.

"Mom. Don't!" Forge says.

"It's a simple question." Sophia raises her brows.

"Ava and I have talked about it," Forge says.

"I'm sure you think it's silly, Ava." She looks over at me. I don't say anything. I don't want to get in the middle of this. I don't know much about the oath except that it is in place and I dislike it. It prevents us from being together. At least, it's one of the things. That's all I know.

"Please can we drop it, mom?" Forge pleads. "Otherwise I'm going to ask you to leave and you just got here."

Sophia breathes out. "Fine. You know my feelings on this."

"I most certainly do," he sighs. She winks at me and I can't help smiling back.

"I want to know all about you, Ava. Apparently, you have my son all tied up in knots."

I hear Forge make a groan of frustration. I have to hold in a laugh.

"Trident said that he's never seen Forge like this, but enough of that. Where are you from? How did you meet Forge?" She links her arm in mine and we follow Forge to the kitchen.

"I thought Tri told you everything," Forge mutters.

"Not everything. Besides, some things are best heard in person. Now, tell me how you met my boy."

Forge rolls his eyes. He's not scowling or frowning. He pulls out a chair for his mother. "You two can sit, I'll rustle something up." He pulls out another one for me, his eyes softening as they land on me, making my heart lurch in my chest. We're sitting at the large island in the center of the kitchen.

I tell Sophia all about how I met Forge. She laughs hysterically when I tell her all the names I called him. We touch on Sly and some of the things that happened, but she quickly steers the conversation away from all the nastiness. I appreciate it. It's nice just to relax. It almost feels normal.

In the meantime, Forge puts a couple of plates down in front of us. He's made BLTs. He opens another beer for me and pours a glass of chilled, white wine for his mother.

I'm not sure how it happens, but the conversation turns to my previous relationships. I tell Sophia about my high school sweetheart and about how we drifted apart in our senior year. She's so easy to talk to. Before I know it, I'm telling her about my ex, Matt.

My cheeks heat when Forge sits across from us. We're friends, I tell myself. We're never going to be more, and besides, I can talk about this stuff. It isn't a big deal.

"How long were the two of you together?" Sophia asks, taking a bite of her sandwich. The lettuce crunches. "This is good," she tells Forge.

"Four years." I pick up one half of my own sandwich. It *does* look good.

"So, he obviously wasn't the love of your life." Sophia takes another bite of her food.

"I thought he was, but it didn't end up being the case. He broke up with me. That was two and a half years ago. I haven't dated anyone since."

"Until now." She smiles.

"We're not dating, mom," Forge interjects; he has already finished his food and is busy wiping his hands on a paper napkin.

"It's a real pity," Sophia says. "I still think that oath you boys took is silly."

"It's not silly." Forge shakes his head.

Sophia's eyes well with tears. "I'm sorry you never got to meet your father and that you are from such a mixed heritage. You are loved though, son. I hope you know that."

"I know, mom." He reaches out and touches the side of her arm. "I love you too."

160 | CHARLENE HARTNADY

My heart is melting.

"I want you to be happy," Sophia goes on; she looks like she has herself back under control. "I think you could be very happy with someone like Ava." She smiles at me. I am reminded of my own mom. I miss her profoundly right at this moment. I wonder if I will ever have a mother-in-law as great as Sophia.

Forge's jaw tightens. He drops the wadded-up napkin on his plate.

"I don't want you to miss out because of an oath you made when you were a pimply teenager." She turns to me. "He wasn't pimply at all, actually. Might have gotten the odd—"

"Mom!" Forge chokes out a laugh. It sounds like he might be a bit embarrassed "Please don't talk about my teenage acne."

Her eyes brighten up. "Why not?" she asks Forge, then looks back my way. "There's a ton I could tell you about my son, Ava." Her face falls. "But you're not my boy's girlfriend, as much as I wish you were."

I want to tell her to confide in me anyway. I want to hear all about it. I wish! I wish really hard. I wish things could be different. I mostly wish that this oath didn't exist.

We finish our food and Sophia tells us she has to leave. She hugs me just as hard as she hugs Forge. "Maybe I will see you again, Ava," she says.

"Maybe." I try not to feel sad since I probably won't. We both know it, since she hugs me again, harder this time. "Silly boys!" Sophia mutters as she lets go.

We say our final goodbyes and she leaves. Forge shuts the door and starts to move away. I go back and turn the lock.

"Your mom is lovely," I say.

Forge squeezes the back of his neck. "Thank the gods my younger brother has a mate. Their second kid is on the way, otherwise, I'd be in deep shit."

"I think she worries about you more than anything else."

He nods. "Yeah, she does."

"She means well."

He throws me a half-smile. "I know." He narrows his eyes. "There's something I have to ask…"

"What's that?" I prompt as we walk into the living room.

"I really shouldn't but it's something you said during lunch and it's staying in my head."

"Ask me."

"Your ex broke up with you?" He's looking shell-shocked. "I find it hard to believe that anyone in their right mind would break up with someone like you."

He's so darned sweet.

"Why did he do it?" He rakes a hand through his hair. "I mean, if it's too personal you don't have to say anything but… I can't help but wonder. A guy would have to be stupid. That's all I can say. It's been playing on my mind since you told my mom, and I…" He shrugs. For once, it's Forge who is babbling.

I find myself smiling. "I don't mind telling you." I sit down on one end of the sofa and he sits at the other. "Matt and I did everything the right way. We dated for ages before we moved in together. We lived together for over two years before he popped the question."

Forge nods.

"I told him right from the start that I couldn't have kids. I have all the parts, they just don't work properly," I say. "My ovaries are non-functioning. At least, they do function, just not enough to be able to ovulate. Anyway, that's boring medical stuff."

"Lyre could probably fix you," he says absently.

I frown.

"Lyre is one of us. He works as a fancy surgeon at the Saint Mary's Hospital in town. His gift involves healing. I'm sure you've heard of the god Apollo?"

I nod.

"I'll introduce you to Lyre. Maybe he can help you."

I nod again. I don't want to get my hopes up. I've seen plenty of doctors and no one has been able to help me.

"I'm sorry." He gives me a small smile before he turns serious again. His green eyes boring into me. "Please go on. You got engaged... to this Matt guy." His eyes grow a little stormy. Maybe I'm not the only one with jealousy issues. It makes me feel marginally better.

I fold my legs underneath myself. I'm wearing the daisy dukes from the first day we met. It feels like forever ago. I feel like I've known Forge my whole life. "Yep. It was fine at first. We got busy planning the wedding and trying to find the perfect venue. Then Matt... he withdrew." I chew on my lip for a second. "It's the best way I can describe it. I asked him if he was okay and he kept insisting that he was. His best friend Shaun and his wife had just had a baby. Matt knew I couldn't have kids. I told him right from the start. No use starting something with someone if they're dead set on having a family." I scratch my knee absently. "Eventually he came clean. It was only weeks before the wedding. Everything was arranged. I had a dress. The cake was ordered. The flowers too. We'd already sent out the invitations." I pull in a deep breath. "He told me he couldn't go through with it. That he had been sure he was fine about not having any children. He had thought he was. Was certain of it. Seeing Shaun, Sandra and their little boy had thrown him. He ended up calling off the wedding."

Forge doesn't say anything. He is looking at me. His body turned towards me. He is hanging on my every word.

"It was a very difficult time. I was devastated. Of course, I'm glad he broke it off before we got married. It could have been worse. We could have been years into the relationship before it broke down. Matt recently got married," I blurt. "His wife is pregnant but…" I swallow thickly. "I'm okay with that. I might even be ready to date again."

I'm not sure why I said that, since it won't be us who does the dating, even though there's huge energy buzzing between us. It's constant. A back and forth that sometimes leaves me slightly breathless and a whole lot needy. Even more achy. I shift in my seat, trying to get comfortable. Our conversations, no matter how they start, always seem to shift to shaky territory.

My words make him glower. Make his jaw tighten. His whole body seems to tense up. Then he smiles. It looks forced. "For what it's worth, I think Matt made a huge mistake. If you really love someone. I mean intensely… deeply love them, nothing else should matter." The way he is looking at me takes more than just my breath. It's taking my sanity.

"I think so too." That's why the break-up hurt me so much. I realized Matt wasn't as deeply in love with me as he should have been. "Your turn," I say. If we're coming clean about things in our life, then Forge has to as well.

He looks confused. "I told you that I've never dated. There are no skeletons in my closet."

"The oath," I say. "Tell me about it… only if you feel comfortable," I quickly add. He doesn't have to say anything if he doesn't want to. Maybe he isn't allowed to. It could be part of the oath. "You don't have to if—"

"I'll tell you about the oath. I told you, you can ask me anything you want to know. Say the word and I'll spill."

I want to know everything.

All of it.

I want to know everything there is to know about this man. I take a page from his book and stay quiet. "We made the oath when we were still teenagers. It was tough growing up different from everyone else. Thankfully, we had each other. We never felt like we belonged. I don't want this to sound like a sob story, but we didn't feel like we were enough. We're not human enough. Not dragon shifter enough and definitely not godlike enough. The only reason Night got to meet Hades was because he can teleport into the Underworld. Hades hasn't shown his own son much interest. Night hasn't spoken about it, but I know he has been deeply wounded. It used to bug him intensely. I think it still does. The rest of us have moved forward."

I see Forge's eyes cloud up. "It's still tough sometimes knowing that the gods couldn't be bothered with their half-blood sons. It's hard on a person being discarded like that."

I nod, my eyes are probably clouding as well. A lump is forming in my throat.

Forge must notice because he says, "You know exactly what I mean."

"Yep," I nod. "My dad left and didn't look back." I play with my ring. The one my biological father gave my mom. Then again, it's not the same. He wasn't a god. He would never have known about my existence. If he had, maybe he would have stayed, or taken an active role in my life. Maybe. The same can't be said for Forge and the others. Their fathers are gods... they would have to have known about their children. Surely?

"We made the oath to prevent more like us being born. Our offspring would belong even less. We have no idea what kind of traits our children would have. It would be true no matter who we took as our mates. If we took human mates, our kids would be more human but still not quite. They would probably have some abilities. If we took shifter mates, they would have more shifter traits, but not as much as pure shifters would. Being a teenager is hard enough without all of those complications."

"So, the oath came about to prevent more mixed-blood children from being born?" I ask, my heart beating faster.

He nods. "The thinking was that if we don't take mates, then we won't be tempted to have children. I know it sounds crazy. Like stupid kids making a stupid oath. It's not stupid, though. Not to us." He looks forlorn and lost. I want to hug him, but I hold back. "We were teased relentlessly by the dragon children and were too strong to grow up amongst the humans. Like I said earlier, we didn't belong. We were fatherless outcasts. I remember as a teenager how the shifter girls wanted nothing to do with us. I was twenty-two when I lost my virginity with a human woman." He's smiling now, trying to make light of something that would have been tough.

I roll my eyes. "I was twenty. Twenty-two isn't that old."

"It felt like I'd waited forever. The rest of the guys…" He pauses. "It was just me at that stage. I hadn't figured out yet that I needed to ditch my boys if I wanted to get lucky."

"It sounds like things have improved," I say.

"They have and they haven't. We're happier in our skins. We've come to terms with a whole lot of things. I can say that I personally have, but we're still outsiders."

I nod. I guess I know to some degree what it's like. My family is gone. I only have one real friend—Trudy, who I can't even contact for fear of endangering her too. Or that's how it was before I met him.

Forge.

I feel like I fit. Like we fit together. He takes my hand and I can hardly breathe. He rubs a finger across my palm. "You can't have kids."

I shake my head.

He leans back on the sofa, looking up at the ceiling for a moment. When he looks back at me his gaze is intense.

Now I'm breathing too hard. My heart is going nuts. His gaze cuts right into me. "If we ever had anything, there would be no temptation to have children."

I shake my head. "Several doctors and plenty of tests later… I can't have children."

"Has it been rough?" He rubs my palm with his thumb again and my nerve-endings are going nuts. Who would have thought such a small touch could do this to me? "Knowing you can't have a baby, I mean."

"How have you felt about it?"

"It's not the same. I technically can have kids…" He raises his brows. "At least I think I can. I'm okay with not going there though. I'm fine." He shrugs. Something in his eyes… it's a haunted look, it tells me he isn't as fine as he's pretending to be. I wonder how often Sophia has seen this in her son. I know what loneliness is. I know what it looks like.

"Not having kids, even if you can have them is the same, I suppose, but it also isn't. Not really. To answer your question… yes… it's been tough." I think back on Matt and everything that happened. "Just when I thought I'd found someone who accepted me, who got me…" I shake my head, my eyes pricking with unshed tears.

"You were let down. You had your heart broken."

I nod. "It hurt, for a long time."

"We could make a go of this… of us." He lets my hand go like he's been burned. He runs a hand through his copper strands. He looks tortured. "I shouldn't be saying any of this."

"Why not?"

"My life is complicated. I would drag you into—"

I snort out a laugh. "I think *I'm* the one with the complicated life. I'm the one dragging you into my shit right now." I turn very serious, closing the distance just a little by scooting up towards him on the sofa. "Besides, if I could choose between complicated and together or simple and on my own… I'd choose complicated every time to be with you."

He half-smiles. It's sexy. "Not this damned complicated." He rakes both hands through his hair. "Life with me would be—"

"Stop being difficult," I push.

"We should wait. See how this pans out."

"Fine." I let it go. I don't mean it though. I'm trying to think about how I can convince him. *What can I say?*

"Okay," he says out of nowhere about half a minute later.

"Okay what?"

"I think we've waited long enough." His Adam's apple bobs as he swallows. His eyes are on me. "I don't want to wait, Ava. I want you... us... all of it." His eyes have me. He has me. If I'm honest, he had me from the start.

We crash together. We're all hands and limbs. Mouths and tongues. I'm on his lap. My body plastered against him. My one hand in his hair. The other gripping his bicep. His hands are on my back, my ass, no, my back... now he's squeezing my thighs and growling into my mouth. "Oreo," he murmurs in his deep baritone. "I've been fucking dying," he says as he kisses my neck, "for a taste."

"Of me?" I'm panting.

"Your pussy." His voice. His dirty words. They send shivers rushing through me.

I groan as he squeezes my breast, raking a thumb over my nipple. They're tight little nubs. Everything feels tight. My skin. Down there. I think I might already be drenched.

"Oh," I half-moan the word. "Is that right?" I push out.

He pulls back. His eyes are glassy with desire. "Are you sure about this, Ava?"

"I'm sure," I say. I want this man. I need him.

"This will mean something to me."

"It'll mean everything to me."

"Good answer." He flips me onto my back. His eyes are all over my body. Like he can't get enough of me. "Fucking dying," he mutters. "Can I take these off?" He touches my shorts.

"Yes." I nod. I want him so badly. In me, on me. In every which way. I can't believe this is happening. I'm a little nervous, though. I have hang-ups. One hang-up in particular.

Forge leans over me and captures my lips. He kisses me until I relax.

Then he pulls back, his eyes are filled with need. For me. He unbuttons my shorts, taking his time. His hands are steady. Then he pulls down the zipper, the sound reverberating around the room. I can hardly breathe. His eyes are on mine. Before he takes them off, he takes his own shirt off. It is a sight I will never tire of. He is beautiful. Forge peels the shorts off of me. He keeps my underwear on.

He opens my legs a little. My heartrate is soaring. I try hard to relax. I'm finding it difficult. I always hate this part when a guy sees me for the first time.

"You okay? Having second thoughts?" he asks, putting me at ease.

I shake my head.

Then he gets onto the floor. He's on his knees. His eyes have moved down. I'm wearing a powder-blue, cotton set. It's plain. Nothing sexy about it. You would never say so though by the way he is looking at me. Forge leans in, holding my thighs. He lifts my shirt slightly, his fingers brushing my belly. It makes me tense up all over again. I wish I wasn't so touchy about my body. I thought I'd be completely relaxed with Forge. I'm not. I'm worse than I normally would be but only because I care so much about what he will think. I hate it when this happens. Why can't I just chill and enjoy the moment? My first real boyfriend told me that guys don't give a shit about the same things that girls do. It didn't make me feel better. It somehow made me feel worse.

Forge places a kiss on the skin of my lower stomach, bringing me back to the here and now. He lets my shirt go. I can breathe again. "I got you," he says as he leans in and kisses me. There. Through my panties.

I make this godawful moaning noise. Like I'm about to die. The good news is, he makes a groaning noise too. Only, he sounds sexy. "Oreo... you have one hell of a center. I'm going to enjoy licking you." He opens his mouth over my core. It's hot.

I make that same moaning, dying noise again. Then his mouth is on me. On my skin. I'm not sure how or where my panties went, only that I'm glad. I'm ecstatic. My back bows off the couch. My eyes are wide. I'm panting and he's hardly touched me.

"Open your thighs wider," he instructs.

"O-okay," I stammer, my voice is shrill.

I thread my fingers through Forge's hair as he leans in, I'm watching him between my legs. Mesmerized. He's eating me out. His head is moving up and down as he licks my slit. His gorgeous eyes lift as he closes his mouth over my clit.

Holy shit!

Holy!

I cry out, sounding agonized. That couldn't be further from the truth. Pleasure is rushing through me, pooling right there where he is focussing. He moves down to my entrance. His tongue is relentless. It's hot and it pushes deep.

I groan even harder. My throat actually hurts. I grip his hair. I can feel that I'm being too rough, but I can't let go. I feel disembodied, I have no control over myself right now. I grip him harder still as he suckles on my clit. A scream is lodged in my throat. *Sucking. Sucking. Sucking.* I don't think anyone has done this to me before. Not like this. It's probably what getting head feels like for guys. No wonder they're obsessed.

My back is bowing again. The pleasure is building. Building. I make a choked cry as he goes back to licking. Both my hands are in his hair now. I'm pulling him. Holding him. I think I might be begging him. I need more. I need it now.

His glorious mouth closes over my clit again. Hot. So hot. Just the right amount of pressure.

I realize that not only am I holding him in both my hands, pulling his hair while I'm at it, but my hips were moving too. They're jerking against his face. I yell as he slides his finger inside me. "Oh god!" I yell. "Oh… oh… oh…" I say with each thrust. He's crooking his finger. He's getting me… there. Right there. "God… oh… god." My voice is deep and hard.

My eyes are wide. Too wide. My breathing is ragged. Too ragged. Forge's mouth is on my clit. There's a coiling sensation deep inside me. I've had orgasms. I've had plenty. With partners and on my own. This is going to be different. This is going to be spectacular. My eyes are beginning to roll back.

His finger thrusts deeper, moving quicker. Still touching me right there. His mouth is on that bundle of nerves. Everything is pulling tight. Too tight.

There is a moment of calm. Everything feels elevated. Like I'm hanging. Then my whole body goes slack. My heart feels like it has stopped. Missed a beat or two. I start to think it isn't going to happen. I'm wrong.

Very wrong!

Everything is tightening back up and all at once. My back is lifting off the sofa. A rush of blinding pleasure is tearing through me. Sheer ecstasy. I don't want this to end.

My muscles are vibrating, my eyes roll right back... my throat hurts. *Shit!* I might have screamed. I come down slowly. Forge won't have it any other way. He continues to tease and to play. At least my hips have stopped jerking.

Forge fingers me more slowly, his tongue is still laving and lapping. I'm still panting. I feel like a boneless heap of flesh. *Crap!* I'm holding onto him like my life depends on it. It takes me a few moments to get my fingers to loosen. Both my legs are over his shoulders. *When did that happen?*

He lifts his head, licking his lips. "Better than I imagined."

"You imagined doing that?" My voice is croaky. I take my legs off his shoulders, placing my feet on the edge of the sofa. My underwear is still pulled to the side where he must have moved it so that he could... do what he just did.

"I definitely imagined doing that. Only about two dozen times," he lifts his eyes, "could be more."

I laugh. It's throaty.

His gaze turns feral. "I know you've been through a lot and we don't have to…" he shakes his head, "take the next step. I can wait. I—"

"Stop." I smile. "I would desperately like to have sex with you now."

"Thank fuck." He exhales. His hair is standing up from me pulling on it. It's so cute. He leans in and kisses me softly on the lips. "We just need to get one thing straight, first." He has the start of a smile tugging on the corners of his mouth. His eyes are glinting with mischief.

"What's that?"

"You shouldn't shout 'god' when you're coming."

I snigger. "I *was* shouting it, wasn't I?" I lick my lips. "I can tell by how dry my mouth is that I screamed it a good deal." I grin. "Should I scream 'demigod' then?"

"Lord would work better." He winks at me. "I'm a lord. If we're going to get technical, I'm the Lord of Fire."

"A bit of a mouthful. I might give 'lord' a try though."

He smiles. I melt. I'm so in over my head it's scary. Sex with Forge is going to destroy me. I know it. I hope he changes his mind about this oath. I hope his friends don't make him stick to it. He gets up. I close my legs, feeling shy all of a sudden. There is a huge bulge in his jeans. "Plain old Forge would work too," he says, drawing my attention back. "I think I'd like you to say my name when my cock is inside you. When you're coming hard." His eyes narrow into mine. His jaw is tight.

So sure of himself. I feel a zing between my legs, like my orgasm never happened. I'm achy and needy all over again.

"I think we should take this to the bedroom. I'm going to get you some water first." He grins. "You're about to scream a whole lot more."

The zing becomes a clench. I nod because I don't trust my voice. I want to scream his name really badly.

I watch as Forge rounds the island. He opens the refrigerator. I'm so happy. I feel like getting up and dancing around the room. I can't believe this. I always saw my infertility as a curse. A huge negative. I always expected it to impact finding the right person. Keeping that person. Who would have…? I'm lost in my thoughts when my life goes to hell.

Sly appears. At first, I think I am seeing things. Having someone materialize from nowhere will do that to a person. It will always shock me to my core.

I pull in a breath and try to scramble away. I don't succeed. Sly's hand closes over my arm. I kick at him, but it does no good. My stomach lurches. He is teleporting us. There is no way for Forge to follow me. I am doomed.

CHAPTER 16

FORGE

I'm a bastard. Not just a bastard. I'm a selfish bastard. I should not be doing this. The moment I hear that Ava can't have children, I get excited. What's wrong with me? It's easy to see she has experienced pain over her condition.

Not only am I dragging her into my fucked up world but I'm damning her to a childless future. Lyre is not just a gifted surgeon, he has the gift of healing. When I told Ava he could help her, I could see she didn't believe me, but the fact of the matter is that he *could* help her. I know it. That's why I'm a selfish prick. If Ava is with me, we can never have children. *She* can never have children.

I should tell her. Make her understand that she could be healed and live a normal life with a normal man. She could have a family. My heart clenches at the thought. There is an ache in my chest. It's longing. I have no business feeling it.

I haven't known Ava long but sometimes you just know. With Ava, I belong. I am accepted. I am me. We could be happy. Thing is, once Sly has been dealt with, her life can go back to normal.

Normal.

Normal.

It's something I have never been. Something I will never be. I'm good with that. It's something I've come to accept. I want Ava to have everything. I want to be the one to give it to her. I can't, though. Not if I uphold my oath.

I have to do the right thing. At least I got to taste her, to hear her come. I watched her too. It was the single most erotic thing I have ever seen. I will hold on to that memory because we can't have sex.

My mind is made up. I will grab the water, then Ava and I are going to talk. I will convince her that I am all wrong for her, even if that's ultimately a lie.

I reach out to open the refrigerator and I hear a strange noise. The noise is coming from Ava, and it's all wrong. It makes the hairs stand up all over my body. My blood turns to ice. I am running as I turn.

I'm too late.

Ava is already gone, and all that remains is the lingering scent of ozone.

I scream her name. I can't believe I allowed myself to become distracted. This never should have happened. I may have cost Ava her life or worse; Sly will make her existence a living hell. *I'm such a fuck up!* This is exactly why we can never be together. I am trying to get my cell phone out of my jeans pocket. I'm thankful I'm still wearing them. When I do, I drop the damned thing and curse. My hands are shaking. I grab it up off the floor and immediately dial Night. I am following our plan. If I am quick enough, we might be able to save Ava. If not—

I don't want to contemplate that. He doesn't answer immediately. "Come on. Come on," I say, pacing. The scent of ozone is barely there anymore. Soon there will be nothing for Night to track.

He doesn't answer but materializes next to me. He's scowling.

"He took her!" I yell. I'm so fucked off. I've never been this angry in my whole life. I'm shaking. Scales have popped up on my chest. My nails have sharpened. My eyesight is more acute. Night doesn't say anything, he just nods once, his stare moving to where Ava was sitting just half a minute ago.

He can still see the trail. "It's weak," he says, confirming my fears.

I grab Night's arm as he starts to teleport. His eyes widen as I do. It's not easy for him to teleport within this realm. It will be even more difficult for him to do it with me in tow. I will let him go if I have to, but I want that fucker. I want to be the one to end him. Night looks at me with understanding, then his eyes harden with resolve.

I've only done this a handful of times. It was years ago. My stomach drops and clenches hard. I squeeze my eyes shut. It seems to take a very long time. Too long. I'm gagging by the time we hit the other side. I stagger and fall. The world feels like it is spinning. I'm trying to look around us. I'm not sure what I'm seeing. Where are we? Night is walking in circles.

"Not here," I hear him say. He might have said more but that's all I pick up.

I try to get up but fall. I'm like a newborn lamb. Ava isn't here. "Where...?" I push out. My mouth is filling with saliva. I think I might get sick.

"Close..." Night says. He's still walking. "I think she's..." he sniffs the air, "close."

I shout her name and pull myself to my feet. Thank fuck the nausea is dissipating. We're in a hallway. It's long. At the end of it is a painting of golden wings. The frame is gold-leafed. I think we're in the hotel of his casino. That prick. I feel everything in me bristle. I fist my hands. They might be here, but they could be anywhere in this building. Time is running out for Ava. I can feel it. I shout her name again, in the hopes that she can hear me and respond. It's all I have right now. That and sheer desperation.

Night disappears and someone screams in the room to my right. A woman. It doesn't sound like Ava. A man yells something across the hall. Night is checking each room. I'm not sure how long he will be able to keep that up. I walk down the hallway, following the chaos. When he can no longer teleport, I will take doors down. I will search every inch of this building until I have Ava.

I throw my head back and roar. I hope that fucker can hear me. I hope he knows I'm coming for him. I hope even harder that I am in time. That he doesn't have a chance to hurt her first.

AVA

I fall onto the floor. Thick rugs. It's like *deja vu*. I'm in a hotel room. It's the same as last time.

No!

No!

No!

Why is this happening? Thankfully the dizziness has dissipated already, but I'm sick with fear. It's gnawing at me. Making my hands clammy and my mind race. How am I going to get out of this? How am I going to get away?

I smell that strange smell. It happens every time we teleport. It's subtle but there. I look around me and recognize the décor. From the colors, to the fabrics and finishes. This is The Winged Palace. Sly has taken me back to his own turf.

"Hey, babe." He grins at me when I turn towards him. He's lying on the bed like he doesn't have a care in the world. His hands are clasped behind his head. "Get your gorgeous ass over here." He pats the bed next to him. "I'm done with games." His stare hardens. "No more waiting."

"Go to hell!" I snarl, getting up. I turn to the door.

Sly is suddenly beside me, he grabs me by the arm. He is so strong. He hauls me over to the bed.

"Get your filthy hands off me!" I try to pull away but he's holding on too tight. His grip will leave bruises.

"I don't like that he touched you." Sly sounds pissed off. "I had to listen to the two of you…" He makes a face. He was listening in? I feel sick. "You're mine," he growls.

"I am not yours!" I shout. "How many times do I need to tell you? How did you even find me?" Am I never going to be safe? Is this going to be my life from now on?

"I watched your cocksucker boyfriend's buddies. It was just a matter of time before one of them led me to you and—"

I stomp down on his foot before he finishes his sentence. I have the information I need. He had Night followed. Maybe even Sophia. Why didn't we think of that possibility? It was careless. If he thinks I'm giving up or giving in, he's wrong. I manage to break free but don't get very far.

Sly backhands me and I go flying onto the bed. The whole side of my face stings. I think my lip might have split. I taste blood. My ears are ringing.

"You are mine to do with as I please." He is undoing his belt.

No!

No!

"You want to rape me? You're a sick bastard!" I yell. "This isn't fair. You can't do this."

"I will rape you if I have to." His eyes are hard. "I want a son," he says by way of explanation. Then he shrugs. "That means we have to fuck." He winks. "It will be fun, you'll see."

"What?" I can't believe what I am hearing. "A son?" *Did he just say that?*

"I want a son. I want a child and it has to be with you. That means that we are fucking... and not just for one night. We're fucking until you become pregnant. Once I have my boy, you can leave." He unclasps his pants and is about to pull down his zipper.

"Wait!" I yell. "I can't have kids." He must be mad. Completely out of it. To choose me, a waitress in his casino. I'm a nobody in his mind. *Why?* "I can prove it. We can go and see my gynecologist. She'll explain my medical problems."

"Of course you can have children." He laughs. "You just needed the right man in your life." He unzips his pants. "Take off the underwear, babe. I wouldn't mind seeing those lovely tits of yours as well." His eyes move to my chest... hungry, almost rabid. Pure evil.

"I'm telling you I cannot have children! You're barking up the wrong damned tree. Take one of your many admirers instead. I'm sure that most of them will not only be able, but quite willing to give you what you want."

"I wish. This whole 'cat and mouse' bullshit has lost its appeal. Then again," he smiles, "it's been a whole lot of fun. I knew exactly where you were the entire time. It was a rush knowing I could have you anytime I wanted. All the while you thought you were getting away." He chokes out a laugh. "The result is a hard-on I can't seem to rid myself of. You're going to help me with that. You *will* become pregnant, Ava." I can see how sure he is. "That isn't just any ring." He looks down at my hand. "You're no ordinary girl. You're special." He leers at me.

"Bruce," I whisper my brother's name. My eyes sting with tears and my throat is clogged. "Did he really kill himself?"

"Forget about Bruce. He was a loser. Your half-brother. Your weaker half, I might add.

"I won't forget about him! He was my only family.

All I had left. Tell me." I know what he is going to say before he says it.

"I organized for that package to go missing. It's in my safe right now."

This man is pure evil. He makes me sick. I say nothing. I keep my eyes on his. Sly grins. It revolts me. "I may have suggested he take his own life. I offered to keep you out of it if he did."

"What?" I yell, tears are streaming down my face. "You made him do it! Suggested? Like hell!" I choke out. "Just like you're giving me a choice now. You are the most vile and disgusting human being I have ever met."

"Not quite human." He winks at me. "That's why it has to be you. Now don't fight too much, babe." He pulls out his penis. It's long and hard. It makes me feel disgusted, sick... terrified. He really plans on going through with this. "I don't want to have to mess up that pretty face of yours." He takes a step towards me.

I'm panicking inside. Hardcore panicking. I will fight. Of course I will, but he's too powerful. Sly is coming for me in one minute, a predatory smile on his face, then, inexplicably, he falls. He comes crashing down as if he slipped on something. There's nothing there though. The moment is so bizarrely comical, it makes me want to laugh, but there's no time.

I take advantage of the moment, jump off the bed and run for the door. Sly grabs a fistful of my hair as I reach for the handle. "Against the wall will work too," he growls, pushing me against the hard surface. He starts to tug on my underwear.

I elbow him.

Sly's phone starts ringing. He swipes out with his leg,

knocking my feet out from under me. I fall. Hard. He shoves my head down into the rug, putting a knee on my back. I can't move. His weight hurts. My bruised cheek is pressed into the floor and it throbs. Thank god the rug is plush.

"Yeah?" He answers the phone as if it's the most natural thing to do while attacking an unwilling woman.

I start to yell, and he pushes harder, turning my scream into a strangled cry. He releases some of the pressure, but I can feel the warning hovering. *Keep quiet or else.*

"You sure?" He pauses. "Which floor?" he barks. "Fuck!" he curses, almost immediately after he ends the call. Sly gets off me and stands up.

I scramble to my feet and back away from him. My head is throbbing. My right knee as well.

"Looks like we've got to go. Won't be long now before you get this." He cups his dick and smirks at me. Then he tucks himself into his pants.

I want to run but I know he'll catch me. I have to think of something else. What though? Someone is here. Maybe it's Night. Maybe Forge was able to get him in time. I have never prayed for anything this hard in my life.

Then he pulls up his zipper; his eyes go wide, as does his mouth. Sly screams. It's like he's in agony. It takes me a second or two to realize what's happened. He has closed his zipper over his semi-erect penis and some of the skin has caught. I look down. A good deal of the skin has caught. *How the hell did he manage that?*

I laugh. I can't help it.

"Fuck you!" he snarls. He lets go of his zipper, putting

his hands in the air. "Fuck!" he yells. "What the fuck!" He doesn't want to touch himself. He's in obvious pain. "Help me!" he begs, his eyes pleading.

I look at him like he's lost his mind, because I think he has. "It's karma, babe." I wink at him. Then I'm running for the door. I can't believe it but Sly comes after me. It doesn't matter how much pain he is in, he is still fast. Not as fast as before but he's gaining on me.

"Bitch!" I hear him growl. I know we will teleport if he touches me. I can't let that happen. I run faster.

I yank the door open. I can feel him right behind me. I push the door to try and slam it, hoping it will hit him in the face. I'm shocked when it slams shut.

I hear him open it. He's coming for me again. He's slow, so he must be in agony. I'm glad! I punch the button for the elevator. It's going to take too long. Sly is nearly on me. I see a door to the right. I pray it's the stairs and not a closet. I glance back at Sly. He's about ten feet behind me and gaining. I don't think I'll make it to the stairwell and even if I do, I won't get far.

Then, without warning, the bronze and crystal chandelier in the hallway falls. I'm not sure if it has pulled out of the ceiling, or if the chain onto which it has been attached breaks, but it falls… onto Sly. I think Sly tries to teleport. For a second he turns hazy, then he is back. For some reason, he can't do it. Maybe pain inhibits him. Right now, he has his dick caught in his zipper and a huge chandelier on top of him. Sly groans.

I don't wait. I turn and pull the door open. Thankfully, I see stairs. It's not a closet. Good thing, since I hear Sly shove the chandelier off himself with a crash. I run down the stairs. I'm moving so fast I'm on the verge of falling.

I have to get away. Sly materializes about half a flight of stairs below me. I yelp and turn around. He's going to get me. I know it. This is where my luck runs out.

CHAPTER 17

FORGE

Night is still working his way from room to room. It's taking a long time. Too long. I'm frantic but I've calmed down enough to be able to think. I find a floorplan in the lobby, next to a fire extinguisher. There is one more floor above us. That's normally where they have the luxury rooms. They might even have a penthouse suite up there. I'm sure the owner of the casino will expect to stay in the best room. A prick like Sly would insist on it. What if Night was slightly off? He hit the right location, just lower than the actual mark. As soon as the thought enters my mind, I know I am right.

I leave Night. It's better if we split up. We'll have more chance of finding Ava. I fucking pray I'm not too late. I sprint to the elevator. There is only a 'down' button.

That, and a slot for a keycard. You need to have a keycard to gain access to the top floors.

Fuck!

I see a door. It must lead to the stairs. It's locked.

Double fuck!

The elevator dings and five security guards emerge. They are all carrying batons. They also have Tasers on their belts. They have been alerted to our presence.

"Come with us," one of them instructs. He has cable ties in his hands. He glances at the guy next to him. "There are two of them," he says. Yep, they have definitely been alerted to our presence, which does make sense but I don't have time for this bullshit.

I punch him in the face. I take out two more of them before anyone can react. Guy number four hits me with the baton. I bob my head out of the way but take a crack to my neck, just up from my collar bone. It hurts like hell, but I'll deal. I punch him in the mouth and he drops like a stone. The fifth guy is trying to get his Taser off his belt. His hands are shaking. I notice that he has dropped his baton. I growl at him, letting my lip curl away from my teeth, which have sharpened some.

He screams, turns and runs away. I notice that his crotch area is wet. I look down. My muscles are bulging. There are patches of green scales on my chest. I almost feel sorry for the guard. I must look terrifying. I pull a lanyard off the neck of the nearest unconscious schmuck. One of the others is groaning and starting to come around. "Thanks," I say and sprint back to the elevator.

The card works. The elevator dings open and I bound in. I'm going up. The doors shut. It seems to take forever but eventually I feel an upward lurch. Another ding sounds. The doors open. I see that fucker. His shirt-tails are hanging out of his pants. He has a bloody nose. There is a chandelier lying on the ground behind him. It's littered with shards of glass or crystal. I'm not sure which and I don't care either. It looks like he's been in a fight. He limps a step and then disappears.

Fuck!

Ava. Where is she? I scream her name. I'm about to run down the hallway when I hear her scream. She sounds desperate and terrified. Every hackle goes up. Adrenaline bursts through my system, making my muscles rope and bulge even more. My nails are sharp.

It takes me a few seconds to orientate myself. To find where the scream came from. The stairwell. She's taking the stairs. Sly is after her.

I snarl as I start to run. I'm fully prepared to break down the door if it's locked but it opens easily when I turn the handle.

Ava's running up the stairs towards me, taking three stairs at a time. That fucker is right on her tail. He is about to get her. He is stretching his hand out. If he so much as puts a finger on her they will teleport again. If that happens, I will have to find Night in time to follow them. That's if he can still teleport. Chances are he doesn't have much juice left.

Sly's eyes go wide and he trips. He tumbles down the stairs. It's a stroke of good luck. It's the break I needed. I reach Ava but don't stop. I've got seconds before that fucker teleports away like the yellow-bellied coward he is.

It's like everything is moving in slow motion. I can't move fast enough. I watch him roll onto his back, scrambling to find his feet. He is dazed. His eyes focus on me. He's going to run. I can see it in his eyes. "Nooooo!" I bellow. I feel this heat inside my chest. It builds and builds. Then it spews forth. *Flames!* They come from nowhere, hitting Sly. I keep roaring, watching as his shirt melts. His hair seems to melt as well. Welts appear on his skin, which blisters and then blackens.

Sly screams, an inhuman, high-pitched wail. Heat engulfs the whole stairwell and the stench of burning flesh and hair thickens the air. When I stop roaring, the flames subside. I leap onto him like an enraged animal. When I look down, my hand is in his chest. I've punched a hole into him. I close my hand around his heart and pull. My eyes are on his as I rip the organ out.

Shock fills Sly's eyes. Then he pushes out a rattling breath and dies. His heart stops beating at the same time. I drop it and wipe my hand on my jeans. I feel nothing. He deserved to die. Even a demigod can't regenerate from this. *Good!*

I turn. Ava is breathing hard. Her eyes are filled with terror. *Fuck!* She just watched me kill someone. It doesn't matter who he was or what he planned. It's very different thinking you want someone dead and then actually seeing them die horribly. We might not need to have that talk anymore. Any feelings she has for me might be gone. She won't be able to look at me the same way. I am a monster.

I see that her lip is busted up and bleeding. Her arms already have bruises forming from where he grabbed her. One of her knees is red and looks like it is swelling. Just like that, I am happy I killed Sly. Ecstatic in fact! I only wish I could do it again, slower this time.

"Forge," she chokes out. Then she's running down the

stairs towards me. She throws herself into my arms.

I catch her. I will always catch Ava. Always. "I've got you," I say, wrapping my arms around her. My throat is thick.

She pulls back. "You saved me! You…" Tears well and then stream from her eyes.

I pull her back against me, holding her tight. I nearly lost her. *My Ava.* I'm in love with her. Completely and totally. I still have to do the right thing by her. I have to let her go. Right now, though, she needs me. I will be here for her until she heals and then… I have to say goodbye. My heart aches. "You're safe now," I murmur.

Ava sobs in my arms for a couple of minutes. I keep holding her, even after she stops crying. I hold her when I see Night appear. He does a double-take when he sees Sly's body. He throws me a look. I ignore him. Without a word, he stuffs Sly's heart back into his chest and teleports away with the corpse. I can see by the look on Night's face that there will be a major debriefing over this incident. I don't know what the fuck just happened. I'm still trying to process it.

Ava sniffs into my chest. "You had flames coming out of your mouth. Huge flames." She pulls back. "It's the most awesome thing I've ever seen." She looks at me in utter amazement. "Lord of Fire," she gushes. "You *do* have a power." She smiles shyly at me, taking my breath from my lungs.

I nod. "I guess I do." I choke out a laugh. I pull her back against me. Now is not the time to discuss this. We need to get the hell out of dodge. Ava has been through too much. I hold her tighter, squeezing my eyes shut for a moment. Just soaking her in. I nearly lost this woman.

I don't want to let her go. Not ever. It took seeing Ava in trouble to bring my power to the fore. It took something so drastic. It was her. It was Ava. My light. My love. I squeeze my eyes shut trying not to think about tomorrow.

CHAPTER 18

AVA

Five days later

I put my hands on his shoulders and feel him tense beneath my touch. It's not right. He should enjoy my touch. I let him go and walk around the sofa. It's time to ramp this up a notch. I sit down on his lap.

Forge throws me a tight smile. He picks me up and puts me down next to him. Disappointment hits. He's pushing me away. Again.

"How are you feeling?" he asks, touching the side of my mouth. "Your lip is healing nicely."

"It's healed up nicely," I correct. "I'm feeling good. Great even." At least I am physically. There is something wrong with Forge. At first, I thought he was just being careful with me after Sly pulled me through the wringer.

I felt bruised and sore. My knee, my hip, my arms all still have bruises. They have turned purple with a tinge of green. The swelling has gone down. I'm still a little stiff but much better. There are things I'm going to have to work through but Forge saved me before anything truly terrible could happen to me. I'm lucky Sly was so unlucky. I think it was the universe standing up for the good guy for a change. Point being, I'm fine. I'm ready to move forward. You would swear I was half-dead by the way Forge is treating me.

Sure, he's been attentive. He insisted that I stay with him in his apartment. He has made all my food. He wouldn't let me get out of bed those first three days. He waited on me hand and foot. He even offered to give me a sponge bath, but I drew the line at that.

Trident has popped in three times. Night also came to see me, bringing flowers from all of the guys. Each of them signed the card. *How special is that?* I told him everything that happened. I had already told Forge. It was easier the second time.

Forge's mom even visited. Sophia came bearing chicken soup. She made me feel so much better. The soup was delicious. Only, the better I get physically, the worse this feeling inside me grows. Forge is keeping me at arm's length. There is something wrong. I asked him yesterday, but he said that everything was fine.

Fine.

Hah!

Not hardly.

When I told him about everything that happened, his face turned red and a vein appeared on his forehead. He ended up hitting a punching bag in his garage for hours.

Forge might have a relatively small apartment, but he has a huge garage with a whole string of cars. They're beautiful, but he barely noticed them as he stormed into the garage. He punched that bag until the sweat poured off him. Other than caring for me so well, it's the only other indication he has given that he still has feelings for me. He hasn't looked at me in that way. He hasn't tried to touch me or kiss me. He hasn't so much as held my hand.

I get the feeling that if I had let him give me a sponge bath, it would have been purely clinical.

I need to know what the hell is going on with him. I need to figure out my future. I need to find a new job and move forward. Is it going to be with him or...? I don't want to contemplate the alternative. "Is everything okay?" I put my hand on his thigh. I'm not normally this forward but I have to be. I want Forge. I want a future with him. I think I am going to have to fight to make that happen. I need to push him into telling me what's going on with him.

When his eyes lock with mine, I know I am going to have to do more than just fight. I am going to have to go to battle. "All good." His Adam's apple works.

"I'm ready," I lean in, my eyes on his lips, "to continue where we left off."

"Your lip is still healing. You can't—"

"I'm fine," I push out. I climb back into his lap, straddling him. This really isn't like me at all. I don't care. Either we move forward, or he is going to tell me what's bugging him. Either way, I can't wait anymore. I won't!

I put my arms around his neck. His hands are at his sides. He is breathing hard.

I lean in, intent on kissing him. I'm wearing a dress. It's pretty. It shows off a hint of cleavage. If I'm honest, I wore it on purpose. It has buttons all down the front and comes to just above my knees. He should be all over me. At least showing some kind of interest.

"We can't do this." He grips my hips and deposits me on the sofa. "I wanted to wait until you were better."

"I *am* better. We can make love. I'm desperate for you, Forge." I sound needy and scared. I hate it. "What's going on?" He has to tell me.

"I don't mean that we need to wait until you are well enough to fuck."

His harsh words make me flinch. His gaze softens. He rakes a hand through his hair and takes in a deep breath. "I mean I planned on waiting until you were ready to talk."

"You're breaking up with me?" There is a rock in the pit of my stomach. At least, it feels that way.

"No." He shakes his head. "I'm ending things before they begin. I could never break up with you. That's just it, once I get inside you, I will never want to leave." He has this tortured look that tells me he still has feelings for me.

"I'm okay with that," I try. "I don't want to go anywhere."

"It can't happen." He shakes his head, moving back as far as he can. Like he's afraid of what I will do. "We can't happen."

"Why not?"

"I meant it when I said that your condition is curable. Lyre has the gift of healing. He can fix you." He finally leans forward. He takes both my hands in his. "He can cure whatever is preventing you from having children. You can have a family, Ava. You can have a normal life."

"I don't want a normal life. I want you, Forge." I squeeze his hands. "You have become my family. You have become my normal. You mean everything to me."

He looks like he is crumbling. Then his eyes fill with resolve. He lets go of my hands. "I can't do it to you. I can't hold you back for me. You will end up hating me."

"You wouldn't be holding me back!" I half-yell. "I could never hate you."

"I *would* hold you back, Ava. Listen to me, you can have kids. You're not listening to me. I know that a family is something you've always wanted. I could see it when you told me about your ex. About what he did. I could see the longing in your eyes. I understand that longing full well, so don't try to deny it."

"Don't put words in my mouth. I'm telling you what I want. I want *you*, Forge." I am getting frustrated and a little angry. I'm trying not to let it take over, since he is trying to do what he thinks is right. "I want—"

"No, I'm not going to let you ruin your life. You will forget me and move on. It has to be this way." He gets up. "I think you need to go home. I'll help you get your things together. The dragon demigods are wealthy. *I'm* wealthy. I'll give you—"

"No, you won't!"

"See it as compensation for what happened."

"No!" I shake my head. My heart is pounding. My chest hurts.

"This is not up for debate, Ava," he growls.

"You're acting like an asshole again. An even bigger one than before."

"I'm trying to help you this time," he snarls.

"Don't do me any favors!" I yell, getting up. "I don't need anything from you. Not a damned thing." I start walking to the bedroom but change my mind and turn around. "No, that's not true, the only thing I need is love. That's all. Love. I don't need anything else but you, but you can't seem to get that into your thick skull. You can't seem to comprehend that I love you. Very much, you asshole. That all I need is you. Nothing else!" I turn back to the bedroom intent on packing and leaving.

"Ava!" Forge calls me, his voice still deep and hard.

I ignore him. I don't want to hear it.

"Oreo," he says, softer this time. His voice has me stopping in my tracks. I turn around. His eyes are glinting with what looks like unshed tears. I can't believe it. Such a beast of a man. So much power, and yet he is filled with emotion. I did this. "I love you too." It's a little choked. "I'm so afraid you'll regret it."

"I won't. I will never regret you." My eyes are also stinging. My throat is clogging.

I don't recall walking over to him, or seeing him walk to me either, but next thing, we are in each other's arms. Our mouths are locked in a searing kiss.

He growls into my mouth causing goosebumps to lift all over my arms. My legs are around his waist. I'm embarrassed to admit but I am dry-humping him. Sliding up and down him like he's a stripper pole or something. Okay, maybe not quite that bad, but close. I'm desperate. I'm panting and moaning. I'm a mess. A turned on… emotional… needy mess. I don't care. It feels like I have been waiting my whole life for this man. That every day has been leading to here and now.

To him.

To Forge.

"Please tell me we are finally going to make love?" I ask as his mouth moves to my neck. I moan as he kisses and nips me there, moving up and down. There might be more dry-humping on my part, I'm not sure. It all feels really good.

"No," he says against my neck.

What?

Did he say no to sex?

I hadn't expected that. Not at all. It wasn't even a real question. It was an assumption. I'm sucking in a breath to argue when he says, "We're fucking, Oreo." His voice is deep and thick. He pulls back and stares deep into my eyes. "There will be plenty of time for making love. I plan on worshipping your body so many times you have no idea. Right now, though," his jaw tenses up and his eyes blaze, "I need it to be quick and hard." He leans in and sucks on my lower lip. Then nips at it.

Sucks.

Nips.

I'm boneless and panting. I think I'm not only wet but gushing. I want all of that and more. I want it all.

"Something tells me you agree." He has gone back to kissing my neck. My ear… I moan. His hands are on my ass… squeezing.

My arms are around his neck. "Yes." It's all I can manage to choke out since I'm humping him again. I think I might come before anything really happens. I'm making these noises too. I still don't care.

"I can take you bareback." He groans hoarsely, like I

just made his day, no, his year.

I make this stupid noise of agreement. "You've never done it without a condom?" I ask, sounding shocked.

"No... never. I can't wait." He kisses me hard for a second or two and then pulls back. "From here on out it's bareback all the way. I'm going to love every second inside you."

More of those weird sounds come out of my mouth instead of an actual reply. He is hard and my clit is loving the rub.

"I might be a little rough." He pulls back. His eyes are blazing. They bore into me. "I won't hurt you, Ava, I swear." He cups my jaw, his thumb tracing my bottom lip.

"I want this." My hips are still moving. My core is still against him. My clit is feeling swollen. My nipples are hard. I'm desperate. He sets me on the coffee table and shoves the sofa out of the way then flips me onto my stomach. I'm now face-down on the table, my knees, on the rug. My breasts are mashed against the hard surface. Gripping my dress in his hands, he pulls it up and destroys my underwear with one hard yank. I hear the fabric tearing.

"Open for me." There is a desperate edge to his voice as he grips my hips. I do as he requests, and he growls. "One hell of a pussy, Oreo," he moans, sliding a finger into me. I moan harder. I love how crass and forward he is. I love what his dirty words do to me.

"So fucking wet for me." He sounds in awe. His voice is a rasp. There is a hint of the animal I know is inside him coming to the fore. I hear it. I love it. Turns me on even more. His finger moves in and out of me... slowly.

My eyes are wide and I am struggling to breathe. It feels that good. His thumb is on my clit. He is moving it in slow circles. My hands are splayed on the table. "I thought we were fucking," I push out. Any more of this and I won't last. I want him so badly I am shaking.

"Patience." He chuckles. It sounds tense.

"Yes, my lord," I tease. "Please, my lord!" I gasp as he plunges his finger deeper into my slick heat.

He chuckles harder, rubbing my clit harder too. I suck in a breath. "It's Forge." He pulls away. "Just plain old Forge," he adds. There is nothing plain about him. Nothing at all.

I moan in frustration as he moves back slightly, releasing me completely. My legs are shaking with the need to come. There is wetness dripping down my thighs. It's never happened to me before. I'm about to say something, when I feel him put his thick cock against my opening.

"Ready?" he asks, closing one hand around my hip.

"Yes," I mewl.

Forge grunts hard as he pushes into me. He's huge. It stings. I whimper, working hard to stay relaxed. Thank god I'm this wet.

God.

Hah!

I want to laugh but I can't. I can't even breathe. I can only feel.

"Keep breathing," he warns. I must have actually stopped then. His voice is choked. "Won't be long and you'll be screaming my name." His finger is strumming my clit as he pulls out, only to push back in. Deeper. He does it again. My mouth makes an 'O.' My eyes are so wide, I don't know if I'll ever be able to shut them.

He pushes deeper and deeper and deeper until he bottoms out, taking his finger off my clit as I am about to come. I moan. I moan hard. His hips are against mine. I can hear him panting. "Fucking tight." He puts a hand on my back. "Don't hold back, Oreo," he growls, his cock is pulsing inside me. Next thing he is crouching over my back. Heat on heat.

Before I can say or do anything, he is fucking me. All out taking me in hard, even strokes. He's grunting with every thrust. I am yelling. Loudly. With every thrust. If someone hears me, they will think I am being murdered… and I am. In a way, I am dying. The old me will be dead when he is done with me.

The table is moving with each thrust. I don't care about that either. My orgasm is there. I feel the coiling. I feel everything.

Forge slaps a hand on the table next to me. Both my hands are flat on the wood as well. I am yelling his name.

Forge is grunting mine. He bites me! Takes hold of the skin at the base of my neck and bites me. Not hard enough to break my skin but hard enough to have me coming so violently I think I might be busting a kidney.

He snarls. I think he is snarling my name. I can't be sure because my ears are ringing from how hard I am still coming. Just as I'm coming down, he picks up the pace and bites me again. I come again… the sound I make is choked. There must be some disbelief laced in there as well. I've never had a multiple orgasm.

Forge gives a startled yell and his hips jerk forward. My ass is shaking with each hard thrust. I can hear how wet I am. He keeps up the thrusts for a time, holding me there. Then he eases off. It's only when he lets my hair go that I realize he had it bunched in his hand. *Jesus H. Jesus. What was that?*

He slumps over me for a few seconds, breathing hard. "Oreos have always been my favorite," he pants out. "Especially the creamy center," he adds, his chest touching my back with every exhale.

I laugh. It comes out strained between hard pants. I just came twice in a row. *Twice.* I'm allowed to be out of breath. "Are you comparing my lady parts to the creamy middle in an Oreo?"

"I would never do that." I can hear that Forge is smiling. "I've always loved Oreos, but your pussy is a million times better."

I smile too, closing my eyes. I want to laugh again but I have no energy left. I've never come with my whole body before. From my head right down to my toes. I knew it would be intense with Forge... I didn't know the half of it.

He pulls out of me after another minute and carefully turns me over.

He looks sheepish. His eyes flit over my face. "I'm sorry. I never meant to bite you like that. It just kind of happened." He sweeps some of the hair off my face.

"It was good," I gush. "Really good. You can bite me anytime."

He shrugs. "Good to know, but..." he pauses, "it might be mating behavior for dragons."

"Might?"

"Is... it *is* mating behavior. Are you freaked out?" He winces.

"No." I mean it. We're meant to be together. It feels so

right.

"Good, 'cause I'm not freaking out at all." He brushes a kiss over my lips.

"It's mating behavior for your dragon side but what about demigods? Is there mating behavior for them too?"

"I have no idea about demigod mating behavior. We might need to have way more sex to figure it out."

"Sounds good to me."

He picks me up. "I want you naked and on my bed."

I tense up.

Shit!

He stops midstride. "You don't mind me getting a good look at the bottom half of your body but…?" He sits down on the sofa, putting me across his lap so that he can look at me. "What's going on?"

"I might not be as…" I breathe out.

"As what…?" He raises his brows.

"I grew quickly when puberty hit. I fleshed out quickly." I'm trying to tell him without saying it. "I… just… it…"

In true Forge style, he doesn't say anything, just keeps those gorgeous green eyes of his on me. There's no judging, no pushing, zero impatience. It bolsters me. "I have bad stretch marks on my breasts," I say, licking my lips. "I've always been quite subconscious about them. My first boyfriend… We were together from high school already… he was my first."

"When you were twenty?" he says, making my heart skip beats because he remembered.

CHAPTER 19

FORGE

She forces a smile and then nods. "Yes, when I was twenty. When I finally got naked and we did... it... he told me after that he was disappointed. He'd always fantasized about me. He'd always thought I'd be perfect because I looked perfect with clothes on." I roll my eyes. "Men think I have such amazing boobs. Women too, but... I have these stretch marks. My breasts are real... all mine. Not that there is anything wrong with breast implants. They're not quite as firm anymore either since hitting thirty last year and..."

I feel my blood fucking boil hearing what that prick said. "Nobody is perfect, Ava."

"I know that," she says. "Of course I do."

"When you were twenty, that boyfriend of yours must

have been what…? I'm assuming older?" Little prick. I wish I had the power to go back in time. I'd rattle the little punk… hard.

She shakes her head. "He was twenty as well."

"Young and fucking dumb," I grind out, trying not to growl. "I bet you he's seen a couple of women since then, and that he compares them all to you. I'll bet none of them comes remotely close."

She smiles. "Come on! You can't…" Her cheeks are turning pink. "You don't know what you're saying."

"I know it!" I'm not just having her on either. Ava is fucking perfect. I don't need to see her naked to know it's true.

"You haven't even seen… me… so… you can't possibly…" she goes on.

"I don't have to see you. I know." My voice sounds gruff. "When that asshole thinks of you, he'll wish he'd tried harder to keep you. I bet he would like nothing more than to get a shot at you again."

Ava frowns. "Come to think of it…" I can see her mind working. "He *did* contact me out of the blue a couple of years after we broke up. I had just started seeing Matt. It was a weird conversation. You might actually be right. I never thought of it that way until now."

"I'm telling you. Besides," I say, "I'm not a breast man anyway. Don't get me wrong, if I were a 'breast man'…" I let my gaze drift down for a quick second and whistle.

"You're not?" She looks shocked.

"I happen to love your eyes. They're beautiful, like the rest of you. Big, expressive, kind. A gorgeous hazel color."

She giggles. "You're an 'eyes man'? That doesn't even

sound right. You can be a 'breast man' or an 'ass guy' but eyes…" She's shaking her head.

"I'm all of the above, Oreo. All of the above."

"You can't be all of the above," she snorts.

"I'm a *you* man. No specific part. I love all those things. I love anything to do with you." I lean in and kiss her. "I love you," I say as I pull away. "There is nothing about you I won't fucking love. I can promise you that. Your breasts will be no different."

She smiles. Then she's pulling her dress over her head and tossing it onto the sofa next to us.

This gorgeous female puts her hands behind her back and undoes her bra. She lets her luscious tits spring free as she tosses the bra as well. I see fear in her eyes. She's acting brave and yet… she's still fearful. I want to slap that twenty-year-old prick because I have never seen anyone more beautiful in my life. Not fucking ever. I'm biased, but it's not that. She happens to be exquisite. "Your ex," I say as I cup her beautiful breasts in my hands, "was definitely trying to get back with you. His little boy ass had no fucking idea what he had." My dick is hard between us. It's fucking throbbing.

My woman gives me the most radiant smile. Not only that, she thrusts out her chest. My hands are overflowing with her curves. Her eyes are filled with heat. I think she can see what she is doing to me. She straddles me. I lift her and thrust into her hot, tight pussy. She's still nice and wet. I have to breathe deeply a few times to keep myself from coming. My balls are tight.

I put my finger on her clit as I start thrusting up into her. Yes, her tits are real, they jiggle with every hard pounding. I am the luckiest man on the planet. I look into

Ava's eyes while I fuck her. I wasn't lying when I said they are gorgeous. She's vocal. We both are. It doesn't take long before she is spasming around me. Her eyes go wide and she gets this shocked look before her expression morphs into one of bliss. Then I am grunting and jerking hard while I give myself over to her. I plant my face between her tits and spend myself inside her. When we are done – and it takes a good while because I pull out as much pleasure from her as I can, I want her fully stated – I put my face in the crook of her neck. I chuckle, still panting hard. My chest is heaving. "I'm sorry. The next round will be slow and gentle. You make my blood boil. Hotter than Hades."

"Have you been...?" She can barely talk. "To... there... Hades." I can hear she has to work to sound coherent.

Good!

"No, only Night can go to Hades." I'm also battling to form words. "No other mortal. I'm mortal... so..." I shrug. "It was just a saying. I will eventually make love to you, Oreo, but I have a feeling it might be a while before either of us cools down enough for that to happen."

"I think so too," she whispers.

My cock is getting hard again. I groan. I can't normally maintain for this long. Her eyes widen with shock.

Then she smiles. Ava starts to slowly ride my cock. "I'm one lucky girl," she says.

Luck.

I chuckle even though she's sliding on my cock, feeling amazing. "I'm the lucky one. I have you." Then I am grunting. Ava is picking up speed and my brain is turning to mush.

CHAPTER 20

FORGE

Two weeks later

I thread my fingers with hers as soon as she gets out of my car. I can see that she is nervous. "It will be okay."

She pushes out a breath. "I hope so." Ava looks pale. Her eyes are bloodshot. We both tossed and turned last night—neither of us got much sleep.

"It's not like I'm going to ever break the oath."

She nods once.

"They will accept you. They will accept *us*. I know it." I put my arm around her shoulders.

"What if they don't?" Her brow is furrowed. Her hazel eyes look huge and beautiful. So fucking beautiful. "What if they make you choose? I don't want you to ever have to choose."

She's so sweet. So kind. My heart swells with emotion. "They will accept my decision. They will accept you. I'm sure they already have."

"I'm not so sure. We waited too long." She gives me a tense smile.

"Yeah, we did." I bob my eyes. "We were getting to know one another."

She finally cracks a real smile. My heart warms. We spent the last two weeks holed up together. We fucked every day, several times a day, but we also talked. We talked so much and about everything. My love for this woman grows more with each second. Each heartbeat. She is mine and more importantly, I am hers. I finally belong. I finally fit. I will always choose Ava, just as Ava will always choose me. My boys will see that, and they will accept it.

I got a message from Bolt yesterday telling me they want a meeting with us. The guys messaged me often. Firstly, wanting to see how we were, and then wanting to know what the fuck was going on. I was bad. I ignored them. The message yesterday was more of an order than a request. It is time. They need to know what the fuck is going on. Like I told my woman, I'm sure they know already. This will be a formality.

The door to Night's house opens before I ring the bell. He is frowning. Looking pissed. He looks down at where we are holding hands. His frown deepens as he sniffs the air. He can scent what we've been up to, namely fucking like rabbits. We haven't made love yet. I know the day is coming and I look forward to it. I look forward to all of it... all of what is possible at any rate.

Night doesn't say anything, just turns and walks down the hallway. He turns right and enters the conference room. Just as before, everyone is sitting around the table. The sun went down an hour ago, so Samuel is here as well. Even Lyre. They're all here. My mouth is dry but I'm fine.

Jarrod gives Tri a hundred buck note. My best friend is grinning. He stuffs the money into his pocket. They were obviously taking bets. Tri was right on the money. Ava and I are officially together.

"You are going to break our oath." Night sounds disappointed. "If you fall, others will fall too. You've started something, Forge." He rubs a hand over his face, looking defeated.

I pull out a chair for Ava. She sits down. "Hello to you too," I say.

No one says anything, so I sit next to Ava. "Our oath was constructed to prevent more mixed-blood children from being born," I continue. "Ava can't have children. We have made the decision... *she* has made the decision to keep it that way." I look at Lyre when I say that part. I know what he will be thinking.

"The oath will never be broken, and we can be together."

"Our oath specifically said no partner. Therefore, no mate. Therefore, no children. That means you have already broken our oath. I'm going to assume that the two of you are now together, already making plans for the future. Plans that involve a wedding?"

We have talked about it. I haven't popped the question. It's far too soon for that. Too much has happened. Besides, we want to enjoy our newfound relationship. I love having a girlfriend. I *will* marry this woman one day in the not too distant future. Night and the others don't need to know any of this, however. I'm sure they can see what Ava means to me. "The whole reason the oath came about was because of —"

"To prevent more fucked up individuals like us from being born," Rage interrupts. "If your woman is incapable of having children then I don't think it's too much of an issue."

"There is that other piece of news that's come to light," Bolt adds, looking at Night.

Night looks completely out of sorts. I'm not used to seeing him like this. He leans forward and then sits back again. I can see he's thinking things over. He looks like he has more energy buzzing inside him than he knows what to do with. "I don't like it." He shakes his head. "Ava can't have kids but what about the next female?"

"There won't be a next one," I growl. "Ava is my future."

My beautiful girlfriend puts her hand on my thigh and squeezes. I have to work to stop myself from smiling at her. I find myself smiling often lately. Sometimes for nothing at all. It feels good.

"I'm not talking about you," Night says to me. "We can all see that you are taken with Ava. It's too risky for the rest of us to take mates." He is talking to Bolt now. "To have kids. We need to stick to our original oath." He is addressing everyone in the room. "I'm talking about the rest of us. Who will be tempted to break the oath next? The two of you look so fucking happy," he goes on, looking at us like we're stricken with the plague. "You make the rest of us want the same. You make us turn weak. Not me!" he quickly adds. "One of *you*, maybe." He glares at the other demigods.

"I disagree that we still need to stick to our oath," Bolt says. "I don't want to take a mate myself." He makes a face, like the thought disturbs him. "But some of the others..."

Jarrod nods. Samuel does too, like he's thinking about it.

"Nah!" Tri shakes his head. "There are too many women out there who need me. I can't settle down with just one," he smirks.

"Look at what the two have you have done!" Night growls. His eyes are tortured.

"Wait a minute." I put up a hand. "Nothing has changed. I just happened to fall in love with someone who can't have children. The oath should still stand. I know I'm a prick for saying that, but it's true."

"I always thought I was the unluckiest person on the planet," Ava joins the conversation. "Turns out that's not true." She takes my hand and squeezes. I have to smile at her. I can't help it.

"Actually, it's a little of both, Oreo." Trident chuckles, bringing us back into the conversation.

I growl low. Tri knows I hate it when he calls Ava that. He can be a real dick.

"Don't be so touchy, Forge," he says, grinning.

"Ava is a bit of both," Rage says.

What are they talking about? "Why do I get the feeling we're missing something?" I look at each of them in turn. I can see that they're keeping something from us. Something important.

"You're not entirely human, Ava," Night blurts out.

I frown. I frown hard. *What the fuck?*

Ava chokes out a laugh. "Wait… what?" She looks at me. She's confused and shocked. "Of course I'm human. What else would I be?" She shakes her head.

"We'll start with your scent," Night begins.

"Not human at all," Trident says. "Oreo." He winks.

I growl again, deeper this time. My whole chest vibrates. He needs to cut the crap. This is serious.

"Easy!" Trident puts up a hand. "I'm making a point this time."

"It's human, just different," I agree; it wasn't a stretch to consider the possibility that she wasn't entirely human. I admit that the thought had crossed my mind once or twice since meeting her.

"Think about the things Sly said to you, Ava," Night continues. "He told you he had been searching for you for a long time. Said he had to procreate specifically with *you*. He said you were special."

"I wouldn't listen to a thing that came out of that fucker's mouth," I object.

"We believe he wanted to have a son with a woman who also descended from the gods." Bolt is leaning back in his chair. "Same as him. Sly wanted a son with powers. He didn't want to take a human mate."

"What am I then?" Ava asks, looking shell-shocked.

"We're pretty sure you're descended from the goddess Tyche," Bolt says, in that deadpan way of his.

"No way!" Ava shakes her head. "Surely I would know if my mother was a demigod?"

"Not your mother," Night explains. "We believe

your father was a demigod. That his mother was the goddess Tyche."

Her mouth drops open. She's looking down at the table. Her mind is racing a mile a minute.

"How would you know that?" I ask. This now seems farfetched.

"While you were all cozied up with Ava," Night rolls his eyes, "in a sex-drunk haze—" he adds.

"That's unnecessary," I say, even though it's true.

"While you were busy," Bolt half-smiles, "the rest of us got to talking. Night did the research. It was he who figured it out, although the rest of us quickly agreed."

"It's your ring, Ava," Night says. "After everything that happened this last time around, I figured it out. I didn't say anything because I wanted to be sure first. All the gods wear rings similar to that one." He looks at her hand. "Hades… my father has one. It has the same blend of white and yellow gold. It's heavier set with a different pattern. Yours is feminine, with a diamond, that's why it didn't click at first, but it's ultimately the same. I believe that ring belonged to your grandmother."

"A goddess?" Ava whispers.

"Yes." Night nods. "You are a quarter god and three-quarters human."

"I don't have any powers, though. I'm human," she insists. She's fiddling with her ring, rolling it around on her finger.

"We believe that you *do* have powers, they're just subtle," Bolt steps in.

"We believe your powers have increased since you and Forge got together. The same is true for you." Night looks my way. "That whole 'fireball out the mouth' thing." He raises his brows.

"I can't believe you have such a great power," Tri grumbles. I can see he's stoked for me. He is pretending to be annoyed.

I haven't tried using my power again but there is a different feeling inside me, inside my chest, that tells me I will probably be able to breathe fire again if I want to. I am now truly the Lord of Fire. I nod in agreement. I can't think about my powers now because Ava... fuck! A descendant of the gods too. No wonder we felt such a connection. It makes sense to me now.

"I don't have powers," Ava is talking more to herself. "I would know if I did. Surely I would know?" she is asking me.

"The goddess Tyche is the goddess of luck and fortune. Your high rollers in the casino liked having you serve them and called you their lucky charm because you *were* a lucky charm for them... to a degree."

"I helped them win?" Her eyes are wide.

"Yes," both Night and Bolt say, "you may have helped one or two of them along a couple of times."

"But Tyche can also be responsible for bad luck," Trident snickers. "Like when Sly fell for no reason and then proceeded to zip up his cock." He all-out laughs. "I'm sorry. I don't mean to bring up bad memories. I sure wish I could have seen that."

Ava smiles. "Actually, that happens to be a fond memory of mine. One I will treasure."

"Then the chandelier fell onto him," Night adds. Even he is smiling. My sweet Ava took a demigod down, all on her own. *I fucking love it!*

"Yeah," Ava is thinking it through. "It did fall for no reason." She nods a few times.

"Not for no reason." Night shakes his head. "*You* did that."

"He also fell down the stairs when he was coming after me." Ava is thinking it through.

"That's a lot of accidents for one person to have. Too many maybe," Lyre says. "It was seriously bad luck." He winks.

"It still seems bizarre," Ava muses. "I lived a normal life. I felt human."

"That's because you mostly were," Night explains. "We think that being with Forge brought your powers out. Maybe even being in a tough situation helped them along. We're not sure about the details." He shrugs. "We may never know for sure. My father won't tell me anything." He glowers for a moment.

"So, it would seem that it might be possible for us to have children with humans. It seems that the blood becomes more diluted, leaving them mostly human. Look at you, Ava." Jarrod says. "Maybe we don't need the oath anymore."

"Here we go again. This is a giant fuck up." Night stands, still resisting. "We don't know any of this for sure."

"It makes sense that Ava is a child of a human and a demigod," Jarrod throws back at Night. "It took us a long time to figure out she's not human, and we should be more attuned than anyone. We could lead normal lives. Have children who are accepted."

Night snorts. "Take off the rose-colored glasses. We. Are. Not. Normal. Our kids wouldn't be either. It's a fact!" he practically yells.

"Night is right," Rage says. "We're *not* normal. We can't live normal lives. Forge has fallen in love. It's happened." He makes a face like it's a terrible thing. "We can't ask him to give his female up. What's done is done. The only saving grace is that she can't have children."

"I would never give Ava up!" I say. My whole body goes tight at the thought.

Night's jaw tightens. His whole body bristles. "No children. You can never have them. You both need to swear." He knows, just like I do, that we can go to Lyre any time and heal Ava. At least, I think we can... but I won't. As much as I would love a family with this woman... my woman, I can't. *We* can't. I know she agrees because we've talked about it at length.

"I swear," Ava says.

"So do I." I take her hand and lift it to my mouth, brushing a kiss on her knuckles. I still feel guilty about this part. I feel selfish.

She squeezes my hand, reassuring me. Thing is, Ava is a strong woman, capable of making her own decisions. If she wants to give up on a family for me, I won't stop her. I will spend the rest of my life making sure she never regrets her decision.

"As far as I am concerned," Night intones, standing up from his chair, "the oath still stands for the rest of us. This changes nothing." His voice is laden with emotion. Anger and frustration are at the fore. I think there might be some pain thrown in at the back. Then he turns and stalks out.

CHAPTER 21

AVA

Two weeks later

I push my plate away and pat my belly. "I'm stuffed," I groan. "You are an amazing cook, Sophia." I smile at Forge's mom, and she smiles right back.

"There had better be room for dessert in there," she says, looking down at where my hand is still holding my distended belly. At least, it feels distended. Especially after eating so much. It isn't, though. Sophia cooked us a roast dinner with all the trimmings. I ate far too much. I feel slightly ill, but it was worth it. It's been a while since I had a home-cooked meal like this one. My eyes sting for a second as I think about my own mother and Bruce. I still get teary when I think about him. About what happened. What Sly did. It's going to take time to work through everything that happened. I will never get over his death but maybe one day I will learn to live with it.

"I know how you feel," the beautiful woman across from me says, pushing her own plate away. She pats her belly as well. Hers is distended for real since she's pregnant and quite far along.

Her husband, Colton, is sitting next to her, he throws her a loving look. He is cradling a sleeping young boy in his arms. The little boy is called Luke and he's three years old; he's Forge's nephew. I know I have no business feeling this way, but there is this pang I get when I look at them. They are a beautiful family. I wonder to myself if Forge feels it as well.

I pull myself out of such dreary thoughts. I know it is normal, so I won't be too hard on myself. We are having lunch with Forge's family on their ranch. I note that Forge's brother looks nothing like him. He has blond hair and blue eyes like his mother. He's not nearly as built, not nearly as gorgeous, but then I'm biased when it comes to Forge. Looking at him still makes my belly tighten and my mouth go dry. I have a feeling it will always be this way.

Forge puts his hand over mine. I look his way and he winks at me. "What do you say we go for a walk?" he asks me. "Work off some of that lunch to make room for dessert? I think it's key lime pie. My mom makes a mean pie." He looks over at his mother, who beams.

"Sure, there's no rush," Sophia says, still beaming.

"I can second that," the beautiful woman, putting her hand up. Her name is Ariana. She is radiant and glowing. Everything the magazines mention when describing a pregnant woman. She heaves a sigh. "I think I'll have a lie-down. My feet feel like they are swollen. Pity I can't see them." She laughs.

"I'll bring Lukie," Colton says. "Thanks for the lunch, mom. Delicious as always." He and Ariana stand. "Enjoy working off lunch," he says to Forge, grinning.

He doesn't think…? No! Does he think we want to sneak off to go and have sex? My cheeks heat.

Forge and I also stand. "We'll help clean up first," I say.

"No, you two lovebirds go on," Sophia urges. "I like doing dishes. It relaxes me."

"You sure, mom?" Forge asks.

"Absolutely, I'm so happy you are here, Ava." Sophia stands as well. "I know you're going to take good care of my boy."

"Mom," Forge warns halfheartedly. I'm sure he knows his mother is just… being a mother.

"I'm not saying anything bad." Sophia shakes her head. "You need to take excellent care of Ava here as well. That's what being in a relationship is all about. Taking care of each other through good times and bad. I'm so glad you gave up on that silly oath. I'm hoping the rest of the boys come to see that."

"It's not silly, mom," he says, sounding somewhat deflated. "Things just happened to work out for Ava and me." We haven't told Sophia that we don't plan on ever exploring having children. Forge says she won't understand and that she won't take it well. We both hold our breath, hoping she won't push. It is a conversation we need to have, but not yet.

"I'm just so happy for you, son." Sophia is smiling broadly, her eyes are glinting like she might want to cry.

"I want the same for the others, that's all." Then she turns to me. "When you get back, we're going to talk all about Forge. I have a couple of juicy tidbits for you. Like the time when he—"

"Mom!" Forge warns. "Don't you dare."

"I haven't said anything yet." Sophia laughs as well. "I promised Ava I would spill, and I will." She bobs her eyebrows.

"Yes," I say. "I really want to know everything there is to know." I'm grinning at Forge.

He's trying hard not to smile. "Okay, Mom." Forge breaks down and chuckles. "You can tell my woman anything. I don't mind."

Sophia narrows her eyes a touch. "Can I tell her about the stash of socks you kept under your bed as a teenager?"

His mouth drops open and he shakes his head. "No way! Mom! You can't—"

"What about what was actually inside the Sports Bloopers DVD case?"

He pulls in a breath, sounding shocked. "You knew what was in there?" He looks shocked too and I'm intrigued.

"Of course. I'm your mom. It's my job to know things." She laughs.

Forge shakes his head. "Now I'm scared," he mutters.

"You should be." She picks up an empty plate.

"You sure you don't need help?" he asks.

"I'm good." She picks up a dish.

"We'll see you in a bit then," he says.

Sophia nods.

Forge takes my hand and we go outside the back door. "Okay, so, I have to ask, what was inside the Sports Bloopers DVD case?" I press after we have been walking for a few minutes. It's a beautiful day. The sun is high. There isn't a cloud in sight.

He looks at me sideways, his hand closing a little tighter over mine. "Porn." He grins but quickly turns serious. "I'm shocked my mom found it. I thought it was the perfect hiding place, since she doesn't watch sports."

"Porn?" I choke out a laugh. I had expected as much.

"I was twenty-two before my cherry was popped, remember? That's a long time to wait and a ton of testosterone in one body."

"I'm pretty sure I can guess why you had random socks under your bed." I snort out a laugh. "That's so gross."

He laughs as well. "I'll admit that it is pretty gross. The things we did as teenagers." He makes a face.

We walk for a few more minutes, just enjoying the day. "I want to show you something," he says, letting my hand go.

I watch as Forge pulls his shirt over his head. Then he pulls his shorts down, until he's standing in front of me, completely naked. "Not that I'm complaining..." I give him the once-over, "because I'm really not, but I've seen you naked. It sounded like you planned on showing me something I've never seen before."

He lifts a brow. "You said you wanted to see me in my dragon form, smartass." He lifts his brows. His eyes are glinting.

I suck in a breath. My heart beats faster. "I do! I absolutely do."

"I have to warn you, it can take a while after shifting back for my human side to get back up and running."

"What does that mean?" I don't know why but the idea of him being more animal than human turns me on. "You will look like a human once you turn back, won't you?"

"Oh, I'll look human, but my animal instincts will be front and center. I'm afraid that after all this talk of porn… That, and knowing about all the goodies you're hiding under there." He tugs at my dress. "I might not be able to resist you, Oreo. Do you still want to see me in my dragon form?"

I'm liking the sound of this more and more. "I think I can handle you in beast mode." I wink at him.

Forge throws me this sexy half-smile that—I'm not afraid to admit – makes me a little wet. Then he takes a couple of steps back. I'm reminded of what Trident said way back when I first met him, that shifters are big in their dragon form. Then I watch as something magical happens. My beautiful man grows and changes into an even more beautiful, majestic creature. His limbs stretch. Scales sprout. Wings and a tail slowly grow before my eyes. His jaw elongates. I just stand there gaping.

"Wow!" I finally say, completely in awe. He is huge once he has completed the shift. Tall. So powerful. His eyes are still the same green.

He arches his back and roars. Then flaps his wings. Next thing, he's lifting up and up. Instead of taking to the sky like I expect, Forge stretches his claws out in my direction. I have a feeling…

I start to shake my head. "I don't think—"

Forge picks me up and heads into the sky, wings

flapping noiselessly. It is all so graceful and effortless. I grip his claws. My heart is going nuts. I'm both petrified and exhilarated. Adrenaline is pumping through my system. It's so beautiful up here. There are mountains, streams and rivers. All of these lands belong to the shifters. It's still on the edge of town, so not too far from civilization.

Humans are not welcome on these lands unless invited... and this is why. The dragon shifters can be in their animal skins without exposing themselves. He eventually descends. We are in a large clearing in a wooded area. It's so beautiful out here. I hear the birds and the insects, the rustling of the leaves in the trees as the wind picks them up.

When I turn back around, Forge is almost back in his man form. There is skin where his scales were. His eyes are so intense. His whole body looks poised and tense.

Forge growls low, his eyes on me. If I didn't know better, I would think he was going to take me apart, limb from limb. "Did I tell you how good you look in that dress?" His voice is deep.

I smile. "You did." I can see that he is barely holding on. I love that I do this to him. He is running on instinct right now and he wants me. I've never seen such unbridled desire before. It makes me shiver. It makes my nipples tighten and my blood run hot.

"We have a little while before I will be able to shift back," he says. "I wonder what we could do to pass the time."

I smile. "I wonder."

"Any ideas?"

"I have one or two," I say.

He nods, his Adam's apple bobs as he swallows.

"We're in the middle of nowhere." I look around us.

"No one will hear you scream." His eyes narrow in on me.

"How lucky are we?" I say, pulling my dress over my head.

Forge growls low, his eyes are feral. They might even still be slitted.

I pull off my panties and unclasp my bra, throwing all my garments over a nearby branch.

Forge's gaze is on me. "I want you on your knees." His voice is rich and commanding.

I look around, finding a softer looking mossy patch, under a nearby tree. Forge just stands there watching. I go over there and drop onto all fours.

Forge snarls. I turn to look at him and he is fisting his hands. His muscles are roped. It looks like he wants to pounce on me.

Good!

I lift up my ass, sticking it in the air at him. "Are you going to bite me?"

"I think that might be a distinct possibility." He's closer.

I'm panting in anticipation. This is how it is between us. *Explosive! Next level!* Unbelievable also comes to mind.

Forge drops down behind me. He is breathing hard as well. He doesn't waste time. He leans over me and starts to rub on my clit. "You wet, Oreo?"

I moan. "You know I am."

He pushes a finger into me and I groan, shutting my

eyes. I bite my lower lip. So good. I'm already nearly there. It doesn't take much with Forge.

"Good and wet." His voice has changed, it's filled with desperation. "I'm going to fuck you now." He sucks on my earlobe, his finger is back on my clit.

"No lovemaking?" I tease.

"Maybe one day when we are old and grey." He gives a tense laugh.

Forge is crouched over me. He kisses my neck. "I'm desperate for you." His voice is a husky rasp. He cages me in with his massive body. He growls hard as he thrusts inside me, bottoming out in one go.

"Oh, god.! I yell, feeling him everywhere and all at once.

"What's that, sweetheart?" His thrusts are now short and punchy, taking my breath away. "What did you call me?" he demands roughly, his thumb is on my clit using firm strokes.

I'm barely able to breathe. "Lord!" I yelp. "Forge... Ohhhh...." He's taking me deep. I have to clutch the tufts of grass to keep from being pushed into the mossy earth. It's wild. It's rough. As always, he's taking my breath away. I'm already feeling that coiling sensation. My whole body is preparing to let go.

His teeth are biting down. His hand is closing on my hip. His finger is frantic on my clit. I am screaming as my orgasm takes me. He is jerking into me. I can feel him coming inside me in hot spurts.

"Fuck!" he growls. "Ohhhh fuuuuck!" He is still jerking, his movements slower.

My neck is stinging. I put my fingers there.

"I'm sorry," he whispers. "My dragon has decided he

wants to mate you."

"That's good," I heave out. "We'd be in trouble…" I am struggling to catch my breath. My body is humming from coming so hard. My legs might actually be vibrating. My hands are shaking. "We'd… be in… trouble…" I pant, "if your dragon side wasn't all in."

Forge rocks into me. He is already hard again, or still hard, I'm not sure which. "Oh, he's all in, Oreo. All fucking in!"

My knees and hands are dirty when we go back to Sophia's house. Either nobody notices or nobody says anything. I go and wash up, praying that it is the former. The key lime pie is superb. The stories both Colton and Sophia tell us about Forge are too. They all make me feel so welcome. Like I am already one of them. My heart is bursting with love.

CHAPTER 22

AVA

Three weeks later

I feel sick to my stomach as I push open the door.

"Go away," my boyfriend growls. He isn't looking my way. He's busy working. I shouldn't interrupt but I have to. My stomach clenches.

"It's me," I call, closing the door. I try to sound upbeat.

Forge comes out from under the hood and drops the wrench he is holding onto the table next to him. It lands with a clang. He is smiling. "My gorgeous Oreo." He walks over to me and picks me up. "You've come to help me christen the other workbench." He points at the bench on the other side of his workshop.

I popped in the other day and we ended up having

sex… on his main workbench. There are two of them in the shop. The thought of hot, sweaty sex on bench number two still makes my clit tingle and my nipples tighten, even though I am nervous. We have plenty of sex but still can't seem to get enough of one another. I'm sure things will slow down at some point but for now, we are enjoying each other too much for that. Hopefully, he will still feel like christening the other bench when I am done with my confession.

"We could do that." I smile. "I just wanted to — "

"While you're here…" He kisses me. A couple of soft brushes of his lips to mine. *So sweet.* "There's something I want you to see." He looks excited. Like a schoolboy. He puts me down and takes my hand. "This way." He leads me to the far section of his workshop.

My mind is racing. I have to tell him. This can't wait.

He picks up a tarp and pulls it aside. My eyes go wide. I can't believe what I am seeing. "Miss Sunshine!" I say, sounding shocked. I *am* shocked. "Wow!" I gush. "She's beautiful. I thought you said you didn't have time to fix my car." I narrow my eyes on him.

He grins at me. "I lied. Of course I lied. I thought you would have realized what I was up to." He chuckles. "Actually, I can't believe how shocked you are. It isn't finished but I thought I'd check that you're happy before carrying on."

"It's beautiful! She's gorgeous!" I touch the paint. "You've done such a great job." The mustard yellow is gone. It still has yellows and golds. But there are also oranges and red tints too. I recognize the design. It's the same as the tattoo on his chest. The one of all the flames I love so much.

"I thought you could still call her Miss Sunshine. I didn't think you'd want to change her so much that you'd have to change her name." He shrugs. I realize that he's shy. Not sure if I'm happy for real or just humoring him. "We could get you something new… you can drive whatever you want now." He gives a one-shouldered shrug.

It means so much. I can't wait to tell Trudy. My best friend will love this. My eyes well with tears. My car has been transformed. It's been a labor of love. She is the sun now. She's incredibly beautiful. I can't believe it. "No!" I choke out. "I love it so much. I love you for doing this."

"I still have to fix the interior," he adds, still looking unsure. "Leather seats. Better finishes. You'll need a decent sound system and —"

"I'm pregnant!" I blurt.

"What?" Forge growls. His eyes darken.

"I'm sorry." I burst into tears. "I'm so sorry. I don't know how it happened." I cover my mouth with my hand.

"I'm pretty sure I know how it happened." Forge puts an arm around me. His features have softened but his eyes are still filled with worry.

"I… I'm… I can't…" I'm all over the place. "I was sick… nauseous and my breasts were tender. I couldn't ignore the signs. I took a test. I thought I was crazy. I'm not crazy." I'm clearly and visibly panicking.

Forge pulls me in for a hug. "I've got you."

"How did this happen?" I say, still sobbing into his chest. "I mean… I know how it happened, but… I can't have kids. How did I get pregnant?"

"You needed to be with the right guy," Forge says.

"Isn't that what that prick said?" His voice drops a couple of octaves. By 'that prick' I know he means Sly. Sly was adamant that I could get pregnant with the 'right guy.'

"Maybe you needed to be with someone like me," Forge goes on. "Someone like us… with the blood of the gods in their veins." He looks like he's thinking it through. He looks unsure. He doesn't look happy.

Oh no!

I cry harder, burying my head back in his chest. "What is Night going to say?" I'm panicking as I come up for air. "What about the others? This is a disaster, isn't it? We swore not to have children and now—"

"I don't care about any of that." Forge pulls away. He dries my eyes with his thumbs. "I love you, Ava. Somewhere, somehow, the universe decided that we were going to be parents. It doesn't matter what anyone says or thinks. Only *we* matter. How we raise this child matters. I see that now." He plants a kiss on my lips. He is smiling. Smiling more brilliantly than I've ever seen him smile. "I'm going to be a father." He gets down on his knees in front of me. He puts both his hands on my belly. "You are going to be an amazing mother and we will be okay," he murmurs. "We will be great, just you wait and see."

The End

AUTHOR'S NOTE

Charlene Hartnady is a USA Today Bestselling author. She loves to write about all things paranormal including vampires, elves and shifters of all kinds. Charlene lives on an acre in the country with her husband and three sons. They have an array of pets including a couple of horses.

She is lucky enough to be able to write full time, so most days you can find her at her computer writing up a storm. Charlene believes that it is the small things that truly matter like that feeling you get when you start a new book, or when you look at a particularly beautiful sunset.

BOOKS BY
THIS AUTHOR

The Chosen Series:

Book 1 ~ Chosen by the Vampire Kings
Book 2 ~ Stolen by the Alpha Wolf
Book 3 ~ Unlikely Mates
Book 4 ~ Awakened by the Vampire Prince
Book 5 ~ Mated to the Vampire Kings
(Short Novel)
Book 6 ~ Wolf Whisperer (Novella)
Book 7 ~ Wanted by the Elven King

Demon Chaser Series (No cliffhangers):

Book 1 ~ Omega
Book 2 ~ Alpha
Book 3 ~ Hybrid
Book 4 ~ Skin
Demon Chaser Boxed Set Book 1–3

Shifter Night Series:

Book 1: Untethered
Book 2: Unbound
Book 3: Unchained
Shifter Night Box Set Books 1 – 3

BOOKS BY THIS AUTHOR

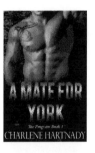

The Program Series (Vampire Novels):
Book 1 ~ A Mate for York
Book 2 ~ A Mate for Gideon
Book 3 ~ A Mate for Lazarus
Book 4 ~ A Mate for Griffin
Book 5 ~ A Mate for Lance
Book 6 ~ A Mate for Kai
Book 7 ~ A Mate for Titan

The Bride Hunt Series (Dragon Shifter Novels):
Book 1 ~ Royal Dragon
Book 2 ~ Water Dragon
Book 3 ~ Dragon King
Book 4 ~ Lightning Dragon
Book 5 ~ Forbidden Dragon
Book 6 ~ Dragon Prince

The Feral Series
Book 1 ~ Hunger Awakened
Book 2 ~ Power Awakened
Book 3 ~ Hate Awakened

BOOKS BY THIS AUTHOR

Water Dragon Series:

Book 1 ~ Dragon Hunt
Book 2 ~ Captured Dragon
Book 3 ~ Blood Dragon
Book 4 ~ Dragon Betrayal

Earth Dragon Series:

Book 1 ~ Dragon Guard
Book 2 ~ Savage Dragon
Book 3 ~ Dragon Whelps
Book 4 ~ Slave Dragon
Book 5 ~ Feral Dragon
Book 6 ~ Doctor Dragon

Excerpt

ROYAL Dragon

THE BRIDE HUNT

CHARLENE HARTNADY

CHAPTER 1

They were damned either way. Whether the lesser
kings accepted the proposal or not.

Damned.

The word rolled around in his mind. It made his gut
churn and left a bad taste in his mouth. Coal looked at
each of the four males, from one to the next. All of them
were powerful specimens. Pure royal blood ran through
their veins. Their golden chest markings were testament
to that. As was his own. He felt such pride at being a
royal prince, at being a fire dragon.

Granite, the earth king had dark hair and even darker
eyes, like polished onyxes, much like his own. There
were flecks of black within his chest marking, to show
that he was an earth dragon. Of his personality, it was
known far and wide that he was both strong and a
hothead.

Then there was Torrent, the water king. His hair was
so light it was almost white. His eyes as blue as the ocean
itself. Flecks of green could be found in his golden chest

markings to represent their element familiarity. The male was excessively arrogant but likeable, an odd combination.

Thunder had eyes the color of amethyst jewels. As the air king the blue flecks within his golden markings were definitely prominent. Though normally calm, the male looked agitated at the moment. This meeting needed to run smoothly. Coal only hoped that the males would accept the proposal put forward by his brother, the fire king. Blaze was the strongest of the dragons. He had eyes the color of emeralds. He, like Coal and the rest of the fire dragons, could breathe fire, which gave them a superior advantage over the others. Their golden markings were pure.

The air king held the platinum goblet with such a grip that Coal was sure it would crush at any moment. His face was red. Scales were visible through the golden tattoo on his chest, making more blue bleed through. A sure sign that he was moments away from changing.

"No," Thunder growled. The word was accompanied by a billow of smoke. It left his mouth in a lazy, curling tendril, at complete odds with the male who expelled it. The air king was fire breathing mad. Such a pity for him that a bit of useless smoke was all he could produce. Thunder had better watch his step. Blaze looked relaxed as he leaned back in his chair, but Coal knew better. His brother was not as calm as he seemed. The slight tic in his jaw was evidence of that.

The air king clenched his teeth together for a few long moments, clearly trying to get himself back under control. *Best he do that, and quickly.* Blaze would not tolerate such outbursts, even from another king. "You can forget about having one of the air females. The agreement was, your sister for one of my tribe. A fair trade."

The earth and water kings moved restlessly in their chairs, as did the princes at their sides. They were not privy to the arrangement that had been made between the fire and the air kingdoms. Had the agreement worked out, it would have put both fire and air at the top of the food chain, with their own tribe, fire, as the solid leaders over the four kingdoms. As it stood though, they were still at the head of the game despite the deal falling apart at the last minute.

Blaze twisted the ring on his finger. "I will agree to the three of you taking human mates on the condition that I get to have one of the fertile dragon females." His green eyes blazed. He dropped his hands back at his sides. There was not a single sign of tension in his body. Not true. There it was again, that tic. Only, you had to know where to look and if you blinked once too often you might miss it.

Thunder laughed. There was no humor to the sound. "You are an arrogant bastard." The male turned serious in an instant. "We are going to take humans whether you like it or not."

"Do that, and I will destroy you." Blaze's voice was even. "That goes for all of you." He let his gaze go from one king to the next before returning to Thunder.

The other two kings didn't say a word. Although Coal wasn't sure if it was because they knew their places. Something was brewing and it was clear that these three had discussed this amongst their selves at length.

Thunder leaned forward in his chair. "You are going

to single handedly destroy our species. Just because some human female broke your heart doesn't — "

"Say one more word and I'll kill you, so help me..." Blaze stood, tension radiated off of him. On the upside, that pesky tic was gone. He and Thunder stared at each other for what felt like a long time. Coal had to work to remain outwardly calm. To refrain from fidgeting like the others. He was the fire prince and heir to the throne, should anything happen to Blaze.

"This is how it's going to go down," Blaze said, his voice still calm and even. "I'm going to take one of your sisters. The rest of you can take humans, if it works out, we'll allow more of our males to take them as well." He sat back down.

Thunder shook his head. He ran a hand through his hair. His blue eyes were bright and filled with a multitude of emotions including anger, frustration and longing.

"Deny the males human females and it's a sure fire way to an uprising. Do you want to be overthrown by your own dragons?" Granite's deep voice reverberated around the large room.

"It wouldn't happen. One example and the coup attempt would be at an end." Blaze narrowed his eyes. "We need to make it clear that their turn will come. Patience."

"Their patience is waning." Granite's brother, the earth prince, piped up. "Our males get two opportunities per year to be with a female. They are driven to mate and to reproduce. The testosterone in the air is nauseating. I haven't been with a female for months so I can relate." His neck muscles bulged. He was a second prince, as was the case with the water prince. It was puzzling that he was here. It was protocol for the first princes to be present at such occasions.

"I thought I could scent something odd." The earth king choked out a laugh and some of the tension in the room eased. Even Blaze managed a half smile.

"It's enough to drive even the most level headed male completely insane." Granite took a sip of wine from his goblet. "They will not wait."

"What do you propose?" Blaze cocked his head and raised his brows.

"We need to stick with tradition. All of our males need to be afforded the same opportunity despite their standing within the tribe," the earth king said.

"The hunt," Coal muttered.

Blaze nodded. He looked like he was deep in thought. Coal couldn't believe that his brother was actually considering this. Human mates. It was absurd. Humans were far lesser beings. So far below the dragon shifter species. They were small and weak. Coal had never once contemplated going on a stag run. Why, when there were two perfectly good females in their tribe and several more scattered across the kingdoms? He was lucky to have been born a prince. Human females for the lessers maybe, but for the royals, it was a travesty.

Lately, he and Scarlet had been spending more and more time together. The female had hinted about wanting to become his mate. They were discussing the possibility. The only downside was that she was infertile. The female had never gone into heat and probably never would. Granite was right when he said that they had a built-in need to reproduce. Coal wasn't immune to this drive but neither did he want a human.

Scarlet would make a good mate. She would keep his bed warm, his hearth lit. He enjoyed rutting her and... making conversation. She was adequately attractive. No sparks flew when they were together but that wasn't important. What more did a male need?

His mind immediately moved to thoughts of emotions. His sister had often spoken of love. Of long lingering looks. Of one's heart beating faster when in the presence of another. Of lust so all consuming that it was impossible to keep one's hands to themselves. She spoke of wanting to know everything about another person. What nonsense. He didn't believe that love truly existed. He certainly didn't need it.

No. Once they got out of this meeting, he would discuss mating Scarlet with Blaze. Surely his brother wouldn't refuse him. It wasn't like he planned on taking her for himself. As the fire king, Blaze was destined for a fertile female. There was no other way.

"Yes," Granite paused for a beat. "The hunt. Tradition and lores cannot be refuted."

Blazed laughed. He shook his head. "You speak of taking humans which is completely against our lores to begin with. Diluting the blood of our species is wrong. Diluting our royal blood is a sacrilege."

"It cannot be helped!" Thunder boomed. "Offer another alternative if you have one. We have no choice." He looked down at his lap, refusing to meet Blaze's gaze for a few beats.

"I agree." The water king leaned forward. "We need to follow this path. Our warriors deserve mates, as do the rest of us."

"Agreed," Granite added. "We are becoming

desperate." He gave a humorless chuckle. Sweat dripped from his brow. There was a nervous tension in the air.

"Taking human mates is the only solution. We cannot take too many at once though, a handful of females. Males who take part in the hunt can win themselves a female. The usual rules will apply including the no fire rule." Thunder looked pointedly at Coal before turning his gaze back on Blaze. "Equal opportunity for all." The fire dragons were the only dragons capable of producing fire.

The idiot actually thought that he, prince of fire, would lower himself and take part in such a hunt? For a human? Hardly a prize. It was absurd.

"Where will we find these females?" Blaze asked. "The vampires advertised in the local newspapers, and females came flocking in droves. We, however, do not possess such luxuries. We need to remain hidden. Humans are not permitted to find out about our existence. We were all but wiped out by the humans two centuries ago and our numbers were strong back then. Humans have always feared us, and rightly so." He looked thoughtful for a moment.

"We may be much stronger but they outnumber us by at least a hundred thousand to one. In today's age, they have weapons of far greater power. We would be doomed. Back to my original question, where will we find these females?"

Granite smiled. "We'll simply take them."

"No." Blaze shook his head. "We're not animals. We're not in the business of kidnapping females."

"Granite is right," Thunder said. "We have no other

option but to take some of these human females. I've had scouts on the lookout for the right ones. Young, strong, fertile and —"

"No." Blaze hit his fist against the table. "How will it look when human females suddenly start to go missing? Aside from the implications, it wouldn't be right. We are an honor bound species, we don't steal females."

"What if the females were in need of rescuing? What if they were lonely, hungry, destitute? We can save the females, offer them a better life and in the process, we can save ourselves as well."

"It's walking a fine line. Just because someone is desperate and lonely, may not mean that they want to become the mate of a dragon shifter. I don't like it."

The water king shifted in his chair. "It's not ideal," Torrent conceded. "Though dragon shifters have everything a female could want. We offer them good lives. Females beg me to take them with me when I return from a stag run. It is the same every time without fail."

Granite shrugged. "Maybe we should forget about the hunt and bring females back with us who express an interest in becoming a shifter mate." He raised his brows.

"We've discussed this at length," Thunder growled.

Coal felt irritated at this statement. Proof that the three kings had met privately to discuss this. Why the need for all the secrecy?

The air king narrowed his eyes. "It would not work. Males would fight over females. How would we decide who is eligible to take a human mate? It would be difficult to regulate. A good number of human females would go missing and this would draw attention. What if a female was deceptive and left a mate and children behind? It could be disastrous."

"Your last two points are probably the biggest concerns." Blaze looked thoughtful for a second. "It's a worry regardless of how we proceed."

"Not if we only take females who are destitute," Thunder said. "My tribe has already earmarked numerous females. None of them have family or even many friends. They would be perfect candidates."

"Perfect candidates to abduct?" Blaze sounded exasperated. "Listen to yourself," he growled.

"To be rescued!" Thunder's booming voice filled the room.

"Let's just say that I agree to this hair-brained scheme. *I'm not agreeing,* I'm just giving the whole thing some thought." He sucked in a breath. "Females would need to be in a bad way and in need of saving. They would need to have everything explained to them and would need to be treated with respect and kindness at all times. Even if a male wins one of these females fair and square, he may not force himself on her. Any male found to be forcing a female will pay with his life. The human would need to agree to being mated and later impregnated. She would need to be a willing participant at all times."

"Females will be afraid initially. It's a given." Granite took another glug of wine.

"If a female doesn't want to be with a male, no matter how hard he tries to win her…" Blaze narrowed his eyes. "Then she will be allowed to leave, to return to her old life."

"No," the air king growled. "She would be able to reveal our existence."

"Let's hope that our males are capable of winning the hearts of these females." Blaze smiled. "To be honest though, I don't like the idea in general, whether they can make them fall for them or not. The bloodlines have to be considered. I'm not ready to commit to a yes to such a widespread mating of human females."

"It's not their hearts that we're interested in." Thunder smiled even wider.

"Females are emotional, humans are so much worse. That's why I'm infinitely glad I'm not taking a human mate. Thunder . . ." He looked the male head on. "Bring your sisters when you return tomorrow. I would like to meet with them. I hope that one of them will agree to becoming my mate."

Thunder's face clouded. He looked both angry and nervous. By the sheen of sweat on his brow and his suddenly pale complexion, Coal would definitely say that he was nervous. "I was very angry when I found out about your sister's pregnancy."

"As was I." Blaze didn't take his eyes off the male for a second. Their sister, Ruby had been promised to the air king. The deal was that Thunder would take Ruby and in return, Blaze could choose a fertile air princess to mate with. Unfortunately, Ruby had other plans and had become pregnant with a vampire male's child. They were mated and happy but things were clearly still heated between the fire and air kingdoms. Thunder had not been happy about the news.

The male in question leaned forward. "I may have made some rash decisions, but you can't blame me."

Thunder's eyes were wide and he spoke too quickly.

Oh no.

Coal could sense that whatever Thunder was about to say was not going to be good.

Blaze nodded, urging the other king to continue.

"I gave my sisters to the earth and the water princes, it…" No wonder the second princes were in attendance. No damned wonder. Coal clenched his hands into fists.

Blaze slowly stood up. The tic was back and with a vengeance. Blaze banged his hands on the table. "You did what?" His voice was low and deep.

If what Thunder was saying was true, then there were no more available fertile dragon females left in all four kingdoms. The fire dragons were at risk. Huge risk. Thunder sucked in a deep breath. "I did what I felt was right. There will be humans and they —"

Blaze threw his head back and roared. At once, the room was engulfed in scorching flames. Chairs crashed and furniture smashed. By the time Blaze was finished, they all had first degree burns. Thunder was missing limbs and only barely alive.

The laundry room was cramped. Clean linen lined the shelved walls. The low hum of washing machines and dryers could be heard in the background. "Room 211 is demanding a clean." Her supervisor looked at her watch. "You've got twenty minutes to get over there and to get it done."

Julie had to refrain from rolling her eyes. She pursed her lips together, holding back a choice response. "I was just there. He had a DND sign up," she finally pushed out. "That's why I called and asked to be given another room to clean." As a temp, she only got paid for the rooms she cleaned and then only after one of the managers checked them once they had been returned back into the system. If there were any errors in any of the suites, a percentage was deducted from her pay. Julie needed to clean a minimum of sixteen rooms per shift. That gave her an average of twenty-five minutes a room. She couldn't afford any errors. Literally.

Callie huffed out a breath, looking irritated. "Well, he's changed his mind." She raised her brows. "Now, do you want to keep arguing or should I give this unit to one of the ladies on the next shift?"

Callie was the best of the bunch. Most of the supervisors treated the temps like slave labor. They got the worst rooms. They had to work like dogs to earn something of an income. It wasn't fun and it certainly wasn't fair but Julie had never had it any other way. This was her life. "I'm on it." She pushed the brake on her trolley and made her way back up the hall.

"Oh and, Julie," Callie called after her.

She turned. "Yeah?"

"Pack up and clock out when you're done. I need to fetch Harry from school today so I can't hang around to wait on you."

"No problem."

"You sure?"

"No sweat." Julie gave a reassuring nod of the head.

"Okay then." Callie nodded back.

Julie continued down the hall. Callie was a single mom. She wasn't really allowed to leave until everyone had checked out but her life was one big juggling act. Rules sometimes had to be broken. Julie understood that more than most.

It was a bit of a haul to the staff elevator. Julie walked as fast as the outdated housekeeping trolley would allow. It had one squeaky wheel and if she wasn't careful the door would open and the amenity drawers would fall out. Every minute she had to work over time to get this room done would be for free. The hotel only paid for time spent on rooms cleaned within the allotted shift and then only if they were perfect. She sighed.

By the end of this month, she'd be up to date with her rent and then she could start saving. Julie had moved plenty as a kid. They were all small towns just like Walton Springs. There had to be more. There was a whole world out there to explore. Big cities. Beautiful views. Breathtaking sunsets. So much adventure just waiting. She was done with small time. Done with small towns.

She'd never flown in an airplane, much less been to another country. Once she saved up enough though, she was leaving. Suddenly the trolley didn't feel as heavy or the lift so slow. One day… one day soon. She just needed to get out of this hole and ahead enough to be able to save. It was going to happen.

Julie gave a double knock on the door. Room 211. "Housekeeping," she announced. There was no answer so she tried again. Maybe the guest had gone out.

She cracked the door open. "Housekeeping." She said again before entering with her spray bottle and cloth in hand. The cumbersome trolley stayed in the hallway. It would be a simple matter of returning to it for new supplies such as bedding and amenities when needed.

"Oh god." She covered her eyes and backtracked. "I'm so sorry," she mumbled.

The guy was middle aged and not bad looking. He had an athletic build and salt and pepper hair. He was also completely naked as the day he was born. Her cheeks heated. *Floor please open up and swallow me whole.*

Why call for housekeeping if you plan on changing just then? Also, when someone announces themselves at the door, respond and ask them to wait.

"Don't be silly," the guy said. "Ignore me, do your thing, I'll be dressed in a moment. We're both adults."

Damn. Was he a weirdo? He must be. Then again, he had a good body. Well muscled. She opened her eyes and he was searching in the closet. His ass was… not bad. *Not looking!* She snapped her head in the opposite direction.

This was weird. He was far too old for her but he had that whole Richard Gere thing going on. His hair had that just showered look even though it was already halfway through the afternoon. Odd! No, he couldn't be doing this on purpose. A guy like him could get a date. Surely. Definitely. She relaxed just a smidgen. He was obviously just comfortable in his own skin.

She was tempted to leave and wait outside. Every minute she stood out there would be money lost though. She needed to get up to date with her rent. If she wasn't so damned desperate. Julie suppressed a sigh, she ignored him and got to work stripping the bed. She was sure that by the time she looked again he would be dressed or even better, out the door. First she removed the cover from the duvet, then the sheet from the bed and was just removing the first pillowcase when she looked up.

What the hell!

A squeaky noise came out of her throat.

"Keep cleaning," the guy said. His face had a pinched look. His back was to the closed closet door. He wasn't dressing. He wasn't even attempting to dress. His hand worked his cock. Up and down. In slow easy strokes. Forget Richard Gere, this guy was a creep with a capital C. Gross!

"What the hell are you doing?" She sounded pissed. Which was good, because she felt pissed. Her cheeks felt hot and she could hear the sound of her heart beating. It was as if the thing was in her ears.

"Ignore me and keep cleaning. I won't touch you." His voice sounded strained. Of course it was strained. He was getting himself off. His hand was still going. Tug, tug, up and down. Her eyes tracked the movement in a kind of sick fascination.

"You're some kind of sicko," she blurted. "You like watching people clean?" What the hell! Talk about a strange fetish.

He made a groaning sound that told her she was right on the money. "There's a hundred bucks on the dresser." He pointed with his free hand. "It's yours. Just clean the room and ignore me."

She shook her head. "You are nuts. I'm out of here." No way! Forget it!

"Clean the fucking room and take the money or you'll regret it." His eyes narrowed and his hand stopped tugging.

An icy tendril of fear wound itself around her. "I'm not some kind of..." She grit her teeth. "I refuse to —"

"I said that I won't touch you. Clean my room and do it now. It's what you're being paid to do. There's an extra tip in it for you as well." He glanced at the dresser. "Now be a good little cleaning lady and do your fucking job."

"Fuck you," she whispered as she walked out of the room. Her back prickled and for just a second she expected him to grab her from behind or to attack her or something but he didn't. At the very least she expected an insult to be hurled at her but there wasn't. The door closed behind her.

Her heart pounded. What the hell! She'd only been working for the hotel for a couple of months and although she'd encountered some weird shit, what had just happened was top on the list. She could have done with the hundred bucks but not like that. Forget it.

The guy seemed so normal. Julie shook her head as she pushed the piece of shit trolley. The door on it opened as she arrived at the elevator and she was forced to get on her knees and pick up all the spilled amenities. That was another thing, the temps got the worst equipment. Feather dusters with only half their feathers left. Trollies with only three wheels or like hers, doors that wouldn't close. It was a pain in the ass. She finally made it back to the laundry room just as Callie pushed her locker closed. "What happened?" Her brows were raised and concern shone in her eyes.

Her supervisor was intuitive and a smart cookie.

Julie shook her head. "The DND was still up. I knocked twice but there was no answer, so I hope you don't mind, but I left it."

Callie frowned. "That's weird" — *You don't know the half of it* — "he definitely called and asked for a room clean."

Then she shrugged. "Oh well."

It was on the tip of her tongue to tell Callie what happened but she decided not to in the end. She'd sworn at the guy. It might get her fired, despite the circumstances. She'd learned a long time ago that just because you were in the right, didn't mean that you came out on top. In fact, the opposite was mostly true. She'd checked in with reception and the pervert was checking out this afternoon so none of them would have to deal with him anymore. Julie would try to put it behind her. There wasn't much that surprised her anymore. She'd seen it all.

CHAPTER 2

It took everything in him to bite back a snarl. "What?" Coal felt everything in him tighten. "Didn't you listen to a word I just said?" There had to be some kind of mistake.

Blaze strode over to the large window and allowed his eyes to wander over the fire kingdom. It was vast and beautiful. Rolling mountains as far as the eye could see.

"I heard you just fine." Blaze kept his gaze on the view. "You need to have offspring, Coal."

"Why? You are the king, not I," he stated unnecessarily. "You are the one that needs heirs."

"Yes, but you are next in line. What if something were to happen to me?" Blaze was serious. His gaze was unwavering.

"What could possibly happen to you?" Coal growled. "We are the strongest of the non-humans and you are the strongest of the dragons." More controlled this time. Deep down he knew that his brother had a point but what was the likelihood of him ever having to step up? Tiny to none.

Blaze sighed. "And yet, I am fallible. As are you. It is for that reason that you need to take a mate and to procreate. We need royal offspring, although..." Another dramatic sigh. Blaze shook his head.

Coal didn't care if there was merit to what Blaze had just said. "Brother..." he kept his voice even. "I think that you have this backwards. It is you who needs to take a mate and to reproduce as a matter of urgency. Scarlet and I have discussed this at great length and—"

"And nothing." Blaze sounded almost bored. It infuriated him.

"I wish to take her as a mate." He clenched his jaw.

"Scarlet is infertile. There are no fertile dragon females left and it puts us in a precarious position. The earth and water princes have the last fertile shifter females and will, as we speak, be trying for offspring. It is a given that they will bear royal dragons."

"Yeah, but their offspring will not be heirs to the throne. The kings from each tribe will take part in the hunt and we have no idea if human females can bear royal dragons."

"Exactly," he growled. "No royal dragon has ever mated a human." He shook his head and suddenly looked much older. "It isn't right but what choice do we have?"

"I am sure that a royal mating with a human will be successful," Coal said. "We won't know though until you take one and try."

Blaze shook his head. "I'm considering taking a vampire female."

"What?" Coal could hear the disbelief etched in his voice. "You can't. A half breed would never be accepted as king." Although, according to the lores, mating humans would result in diluted blood. Offspring from humans always had all of the dominant features of the non-humans. This was the main reason why human women were being considered instead other species.

"I know that but I might not have a choice. Ruby birthed a royal child. Her daughter is a fire breather."

"We don't know if the little one will be capable of shifting. She might breathe fire but she also drinks blood." He wanted to call his niece an abomination but couldn't bring himself to do it. She was a gorgeous little thing. "A child like Tinder would never be accepted. Not by our fire tribe and certainly not by the other kingdoms. It's madness."

"That it is." Blaze nodded his head. "It might be the only way though. If humans are not capable of bearing us royal young, we might need to consider that route. Not all of the royals will end up with a human after the first hunt and those that don't might just be in favor of trying this alternative. Especially if humans can not bear royal young. You will see how quickly a half breed will be accepted then. I need you to win one of the humans." His brother wanted him to play guinea pig. Wanted him to take a human so that they could find out if the resulting child of the union would have golden markings.

"No." His breath was hot but he managed to keep smoke from clouding the conversation.

"I'm not asking you, Coal. You need to do this for — "

"A puny, little human. They're not much better than rats."

Blaze laughed. "You've never been on a stag run. You've never even breathed the same air as a human. How do you even know that you wouldn't like them?" He laughed some more. "I have a feeling that once you have a taste of one, you will fall flat on your face."

Coal growled. He couldn't help himself. "Humans are low on the food chain. I would never fall over anything to be with one and I don't have to meet one to know that to be true. I've never had, nor will I ever have, any desire to go on a stag run." No way! Twice a year, all of the males sought out human companionship. It was a rut fest. The males got more and more excited as the date neared. They talked endlessly about the females that they would bed. Once the stag run was over, they talked endlessly about the females that they had bedded. On and on. Waste of time. Coal had been quite happy with the dragon shifter females and had made his mind up about Scarlet, thank you very much.

A human... forget it. "You would force me to mate with something I consider to be more like food than an equal? No."

"I need to know if royalty can breed royalty with a human. I need —"

"Ask Inferno, he loves humans. He would be more than willing to mate one and —"

"Our brother is still a pup. There is no way he can stand up against the kings, the best warriors our species has to offer, and actually win. Not without using fire. No way in hell! You on the other hand will cream them. You will be victorious. Our tribe needs you to bring a female home and to impregnate her as soon as possible. If she bears gold, I will follow suit and if not I'll take a vampire female." Blaze touched the gold design embedded in his skin. It was proof of his royal blood. Lesser dragons had silver markings. They were born that way.

Coal felt horror and dread at the thought of a human female. Humans were primitive beings. It was like asking a lion to mate with a gazelle. It wasn't done. It wasn't right.

"The fire tribe is still on top but that won't be the case for much longer if the princes from the other tribes breed royals and we are unable to reciprocate. Do you understand the ramifications of that?"

All too well.

"I can't," he croaked. "You can't ask this of me. Anything but this."

"If there was another choice, I would take it. There are no other options. You need to win the hunt and then win the female. Do all you can to get her to accept you and to agree to mating with you. All I ask is that you enter into this with an open mind. You might just be pleasantly surprised."

Like hell he would.

The next morning…

The bus had arrived early. Okay, only by about a minute, but early nonetheless. Julie had run after it for about a half a block but the driver hadn't stopped. The next bus was late by four minutes. Go freaking figure. Now she was being summoned to the Executive

Housekeeper's office, for being five minutes late. Really?

This day couldn't get too much worse. She'd be assigned the worst rooms, the worst trolley. This sucked.

Julie pulled in a deep breath. She smoothed her uniform down, put a smile on her face and opened the door.

"It's about time." Gretchen Harridge was a middle-aged, severe woman. She reminded Julie of a nun, but only if said nun was seething with underlying aggression. She had yet to see the woman smile, even once.

Her hair was cut short and her face devoid of all make-up. Her mouth was upside down in appearance. Her eyes were on her laptop. She continued to type for a few minutes. Julie remained standing at the head of her desk.

At long last, Miss Harridge removed her glasses and raised her eyes to Julie who tried not to take a step back. The older woman shook her head slowly.

It was only five minutes. This woman needed to take a chill pill. *Suck it up, Julie.* "I apologize for being late. This is only the second time in all the months I've been employed at Lofty Heights Hotel. I'm reliant on public transport."

"Take a seat." Mrs. Harridge pointed to the old, linoleum covered chair in front of her desk. Her office was cramped. As with most hotels, the housekeeping department was in the bowels of the hotel. The laundry, staff change area and housekeeping office had been squeezed into a small space, not much bigger than a hotel room.

Her desk was covered in stacks of paperwork and open files. The shelved walls behind her were filled with more of such files. They were labeled things like orders, staff, room checks and maintenance.

Mrs. Harridge cleared her throat. She sighed. "We have to let you go," she said, without batting an eye.

Julie narrowed her eyes. "What do you mean?" She tripped over the words. "I do a good job, I'm conscientious. Callie was planning on putting me forward for a permanent position, when one became available, that is." She huffed out a breath when she realized that what she was saying was having no affect on her department head. None whatsoever.

Mrs. Harridge looked at her, deadpan. Her glasses still in one hand. It was like she couldn't wait for Julie to leave so that she could carry on with her work. It didn't matter to her how this news would affect Julie.

"Why?" Julie finally asked. She swallowed hard, pushing down the panic that threatened to overwhelm her. If she lost this job, she wouldn't make rent, again. If she didn't square up with James, her landlord, by next Tuesday, she was out. So far she'd been on track to do just that. It had meant living on beans and toast, but hey. She was doing it. Now this. If she didn't find a way to change Mrs. Harridge's mind, she was going to end up homeless. In just a few days, she'd be out on the streets.

Panic churned her gut and turned her hands clammy. She fought not to squirm in her seat.

"Did you, or did you not, swear at a hotel guest?" She cocked her head to the side.

No.

God no.

It was the pervert from room 211. He'd actually gone and filed a complaint about her. "Um... what?... no..."

She shook her head. "That can't be right. He didn't..." Anger welled up in her. "I can't believe he actually filed a complaint about me. The bastard."

Mrs. Harridge looked taken aback. She leaned forward on her elbows and finally let her glasses go. "You just called a hotel guest a bastard. Well, at least this proves that you did swear at him. Don't even try and deny it now."

"He's a pervert. He was naked when I opened the door," she blurted. Oh great. Now she had made it sound like she'd walked in on him.

Her boss cocked her head and raised her brows. "All that tells me is that you didn't follow correct procedure. It certainly doesn't make him a pervert."

Shit! "I knocked and announced myself, three times. He called moments earlier requesting a room clean. I entered. I most certainly followed procedure, to the letter." She wasn't going to just accept this. Forget it.

"You saw him naked and swore at him." Her superior gave a small shake of the head, looking taken aback.

It sucked to high heavens that Mrs. Harridge immediately took the side of the guest. The customer might be king but that didn't mean that he was always right. "He told me to clean his room. Said to ignore him. It was almost the end of my shift and he seemed like an okay guy so I got to work." She pulled in a deep breath. "I should have left. It turns out he was a major pervert. He started . . ." She wasn't a prude but the way her boss glared at her made her feel like she was the pervert, not him. "He started to touch himself... inappropriately. I asked him to stop. He didn't. Instead, he offered me money to clean his room while he touched himself. I'm sorry, but I'm not desperate or depraved. There was no way I was staying in that room for a second longer. No damned way. It was sick. He swore at me. I was just defending myself."

Mrs. Harridge picked up the phone on her desk. "Please, can" — she put her glasses on and peered at the screen — "Susan Jones come to my office?" Then she replaced the receiver in the cradle.

"I swear to you that…"

Mrs. Harridge held up her hand. "I've heard enough. I need to speak with Susan and then we can conclude." She turned back to her computer and continued typing.

It was the longest seven minutes of her life. She felt like a naughty school girl. She could tell that Gretchen Harridge was not interested in what she had to say. Hell, the woman had fired her before hearing her side of the story. What the hell was she going to do?

Even if she found another job today, there was still no way she was making rent on Tuesday. James had been clear about any more non or part payments. He wanted the total outstanding by Tuesday, no excuses.

That bastard from room 211 had totally lied and strung her out. He'd said that she'd be sorry. She wasn't though. Julie would rather be out on the streets than taking handouts from a lowlife pervert.

There was a light knock on the door before it opened. "You called?" Susan ignored her completely. "How can I help?" Susan was one of the permanents.

"You cleaned room 211 yesterday afternoon?"

Susan nodded. "The gentlemen complained that he had asked for a room clean. The room attendant that showed up originally, swore at him and left without doing the room. I went and sorted it out. He was quite upset. I had him direct his complaint to the shift supervisor, as per company policy. He was happy when I left and accepted the apologies put forward. He was given a free night at the hotel for his troubles when he checked out that same day."

The bastard! Julie had to bite her tongue to stop herself from saying her piece.

"Excellent, Susan. Thank you for your time and thanks for coming in this morning to clear this up."

"Anytime. I'm glad I could help." Susan finally looked her way. Her smile tightened and her eyes narrowed just that little bit.

"You can go now." Mrs. Harridge nodded and gave the barest ghost of a smile to Susan.

Once the door closed, she turned back to Julie. "Please be sure to return both sets of uniforms by the end of business tomorrow. They should be laundered to hotel standard. Should there be any damage, the cost will come out of your last paycheck. Should you not return your uniform on time, the charges for them will be deducted from your wages. I'm disappointed."

"He was wanking off in front of me. I didn't do anything wrong. He's the one that you should be disappointed in, not me." She rose to her feet. "I don't want to work for an establishment that doesn't look after its employees anyways." She didn't wait for a reply. Julie turned and walked from the room. She didn't slam the door behind her even though she was sorely tempted. She wouldn't give that beady eyed, troll the satisfaction.

She was a temporary employee, there was nothing she could do. It would be her word against his. She already knew how normal he looked. How clean cut and good looking. Asshole!

Maybe James would give her one last chance. She could only hope.

Five days later…

To think that everything she owned in the world fit inside this suitcase and the backpack on her back. *Everything.*

Julie huffed out a breath as she walked. She wasn't sure what she was going to do. There weren't many options. Shelter, bus stop or alleyway. At least the weather forecast was mild with no rain predicted for the next couple of days. The only person she knew well enough to help her out for a couple of nights was Cloe but she wasn't welcome at her house anymore.

Julie wasn't any good at keeping her mouth shut and when she'd spotted telltale bruises on her friend's arms, she'd said something about it. Especially since this wasn't the first time she'd seen bruises on her friend's body. The first time was a split lip. The second was bruises around her neck, which she'd tried to cover with a scarf in the middle of summer. Enough was enough. She wasn't about to stand by while Cloe got beaten to a pulp.

The two of them had shared one of her many foster homes together. They hit it off immediately and had stayed in touch since but apparently calling her out on her abusive husband was a no no. A hard line. Hopefully her friend would see the light and hopefully it wouldn't be too late.

The one other person she had cherished was Lucinda. One of her foster moms. One of the few really good ones. Only Lucinda was more like a granny than a mother. She could still recall how standoffish she had been to her foster mom for the first couple of months. Lucinda had given her, her space. The only thing she had insisted on was that they ate dinner together every night. She'd thrived under the woman's care. One day Lucinda became ill and three months later she was dead. It had been a particularly aggressive cancer.

Julie swallowed down a lump that formed in her throat. She still missed that woman.

Her suitcase was ripped from her hand. A young guy sprinted away with her belongings. Almost everything she owned.

"Hey!" Julie cried. "Stop!" She shrieked, sprinting after the punk in the hoodie. After an hour of lugging the thing, her arm felt dead and her legs didn't feel much better. Thing was, there wasn't anything of real value in there.

Still, that was it. All of it. Her clothes. Her shoes. Her life. Most of it was in that bag. The last few bits and pieces were in the backpack on her back. Everything else was in there.

The guy was much faster than her, but she was determined. Julie picked up speed. A low growl of anger and frustration was torn from her. Her arms pumped at her sides and her lungs burned. She wanted to shout at him again but she didn't have the strength to both run and call out.

Bastard.

Little asshole.

At first he pulled away from her. Now she was keeping up with him. Pretty soon, the tables were going to turn and then he'd be sorry, he'd be worse than sorry. Julie ignored the voice inside her that begged her to stop. She ignored her fatigued muscles. She ignored every thing and… tripped.

No.

Julie tried to right herself. She staggered. For a moment there it felt like she might just be able to stay upright, then she plummeted down, down. The pavement raced to meet her. Make that the solid edge of the pavement sprinted towards her. She tried to twist away. There was blinding pain as her head hit hard. Almost immediately, darkness descended.

Out Now!

Printed in Great Britain
by Amazon